*Chase caught her by the wrist.
"Come here, Dev. I want to
hold you."*

Devon gave him a forced smile and tried to pull free. "What you want isn't always what you get."

He didn't argue with her. He simply gave her arm a sharp tug, tumbling her across him, then locked her in a tight embrace. "No back talk," he said, his voice suddenly gruff. "Just shut up and let me hold you."

She remained rigid in his arms for an instant. Then the tension went out of her, and she slid one arm around his back and pressed her face against his neck.

Chase leaned his head back and closed his eyes, a sudden tightness in his chest. Hard, cold reality was closing in on him. They couldn't keep marking time like this. Something was going to have to give.

He hoped like hell it wouldn't be his heart.

Dear Reader,

The weather's hot, and here at Intimate Moments, so is the reading. Our leadoff title this month is a surefire winner: Judith Duncan's *That Same Old Feeling*. It's the second of her Wide Open Spaces trilogy, featuring the McCall family of Western Canada. It's also an American Hero title. After all, Canada is part of North America—and you'll be glad of that, once you fall in love with Chase McCall!

Our Romantic Traditions miniseries continues with *Desert Man*, by Barbara Faith, an Intimate Moments-style take on the ever-popular sheikh story line. And the rest of the month features irresistible reading from Alexandra Sellers, Kim Cates (with a sequel to *Uncertain Angels*, her first book for the line) and two new authors: Anita Meyer and Lauren Shelley.

In months to come, look for more fabulous reading from authors like Marilyn Pappano (starting a new miniseries called Southern Knights), Dallas Schulze and Kathleen Eagle—to name only a few. Whatever you do, don't miss these and all the Intimate Moments titles coming your way throughout the year.

Yours,

Leslie J. Wainger
Senior Editor and Editorial Coordinator

Please address questions and book requests to:
Silhouette Reader Service
U.S.: 3010 Walden Ave., P.O. Box 1325, Buffalo, NY 14269
Canadian: P.O. Box 609, Fort Erie, Ont. L2A 5X3

AMERICAN HERO

# THAT SAME OLD FEELING

## Judith Duncan

Published by Silhouette Books

America's Publisher of Contemporary Romance

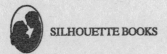 SILHOUETTE BOOKS

ISBN 0-373-07577-4

THAT SAME OLD FEELING

Copyright © 1994 by Judith Mulholland

This edition published by arrangement with Harlequin Enterprises B. V.

Printed in U.S.A.

**Books by Judith Duncan**

Silhouette Intimate Moments

*A Risk Worth Taking* #400
*Better Than Before* #421
*\*Beyond All Reason* #536
*\*That Same Old Feeling* #577

\* Wide Open Spaces

---

## JUDITH DUNCAN

is married and lives, along with two of her five children and her husband, in Calgary, Alberta, Canada. A staunch supporter of anyone wishing to become a published writer, she has lectured at several workshops for Alberta's Department of Culture and participated in conventions in both British Columbia and Oregon. After having served a term as 2nd vice president for the Canadian Authors' Association, she is currently working with the Alberta Romance Writers' Association, which she helped to found.

# Chapter 1

*September*
*Casper, Wyoming*

To the good people of Bolton, Alberta, Chase McCall was something of an enigma. Tall, dark and handsome, he was all speed and danger and as wild as the broncs he rode, with no apparent regard for caution and even less regard for his old man's money or opinion. He was all brash and dash, like the black and chrome truck he drove, and he walked with the cocky swagger of a man who liked living on the edge. He had danger written all over him. With eyes like the devil and a smile like sin, he spelled trouble, and fathers made sure their daughters were at home when he came to town.

The battles between him and his father were legendary, as were most of his hell-raising escapades, but in spite of his wild, wild ways, it was common knowledge that Chase McCall was a man of his word, a man who never backed away from a fight. It was also common knowledge that he was close to his half brother, Tanner McCall, old Bruce's bastard son by an Indian woman—a son Bruce had abandoned and ignored long before Chase was even born. In fact, some said it was because of Chase's refusal to bend to his father's demands to keep away from Tanner that Chase left home at eighteen and never went back. The good people of Bolton often speculated, now that old Bruce's health was starting to fail, if Chase would ever come home.

Chase didn't give a damn what the good people of Bolton thought. He'd had a bellyful of his old man's power, his money, his bought-and-paid-for influence, and the only way anyone would ever get him back on the McCall ranch was in a pine box.

Now thirty-six, Chase had a freewheeling life-style that suited him. An ex-rodeo bronc rider and all-around Canadian champion, he had retired from active competition after a series of injuries that damn near wrecked both his shoulders. Tied to the action in the chutes, he started a business as a stock contractor, supplying rough stock for major rodeos across the U.S. and Canada. He was a rodeo junkie. He had started going down the road when he just turned nineteen, and he'd never had any regrets—except one.

But lately he'd been caught in a strange restlessness that had nothing to do with moving on. He wasn't sure what was picking at him, except that he had this itch that wouldn't go away. And a chance encounter at the stock sale hadn't helped. He'd run into Martin Blocker, an old neighbor from home, and that meeting had kicked off all the same old feelings about Bolton, about his old man, about the Bar M Ranch. About his one regret. And that itch of dissatisfaction turned into a black, hungry mood.

And that mood was why he was stopping off in Casper, Wyoming, instead of booting it through to his spread in Colorado. He was going to find himself a jug of Jack Daniel's, a dingy motel room, a down-on-your-luck country music station, and then he was going to drink himself under the table. Flipping on the turn signal, he checked his side mirror and pulled over onto the shoulder to make the right-hand turn for the motel. Yeah, a meeting with old Jack would take the edge off. Or he could say to hell with the bottle and go to the big quarter horse show Martin had mentioned. It would certainly go easier on his damned head. In more ways than one.

Chase sat off from the crowd clustered in the middle of the stands, his legs stretched out in the aisle, his arms resting on the backs of the empty seats on either side of him. Amusement flickered in him as he watched two buckle bunnies hanging around the contestant gate below him, flirting with a couple of young bucks on horses. Some things never changed. He'd seen enough of that kind of action when he was still chasing points on broncs—young studs feeling their oats, pretty girls on pretty horses strutting their stuff. One looking for a gold ring, the other hoping for a little action. No wonder he'd turned into such a black-hearted bastard.

A voice came over the PA system announcing the parade of champions, and Chase shifted his attention, cocking his ankle across his knee. He watched the female standard-bearers enter the arena, remembering a day when he would have been checking out the fannies in the saddles instead of the horseflesh under them. He grinned to himself. Hell of a thing, getting old.

Reconsidering the Jack Daniel's and dingy motel room, he slouched farther down in the seat and folded his arms, his Stetson pulled low over his eyes. Sometimes a man had to do what a man had to do. His interest sharpened when the reserve champion for the halter class was led in. A damned nice-looking colt—had one hell of a lot more potential, he thought, than the champion. He watched as the horse was led around the ring, mentally recording the bloodlines and the stable. Might be worth checking into later. He watched several of the other top horses enter the ring, his mind stuck somewhere between neutral and low gear, absently acknowledging that the show photographer knew what she was doing. The winner of the reining competition was an-

nounced, and Chase swung his attention to the back of the
arena, everything slamming to a dead stop when the horse
and rider moved from the shadows into the light.

The black stallion entered the arena in a showy, collected
trot, its neck and tail arched, the perfectly proportioned
head held with an arrogant stillness, the white socks and star
in startling contrast to the gleaming black hide. This was
blue-ribbon, championship horseflesh. The announcer read
off a list of championships held by both the stallion and his
progeny, and it became clear that this wasn't only championship horseflesh—this was championship horseflesh that
bred championship horseflesh.

But it wasn't the stud with the eye-catching conformation that made Chase go dead still. It was the rider.

Feeling as if something had just slammed into his chest,
he riveted his gaze on her, his pulse suddenly heavy. She was
right out of his fantasies.

She sat astride the stallion in flawless equitation, her body
still, almost as if she was the source of the collectedness that
was apparent in her mount. She sat deep in the saddle, her
long, long legs equally still, her body moving with the ease
of a conditioned athlete, her hands controlling the spirited
horse with an ease born of experience. Her black hair was
caught in a sedate twist at the nape of her neck, and she
wore her black Stetson with a wide silver hatband low over
her eyes, obscuring her face but revealing a defined jaw-
line. She had on a white silk blouse, the silver beadwork
across the shoulders glinting in the light, those long, long
legs encased in black suede shotgun chaps with engraved
silver buckles and conchos down the sides. Black and white.
Horse and rider. Spiked with silver.

Experiencing a sudden sharpening of awareness, Chase
watched as she reached the center of the arena, his jaw
tightening as the horse exploded into action. She took the
stallion through a reining pattern with such finesse, such
speed, that the audience went crazy, and Chase clenched his
jaw tighter, focusing solely on her as she put the horse

through the challenging pattern. Her long-sleeved white blouse and black suede chaps made him think of white sheets and long black nights. Forcing himself to stay slack in his seat, Chase watched, intrigued as hell. Black and white. Grace and elegance. Skill and horsemanship. But it wasn't the grace and elegance stamped into every line of her body that intrigued him, it was the sensuality he saw in her light, light hands—how she handled the horse with the slightest touch—that stirred something inside him he hadn't felt for a very long time.

He watched her legs, watched the barely discernible movements that cued the horse—the touch of a spur, the smallest shift of her calf, the tightening of her thighs—and the stallion responded, and Chase finally had to look away, his own body responding. *Too long in the hills, McCall,* he thought. *Too damned long.* His arms folded, he stared at the toes of his scuffed boots, contemplating life. A hell of a thing, abstinence. The Jack Daniel's would have been a damned sight less disturbing.

Keeping his thoughts in check and eyes averted, he waited until the last of the horses left the ring. Then he quickly rose and slipped out the nearest exit, dodging the two buckle bunnies he'd noticed earlier. Pulling up his collar against the early fall chill, he pushed open the heavy exit door, angling his hat lower over his eyes. Dead leaves and bits of garbage rattled across the pavement as he headed toward the main parking lot. He was beginning to feel damned black—right from the inside out. A horse whinnied nearby, and there was a commotion as someone tried to load an animal that did not want to be loaded. He turned to see what was going on, but his attention got snagged on a white silk blouse and a black hat moving through a jam of vehicles. She was riding across the back parking lot, her body still motionless in the saddle, only now the black was putting on a show—prancing, tossing his head, fighting the bit.

Settling his hands on his hips, Chase watched, and something happened in his gut that made the corner of his mouth lift. Showing off. The damned horse was showing off. And she was letting him. He watched her bring the stud down to a walk as she threaded her way through the jumble of rigs and pickups. Then she reined up and dismounted by a pricey six-horse trailer and a new dual-wheeled truck, both painted midnight blue. Chase stared off at the horizon for a minute, considering his options, then he shook his head, figuring he was some kind of fool.

Turning on his heel, he headed toward the midnight blue rig. The name of the stable was emblazoned on both the truck and the trailer—Silver Springs Training Stables—both units sporting Alberta plates. Grinning to himself, he approached, wondering what in hell he was getting himself into. It had been a long time since he'd stuck his neck into a noose—a damned long time. Leaning against the front fender of an adjacent truck, he hooked his thumbs in the front pockets of his jeans and crossed his ankles, watching as she unlocked the side storage compartment and swung open the door. Her back to him, she turned to the horse and hooked the stirrup over the saddle horn, then began undoing the cinch on the intricately tooled show saddle. A trio of expensively dressed men approached her, clearly interested in the black, and Chase folded his arms and listened as she told them something about the stallion, where he was standing stud and what the breeding fees were.

Shifting his position, Chase braced his full weight against the fender. Grinning the grin that had got him into more trouble than he cared to think about, he fixed his gaze on her and spoke. "Hell of a horse you've got there, ma'am. Full of sass and prance. Looks like he knows a thing or two about good manners. How is he around the ladies?"

Her head came up and she whirled, staring at him, her startled expression accentuating her high cheekbones and almond-shaped eyes. Chase had the sudden urge to snatch off her hat and take the pins out of the thick twist of hair at the back of her neck.

He could see her collect herself. Then she raised one eyebrow and gave him a slow, shrewd smile. "He has manners," she said, her low, husky voice making his gut tighten. "Not as good as some, but better than most." The glint in her eyes deepened. "And his manners are just fine around the ladies."

Holding her gaze, Chase grinned at her. "Better than most?"

She gave him a dry, amused look. "I'd say so."

She dragged off the saddle, the sunlight glancing off the silver inlay, then carried it to the storage compartment and slid it onto a saddle rack.

One of the men separated himself from the trio and closely inspected the stallion, running his hand down his back legs. The horse tossed his head, and she gave him a sharp command. "Duke! Cut it out."

The stud snorted and flicked his tail, and Chase shot her an amused look. "Duke? As in John Wayne?"

She draped the cinch over the seat of the saddle, then flashed him another wry smile. "No. As in His Royal Highness. He tends to have a high opinion of himself."

Chase grinned. "Hell. With what he's sired, I can't say I blame him."

The man finished his inspection and came around the front of of the black. "What's his name again?"

"Doc's Regal Deuce." Then she listed the animal's bloodlines.

The man stood back and gave the stallion another thorough inspection, and she ducked under the horse's head and went to open the tailgate of the trailer, then set the ramp in place. She entered, and Chase saw that there were three horses already loaded in the slant stalls, and he realized she was getting ready to pull out. His expression turning thoughtful, he watched her expertly adjust the inside divider, then reach across to open the side vent. The truck was top of the line, and the trailer provided five-star accommodations for its cargo. She had "first class" stamped all over her. He didn't know what in hell he was doing there. He watched her load the stallion and strip off the bridle, a tight smile appearing when the black shook its head. He knew the feeling.

The gent with the eight-hundred-dollar boots was obviously a prospective customer, and he followed her to the compartment when she went to put the bridle away. There was a brief conversation, then she unlocked the groom's quarters at the front of the unit, and the gentleman followed her inside. Chase stared at the open door for a space, then clamped his jaw in a hard line. He unfolded his arms and straightened, ticked off for getting drawn off the bead. What the hell was he doing here, anyway? He was messing with things he had no business messing with. And he needed that like he needed another hole in the head. Besides, he couldn't stick around, even if he had an engraved invitation. He had to be in Colorado before noon tomorrow—he didn't have any choice about that. Glancing at the clouds starting to form in the west, he kicked a rock out of his path and turned toward his truck. Damn it all to hell, he should have stuck with the Jack Daniel's and the dingy motel room.

He got in the truck and reached for the sunglasses lying on the dash, then turned on the ignition. He was feeling meaner than a one-eyed cat. Realizing that part of his testy mood had to do with the fact that he hadn't eaten since early that morning, he decided to grab a bite. Then he was going to get this rig in gear and find the highway heading south. No more thinking. No more stray thoughts. He was going to put his brain in neutral and his fantasies in park.

He stopped at a restaurant close to the interstate, got himself a table by the window, then ordered himself a T-bone with all the trimmings. The waitress had just taken his order and was walking away when the midnight blue outfit pulled up to the lights, waited for a vehicle to pass, then made a left turn onto the highway. His expression stiff, Chase rested his arms on the table and hunched over, watching it head north, his gut tightening with a feeling that made him want to bust something. He watched it until it passed out of view, then he clenched his jaw and stared at his clasped hands. Focused on keeping it together, he rubbed his thumb along an old scar on the back of his hand, loneliness rolling in on him like fog. Half-forgotten memories started to pull at him, and he tried to block the images from taking shape in his mind, knowing he was going to be in bad shape if he didn't. A face intruded—an exotic face with high cheekbones and almond-shaped eyes, a smile that made his gut tighten, a voice that slid over a man like black satin.

Annoyed by his wayward thoughts, Chase turned his head, forcing himself to check out the inside of the restaurant. He was doing it again, playing stupid head games, getting caught in something that he would have one hell of a time getting himself out of. He was going to sit here and eat his steak, he was going to listen to a little country music on the jukebox—and he was going to keep his butt planted in the chair for at least an hour.

He lasted forty-five minutes. The restlessness finally got to him, nagging at him like a low-grade toothache, and he got up and threw a handful of money on the table, a head of frustration building up inside him. Why in hell hadn't he stayed on the road in the first place? He didn't need this damned distraction.

Settling his hat on his head, he pushed through the heavy front doors, his jaw rigid as he turned toward his truck. He was going to go home, and he was going to tear down that old corral with his bare hands, and he was going to dig postholes for the new one until he was so dead tired he wouldn't be able to lift his arms.

Getting into his truck, he started the engine, then wheeled onto the service road leading to the highway. At the same lights where the blue rig had turned north, he rolled to a stop, waiting for a green, the frustration building to a dangerous level. He signaled for a right turn, a turn that would take him south to Colorado, but images of long legs and long black hair, of a smile that could strip a man of any willpower, pulled at him. The light turned green, and Chase stared out the window, wondering where in hell his sense was. Swearing, he abruptly wheeled into the other lane, beating an oncoming vehicle as he made a sharp left. Damn it, this was brain-dead crazy. She had a forty-five-minute lead, and it would start getting dark in a couple of hours, but what the hell. All he had to do was make one stop on his way out of town.

Settling back, Chase grinned and watched the speedometer climb, the restless feeling turning into something else. He was going to give that midnight blue top-of-the-line outfit a run for its money, and he was going to run Long Legs to ground. And there was only one highway heading north to the Canadian border.

He was two hours out of Casper and minutes away from sunset when common sense finally caught up to him. Disgusted with himself, Chase conceded that he was acting like a dumb ass and that this was one of the stupidest stunts he'd pulled in a dozen years. Not liking the feeling that was sitting heavy in his gut, he called it quits, even more disgusted for getting suckered by reactions that started below his belt. Hell, she could be anywhere between here and Billings, Montana; she could be sitting fifteen miles outside of Casper at somebody's ranch, for all he knew. If he kept this up, all he was going to get out of it was a speeding ticket and a bellyful of frustration. And he could do without both.

Pulling over to the shoulder, he waited for a semi to whip past in the passing lane, then he crossed the median and headed south, irritation eating a hole in his gut. Lord, sometimes he was the biggest fool ever to put boots on.

Twilight settled in over the barren hills as the sun dropped behind the western horizon, and Chase slowed, watching for antelope along the road. That would be all he needed, to hit one of those. Rounding a curve, he spotted some corrals and a campsite off to the left tucked into the cottonwoods along a creek, and a movement caught his eye. He took a second look and stood on the brakes. Backing up, he squinted through the deepening dusk, his mood suddenly altering. "Well, I'll be damned," he muttered, a grin lifting the corner of his mouth. The black was in the smallest corral by himself, and the other three horses were in the one closest to the creek, grazing on the lush grass along the side. Chase braced his elbow on the open window and rested his hand against his mouth, watching the black. It figured.

Checking his side mirror, he eased off the brake, considering his options. Checking the mirror again, he made a snap decision and accelerated, taking the exit leading to the campground. The narrow gravel road circled under the bridge, and it wasn't until Chase crossed the Texas gate that he saw the familiar outfit parked off to the side. Switching off the headlights, he rolled to a stop and raised the window, then shut off the ignition. He sat there, staring into the deepening dusk, his expression sober. Somebody should take him out and horsewhip him for this stunt—he sure in hell deserved it.

Removing the keys, he got out of the vehicle and stuffed them in his pocket, then set the automatic lock and silently closed the door. He had barely cleared his truck when the door to the living quarters in the trailer opened, and she stood in the doorway, the light from inside framing her. The sedate twist was gone, as were the silk blouse and chaps. She had on a yellow tank top and well-worn blue jeans, and her feet were bare. She folded her arms and leaned her shoulder against the door frame, and Chase stopped, hooking his thumbs in the front pockets of his jeans. Looking at her from beneath the brim of his hat, he grinned, then spoke, his voice a lazy drawl. "I figured it wouldn't be neighborly if I didn't stop by and say hello." He started toward her, something thick and heavy happening in his chest, and he watched her, watched her chin come up, watched her recover from the shock of finding him there. His grin softening, he spoke, his voice turning husky. "So, Slash, how the hell have you been? It's been a damned long time."

Devon Manyfeathers held her position at the door, watching him come toward her out of the twilight, the awful tightness that had been sitting in her chest since Casper finally letting go, a different kind of tightness settling in around her heart.

She had nearly lost it when she'd lifted her head and found him watching her in Casper, and she *had* lost it when she pulled out of town. It had nearly killed her that he'd been able to walk away without a backward glance, without even saying goodbye. But here he was, walking toward her with that loose-hipped saunter of his, smiling that full-of-hell smile. She didn't know whether to laugh or cry.

But she'd been in love with Chase McCall since she'd been eleven years old, and after all those years, she knew that wasn't ever going to change. And God, it made her chest hurt, finding him here, smiling that damned smile of his. She had to really work to keep her throat from closing up on her, to keep her vision from blurring. He'd been gone so long. And there wasn't a day went by that she didn't miss him.

Determined not to let him see how his arrival had affected her, she held her pose. "Well if it isn't the proverbial bad penny," she said, her tone dry. "What's the matter, Slick? You have the sheriff chasing you again, or is some irate husband coming after your tail?"

Chase stopped and grinned at her, tipping his head to one side. "That's one thing I always liked about you, Manyfeathers. You never give a damned inch." He lifted his chin toward the living quarters. "Are you going to invite me in?"

She held her position, a smile lifting the corner of her mouth. "Would it make any difference if I didn't?"

Unfolding his arms, he caught the edge of the door and stepped up, aligning his body beside hers in the open doorway. "Hell, Devon. You know me better than that."

She knew what he was doing, and she slid away, heading toward the tiny, compact kitchenette. "I suppose you're going to want some of my supper."

Chase took off his hat and set it on the counter, then started stripping off his jacket, the glint in his eyes turning into a wicked gleam. "I'll take whatever you're offering."

Amusement flickered through her, and she turned her back to him, allowing herself a small smile. His parents had certainly named him right. Chase—he always cut right to it. Keeping her tone dry, she responded. "What I'm offering is some beef stew and a bag of buns. Take it or leave it."

"Is it homemade stew or that canned crap?"

She turned and gave him a long, level look. "Do you always go out of your way to endear yourself to the cook, or are you just being nice on my account?"

He grinned at her and braced his hand on the corner of the tiny closet, holding her gaze with the kind of amused familiarity that made her insides churn. "So you find me endearing, do you?"

She gave him another look of mild rebuke. "If you want to go fishing, McCall, there's a creek on the other side of those trees."

His gaze fixed on her, he continued to grin at her, the glint in his dark hazel eyes intensifying. His dark curly hair was different from the last time she'd seen him—shorter on the sides and nearly touching his collar at the back—and he had a small scar just above one eyebrow that hadn't been there before. There was something a little different about his face, a little leaner, perhaps, the creases around his eyes just a little deeper—maybe, maybe just a little less bitterness. He held her gaze, the expression in his eyes softening, becoming a little warmer, a little more intimate—the look you gave someone you'd known a long, long time. He finally spoke, his voice oddly husky. "You're a real piece of sass, Manyfeathers."

Something in his tone, something in his eyes, set off a fierce ache in Devon's chest, and her throat got so tight that she wasn't sure she could swallow. Of all the things she missed after he left, it was that special, nothing-to-hide friendship she'd missed the most. They were soul mates—

and had been for a very long time. She scraped up a smile. "Turn off the charm, Slick. Are you going to have some of my stew or not?"

He smiled into her eyes. "Is it homemade?"

She rolled her eyes, then let out a sigh of exasperation. "Yes, it's homemade. And since you're such a stew purist, it's even made with McCall beef. We bought a steer from Tanner last fall and had it butchered."

He straightened. "Well, hell. Why didn't you say so right up front?" He went to the sink, rolling back his cuffs, and started washing his hands. "Let's get this show on the road."

Chase was actually pretty handy in a kitchen. He doctored up the stew while Devon made a salad, and she recalled that one wonderful fall when he'd spent nearly a month with her. It had been as close to perfect as she'd ever come—and now it was almost as though he'd never been away.

"So tell me what's happening back home. How are Sam and Marj doing?"

Sam Creswell was the owner of Silver Springs, and next to Chase, the oldest friend Devon had. He and his wife, Marj, had given her a job when she was fifteen years old, and after her mother had taken off, they had given her a home, a place to belong, and she'd been working for him ever since. The two of them were the closest thing to real family she'd ever had.

Devon smiled and shook her head. "He's still the same. He turned sixty-five in the spring and started bringing home travel information on Caribbean cruises and resorts in Arizona. He and Marj are leaving on a cruise right after the New Year—they'll be gone a month."

Chase tasted the stew and dug through the few cans of spices in the tiny cupboard by his head. "And how's Marj?"

Devon sighed and dumped the shredded cabbage into a bowl, scraping off the cutting board with the blade of her knife. "That's one reason Sam started hauling home vacation information, I think. She's been having all kinds of trouble with her arthritis, and she finds the winters really hard to handle. She never says anything, but we hardly ever see her down at the arena once the cold weather settles in.''

Chase adjusted the heat under the stew, then leaned against the counter and folded his arms, watching her shred more cabbage. "That's got to be hell on Sam, watching her lose ground like that," he said gruffly.

She looked at him, caught a little off guard by the gruffness in his voice, and she saw something in his expression that made her change the subject.

"Have you talked to Tanner lately?"

His expression of disquiet remained for a moment, then he gave a noncommittal shrug. "I talked to him a couple of weeks ago. Why?"

"Then you know that Kate's pregnant again."

He met her gaze and smiled. "Yeah. They told me when they were down in July." He shook his head, his expression softening again. "He sure got one hell of a family when he married Kate. You'd swear to God those two boys were his, and that Allison is going to break a few hearts down the road." He handed Devon the bottle of salad dressing she indicated, watching as she added it to the coleslaw. "It's hard to believe that she's coming on two already."

Devon screwed the top on the dressing, then glanced at his face, her insides taking a funny drop when she saw how deep in his thoughts he was. She considered asking him about his parents but decided against it. She'd heard that his father wasn't well, but she wasn't going to get into that after a two-year absence. She knew if he wanted to talk about it, he would have brought it up himself.

She licked a dollop of dressing off her finger, then stuck a spoon in the salad. "Let's eat."

Twilight settled into darkness, and they sat in the small eating nook, the sounds from outside drifting in through the open window above the sink. And Devon hoarded every minute. She told him all the news she could think of; he told her what he'd been up to, what he was doing with his life.

After they finished their supper, Devon cleaned up, and Chase went out to feed the horses and take them down to the creek to water them. She had the dishes washed and fresh coffee made by the time he returned. He closed the door behind him and took off his jacket, hanging it on the hook behind the door, then pulled off his boots in the bootjack. She was standing at the sink, drying the last of the cutlery and putting it in the drawer, and he came up behind her, reaching for two mugs from the cupboard above her head. Devon nearly dropped everything. He didn't touch her, but she could feel the heat from his body, and she braced herself and closed her eyes, sensations washing through her, making her body tighten and hum. He was too close. Too close. And it had been such a long, long time.

Chase poured two cups of coffee, then leaned against the stove, watching her.

Striving to keep her voice normal, she lifted her chin toward the compartment above the small fridge. "I think there's a bag of cookies up there if you want some."

He raised his mug and took a sip, then spoke, his voice husky. "Look at me, Slash."

His tone set off such a reaction in her that she could barely stay erect, and she closed her eyes again, trying to corral her feelings. She heard him set his mug down, then he held her jaw and turned her face toward him, his expression unsmiling, his eyes dark and intent. "Come on, Dev," he said, his voice whiskey soft. "Aren't you going to ask me how come I turned up in Casper today?"

Held transfixed by the intimacy of his touch, she stared at him, her insides balling up into a wad of dread. Dear God, what would she do if this was the final goodbye?

## Chapter 2

Her system overloaded, her pulse heavy, her heart laboring against it, Devon stared at him, sure that if he removed his hand she would crumple to the floor.

Smiling slightly, he stroked her lip again, his voice softer, huskier, more seductive. "Ask me, Slash."

Mesmerized by the look in his eyes, she somehow managed to swallow, her voice so uneven it didn't sound like her own. "How come you were in Casper?"

Chase slid his fingers along her neck, his touch making her shiver; then he rubbed his thumb against her frantically beating pulse point. "I ran into Martin Blocker in Billings," he said, his voice gruff and very low. "He'd seen Sam a couple of days ago, and he told me you were going to be there."

That admission did unbearable things to her heart, and she closed her eyes against the sudden fullness in her chest.

Chase shifted his hold, taking her face in his hands. "Look at me, babe," he whispered. "I need you to look at me."

Feeling as if she was drowning, she opened her eyes, drugged by sensation, paralyzed by his touch. He stared at her, his expression strained. Then he tipped her face up and slowly lowered his head, and Devon made a helpless sound and let her eyes drift shut. Exerting pressure on her jaw, he opened her mouth, then covered it in a wet, deep, searching kiss that drove every ounce of strength out of her body and made her knees buckle.

Gathering her up in a hard, enveloping embrace, he drew her between his thighs, working his mouth hungrily against hers, drawing her hips even closer. Devon couldn't breathe, she couldn't think; all she could do was hang on and ride out the thousand sensations exploding in her. Chase caught her by the hips and molded her flush against him, his mouth wide and hot as he ran his hand under her tank top and up her back. He emitted a low sound of approval when he encountered nothing but bare skin, and he slid his hand up her bare torso, cupping her breast, stroking her with his thumb.

His touch drove the breath right out of her, and she made another helpless sound against his mouth. Chase tightened his arm around her back and dragged his mouth away, his breathing labored. Her heart racing and her pulse thick and heavy, she turned her face against his neck, the warmth of his hand filling her with a heavy weakness.

"God, baby, but you feel so good," he whispered raggedly, dragging his fingers against her hardened nipple. Her whole body trembling, Devon turned her face tighter against the soft skin of his neck, hanging on to him with a frantic strength, the feel of him against her totally disabling her.

Dragging his hand free of her tank top, he slid it under her hair to cup the back of her neck, holding her even closer. "We don't have much room to move in here," he whispered unevenly, his touch meant to comfort as he stroked her skin. He took a deep breath, rubbing his hand up her neck, then spoke again, a hint of amusement in his voice. "And somehow we've got to make it from here to the bunk."

Not sure she was going to be able to stand on her own, Devon loosened her grip, but Chase didn't let go of her. Turning with her, he reached out and turned off the overhead light. Holding her head against him, he backed her over to the trailer overhang. And to the big double bed.

He caught her hair in a thick rope and smoothed it down the middle of her back, then tightened his arms around her, tucking his face against hers. "You're going to have to let go, Slash," he whispered gruffly. "I've got to get a package out of my jacket."

Devon would rather have cut off both her arms than let him go right then—and she knew what he was going to get out of his jacket. She didn't think she could bear having anything between them tonight, not even that. She tightened her hold. "You don't need it," she whispered unevenly. "Not tonight."

Chase went very still, then he shuddered and crushed her against him, roughly turning his face against her neck. "Are you sure?"

She caught the back of his head and tightened her hold, realizing for the first time that her face was wet. Swallowing hard, she caressed his scalp. "Yes," she whispered unsteadily. "I'm sure."

His only response was a long, heavy stroke across her hips; then he slid both hands up her rib cage and under her top. Drawing a deep, unsteady breath, he eased away from her and spoke, his voice very gruff. "Lift your arms."

Unable to step away from his body, Devon did as he instructed, her breath jamming in her chest as he stripped the garment from her. His breathing ragged, he yanked his shirt free of his jeans, and Devon weakly rested her head against his jaw, her whole body starting to unravel as he groped for the snaps on his sleeves.

The instant he was free of his shirt, he roughly whispered her name and hauled her flush against him, and Devon lost a whole piece of reality when he rubbed his chest against her naked breasts. Catching a handful of hair, he twisted her head back, covering her mouth with a kiss that was meant to incite, to ignite, to devastate, and Devon made a low sound. Adjusting the fit of his mouth against hers, he absorbed the sound, running his hands up her rib cage, rolling her hardened nipples with his thumbs.

Devon couldn't stand it. Fighting for every breath against the frenzy inside her, she drank in the moistness of his mouth, drawing his tongue deeper and deeper, and he rolled her nipples again as a frenzy of need seized her. Sobbing against his mouth, she fumbled to release the heavy buckle on his belt, then ran her fingertips up the thick, hard ridge under his zipper and molded her hand against it. Chase grabbed her wrist and yanked her hand away, making a hoarse sound deep in his throat. Dragging her arms around his neck, he tempered the kiss; then, inhaling raggedly, he eased away from her and undid the front of his jeans. His breathing harsh and labored, he rested his forehead against her, as if collecting some control; then he undid her jeans and slid his hands under her panties. His hands splayed wide on her hips, he slowly, slowly shoved everything down, his mouth grazing her collarbone, the tip of one breast, her midriff.

Tipping her head back, Devon clutched his shoulders, her knees giving way when he dragged his hot, wet mouth across her belly. Straightening, he caught her in his arms and dumped her into the bunk, and before she had time to react, he had yanked off his jeans and hoisted himself in beside her. Drawing air through clenched teeth, he dragged her against him, and Devon's senses went into overload when his body connected with hers, the feel of him thick and hard and fully aroused at the juncture of her thighs driving the breath from her. Grasping the back of her head, he covered her mouth with another blistering kiss, his fingers tangling in her hair, his heart hammering against her. Tightening his hold on her head, he wedged his knee between her legs, then pressed her onto her back, and Devon fought for breath as he settled heavily between her thighs. The feel of him. Oh,

God, the feel of him—it was too much. And it wasn't nearly enough.

Drawing up her knees, she tried to slip her hand between them, wanting him inside her, but Chase grabbed her wrist, forcing her arm against the bed. "No, baby," he ground out hoarsely. "Not yet. God, I need to hold you for a while first." His hand still cradling her head, he held her against him, his whole body trembling, and Devon closed her eyes and held on to him, aware of the tears slipping down her temples into her hair.

Chase held her immobile beneath him, his face buried in the tumble of her hair, then finally he took an unsteady breath and raised his head, brushing his mouth against hers with agonizing slowness. Devon tried to move beneath him, to bring his head down to increase the pressure of his mouth, but he resisted. His mouth barely touching hers, he ran his tongue along her bottom lip. "God, but you taste so good— so damned good."

Devon lifted her head, needing more from him, and he supported her as he deepened the kiss, then slowly, so slowly, flexed his hips against hers, aligning the thick, hard ridge of his arousal against her pelvis, and Devon sobbed against his mouth, thrusting her hips up to increase the pressure.

He stroked her cheek with the heel of his hand, his fingers deep in her hair, tasting her, savoring the moistness of her mouth. "Easy, babe," he whispered gruffly. "Easy. Just enjoy it." He made another foray into her mouth, his touch moist and tormenting. "We've got all night."

Feeling as if she was drowning in the thick, pulsating sensations, Devon shuddered and turned her face against him as he worked his way down her neck, his touch turning her boneless. Sinking into the sensation, sinking into the unbelievable pleasure.

He took his time, savoring her neck, the hollow behind her ear, the sensitive part under her jaw, then he returned to her mouth, kissing her with a thoroughness that went on and on and on. Dragging his mouth away, he shuddered and turned his head against hers, the muscles in his back bunching as he flexed his hips against her one more time.

It was too much. Devon cried out his name and arched against him, her body tightening, tightening as she clutched at his back and lifted her hips. Chase thrust his arm under her hips and shifted; then, with an agonized groan, he thrust into her, burying himself in her swollen, wet heat. His whole body went rigid, and he roughly adjusted his hold; then, gathering his strength, he thrust into her again and again. Devon came apart in his arms, the tightness converging into one throbbing center, and on one deep, urgent thrust, that center exploded, and convulsions ripped through her, making her arch and cry out. Clutching her head against him, Chase locked his arm around her hips, thrusting again and again; then he made a ragged sound and shuddered violently in her arms, his release as cataclysmic as hers.

Devon hung on to him and turned her face against his neck, the emotional aftermath as wrenching as the release—she felt raw and was weeping and in a million pieces. As if it took the last bit of energy he had, Chase adjusted his hold, his hand splayed wide at the back of her head, holding her with such absolute tenderness that it made her throat close up all over again. He could turn her inside out, and God, how she loved him.

He held her for a long, long time, until his breathing leveled out and she stopped shaking, until the aftermath softened into something less intense.

Cradling her head against him, he dragged his arm out from under her and reached up, fumbling for the light. He finally located the switch and turned it on, the small wall-mounted light filling the space with a muted amber glow. Bracing his weight on his forearms, he cupped her face, wiping away the traces of tears with his thumbs. Then, with a heavy sigh, he lowered his head and gave her the sweetest, softest kiss. Releasing another sigh, he lifted his head and gazed down at her, a glint of intimate amusement lightening his eyes. "You do pack one hell of a punch, Slash."

Her throat still unbearably tight, she looked at him, trying to blink away the tears. Swallowing against the clog of emotion, she smoothed her hand up his long, muscled back. "I thought we agreed that you weren't going to call me that anymore."

He smiled into her eyes, caressing her cheekbone with his thumb. "I said I'd think about it. I never said I'd do it."

"I was sixteen years old. I think we could give it a rest."

He chuckled and leaned down and gave her a quick kiss. "Hell, it's not every day that a woman gets you out of your jeans with a buck knife."

"Your leg was broken in two places, Chase," she reminded him.

He grinned. "That always struck me as a weak-kneed excuse. Considering where we were headed and what we had planned."

She gave him a chastising look. "What *you* had planned. You lived by your hormones, McCall, and you know it."

A smile still in his eyes, he trailed his thumb against her upper lip. "If you'd been toad-ugly, it would have helped."

She laughed and gave him a quick squeeze. "Toad-ugly. Don't you think you're carrying this good-old-boy thing a little too far?"

"Nah."

He shifted his hips, and Devon gripped him as her expression altered. "Don't go," she whispered, her voice suddenly uneven.

His expression turning serious, he lowered his head and brushed a light kiss against her mouth. "I'm not moving, babe," he whispered huskily. "I'll stay right here as long as you want me to."

She thought about forever. Instead she smoothed her hands up his back and murmured against his mouth, "Do you think you could manage a week?"

Chase chuckled and moved inside her, as he moistened her bottom lip. "I can give it my best shot."

She sighed and moved beneath him, caught in the same old feeling he always, always aroused in her. Like she was sinking into something sweet and warm.

Chase awoke very early the next morning to the gray half-light before dawn, attuned to the familiar weight in his arms before he even opened his eyes. Gently catching her by the back of her head, he carefully repositioned her weight on his shoulder, flexing his fingers to work out the pins and needles, then slipped his arm around her hips. Gathering the thick silk of her hair into one heavy cord, he smoothed it down her skin, the yard-long strands clinging to his hands, as he pressed a kiss against the top of her head. Her hair was something else. In a braid it was as thick as his wrist and dead straight, and so black it looked blue under some lights. But it felt like silk and it glimmered like satin, and he sometimes teased her that she used the same show shine on it that she used on the horses. When he'd first known her, it had reached past her waist, but now it fell midway down her back.

Chase smiled. That was the first fight they'd ever had— the row they'd had over her hair. She'd been maybe fourteen, and he'd wanted her to go out to the gun range his old man had set up on the Bar M for target practice. She'd said she couldn't go because she was going to get her hair cut. He'd yelled at her, saying there was no damned way he was letting Essie Malone loose on her hair with a pair of scissors—hell, she would come out looking like a boy. Devon said she was getting darned tired of dragging all that hair around, and she was going to get it hacked off. After arguing back and forth for twenty minutes, they finally argued themselves into a compromise. He had braided her hair into one long, thick braid and cut it off at her shoulder blades. Then he'd gone with her to Essie's salon and watched as the hairdresser straightened out his mess. Chase grinned, slowly running his hand over the thick, silky mass. He still had that braid somewhere—he'd come across it not long ago.

Shifting his head, he looked at her, lifting a stray strand that clung to her cheek. She wasn't really beautiful, but there was something exotic and unique about her that made men look. But part of that, he suspected, was the way she carried herself, the way she moved. She was tall, a touch over five foot nine, with small breasts and a long, slender body—and legs that went on for ever and ever. But it was how she moved, with the long-legged stride of a runway model, yet with the grace and power of an athlete. He'd spent more time than he could count just watching her walk. He didn't know how others saw her, but frankly, he thought she was damned near perfect.

"If you think I'm moving, you're in for a big surprise, Slick."

He grinned, getting a charge out of how she'd caught him unawares again. He didn't know how she did it—waking up without a hint of warning. He gave her a little squeeze. "That's pretty cute, Manyfeathers, waking up without waking up."

Her eyes still closed, she smiled against him. "It's an old Indian trick."

Amusement flickered through him, and he stroked her hip. He'd bought that line a couple of times when they first started hanging around together, then he found out that the only time she'd spent on a reservation was driving through one. He'd thrown her in the dugout behind the barn when he found out she'd been putting him on. She'd been laughing so hard she hadn't been able to put up much of a fight. Of course, she'd pulled him in with her.

Still smiling, he ran his hand down the full length of her hair. "What time is it?"

She never moved a muscle. "Ten to six."

He grinned again. He was just testing. Actually, he never could quite buy it, but she had this internal clock that was accurate, plus or minus ten minutes. He always figured she would have been one hell of a medicine woman in another place, another time. He gave her hip a little pinch. "Is that an old Indian trick, too?"

He felt her smile again. "Don't start, McCall. Or I'll shove you on the floor."

He wasn't too worried. She'd always been slow to get moving. In fact, he liked her best in the mornings—slow-moving, a little lazy, sexy as hell. Then something always happened around nine-thirty or ten. It was as if her metabolism kicked in, and she never ran out of juice—she just kept going and going until she crashed about six or seven. But he wasn't going to start anything here, either. If she did decide to dump him on the floor, he would have one hell of a fight on his hands—and he could think of better things to do. Another smile softened his expression. He didn't know how many times they'd made love last night, but it didn't matter. It would never be enough. Shifting slightly, he drew her leg completely over his; then he began softly stroking her breast.

She smacked his hand away. "Cut it out, McCall. It's six in the morning."

His amusement intensified, and he trailed his fingers down the side of her breast. "Just ignore me."

"Yeah. Right." With a resigned sigh, she raised herself up on one elbow and shook her hair back, then looked at him, her eyes all smoky from sleep. "I have no taste, do you know that?" she said, her voice husky and sexy as hell. "You always look like something out of a spaghetti Western in the morning." She ran her thumbnail over the heavy stubble along his jaw. "All you need is a serape and a cheroot clenched in your teeth."

He gave her a lazy grin, slowly running his hand up the back of her thigh, liking the way her black, shiny hair fell around her shoulders, liking the way her eyes got all soft and inviting. "What's the matter, Slash? You want me to park my shooting iron at the door?"

She gave him an amused half grin. "God, but you are vain."

Experiencing a thickness in his chest, Chase lifted a swath of her hair. Maybe if he didn't *like* her so damned much, maybe he could let it go. But she made him laugh, and she would do anything he asked of her—except marry him. Disconnecting from that thought, he caressed the swell of her breast with the backs of his fingers. Trying to stay away from all the danger zones, he kept it light. "Why don't you come up here and say that?"

Her eyes got dark, the pulse point in her neck beating, and she gave him a smile that he felt all the way down to his toes. With the sensuousness of a cat, she slithered on top of him, her hair spilling around them as she straddled his hips, then slowly—so slowly—took him into her, her gaze riveted on his, and Chase clenched his jaw, the pleasure so intense it made his whole body respond. Once he was fully inside her, she settled her weight on him, then softly, so softly, she cupped his face in her hands and leaned over and kissed him, her mouth moist and pliant and unbelievably gentle.

When she finally eased away, he slid his hand up to the back of her head and pulled her against him, releasing a very shaky sigh. "I need to hold you, Dev," he whispered unevenly. "God, but I've missed holding you like this." And he had. Sex with her always felt like the first time; it was the best—the absolute best. But this was what filled up the holes inside him, being deep inside her and holding her like this, feeling as if they had become part of one another. And she understood how much he needed that. There was one time, after Gran died, when she had held him all night like this, and he'd never forgotten it. And he never would. He could not have felt closer to another human being than he'd felt with her that night. Or now.

Pulling her hair out of the way, he kissed the base of her neck, then cradled her tightly against him, letting the sensations wash through his whole body. It didn't get any bet-

ter than this. It couldn't. Closing his eyes against the sudden
thickness in his throat, he turned his face against her neck
and tightened his arms around her. He would take all of this
he could get.

He knew when she'd drifted back to sleep. A small smile
surfaced, and he managed to snag the sheet and pull it over
her, tucking it around her shoulders. Closing his eyes, he
listened to the sounds from outside, drawing in the soul-
deep calm she always brought him.

The sky had started to lighten, and he could hear the
horses moving around, when she stirred and straightened
one leg alongside his. "You can start moving anytime,
McCall," she murmured against his neck, her voice thick
with sleep.

Chase tipped his head back and laughed, then hugged her
hard. "God, but you've got nerve. Falling asleep at a critical time."

He felt her smile against him. "You don't know the
meaning of critical." Sliding her hand up his neck, she
moistened his ear and contracted her muscles around him.

Chase nearly went into full cardiac arrest. Lord, but she
knew how to push all his buttons. Grasping her straightened leg, he pulled her knee up, then put considerable effort into a long, hot, wet kiss. "We'll see about critical," he
murmured against her mouth, then moved, slow and delib-
erate. And suddenly it didn't matter that their time was
running out.

The rays of the sun were cresting the horizon when reality checked in. He had a six-hour drive ahead of him, which
he was going to have to make in five. And he knew she
would have been on the road an hour ago if he hadn't been
there. Releasing a heavy sigh, he tucked her hair back and
nestled her closer, his expression sobering. Sometimes he
wondered why they kept doing this to each other—tearing
each other up with brief periods like this, then enduring
long, empty months of grinding loneliness. He sometimes

wondered what would have happened if he'd never gone back after she refused to come with him. Maybe they would both have gone on with their lives. He looked at her, experiencing a twist around his heart. And then again, maybe not.

"You're awfully quiet."

His expression solemn, he smoothed her hair into one long fall. "I've got to roll out of here in an hour or so." He didn't add that it ticked him off just thinking about it.

She shifted her head and brushed a kiss against his chest, then she spoke, her voice husky and textured like satin. "Are you heading back to Colorado?"

"Yeah." Yeah. He was heading south to Colorado. She was heading north to the Canadian border. And suddenly he wanted to put his fist through something.

He wasn't sure how he got out of there without losing his cool. He'd known when he went after her that this was only a temporary thing, that absolutely nothing would come of it. They were like two trains on different tracks—sometimes they got close enough to touch, but an actual connection was impossible. That was why he hadn't been back to Bolton for nearly two years—because the last time he was there, it took him six months to shake the anger that had simmered just below the surface. He didn't know why he'd been ready to bash heads last time, and he didn't know why he felt that way now. He just knew he had to get the hell out of there before he blew sky-high.

It wasn't until he pulled onto the highway and quit watching for her in the rearview mirror that he tried to pick his reaction apart, to sort it out. Part of it—the surface level of anger—was left over from his last battle with his old man. A battle fought over his association with Tanner—and the fact that his father had found out he'd been sleeping with Devon Manyfeathers for several months. It had been one hell of a row. And he'd sworn then that once he walked out the door, he would never go back. And he hadn't. But that was only part of the anger. And he knew better than to go picking through the rest of it. The last time he'd done that, he wasn't fit to be around for nearly a year.

Staring at the white lines flashing by, he braced his arm on the window and rested his hand across his mouth, deliberately shifting his line of thought.

He often wondered why he and Devon hooked up the way they had. She'd been a very mature eleven and he'd been fourteen, and even then, there had been a weird kind of recognition. Like they had known each other forever. Thinking about that first meeting, Chase smiled slightly. Hell, she had set him on his butt the first time he laid eyes on her.

It had been in the spring of the year when Devon and her mother turned up in Bolton and rented a shack down by the river. She'd been tall and quiet, with a sweetly maturing body and that long black hair, and she caught his attention right off, as if someone had settled a rope around him. Chase's smile deepened. Actually, if memory served him correctly, she had snared a lot of attention. And when a couple of his classmates started putting the moves on her, he'd appointed himself as her guardian. And he'd hammered a few faces over the years because a few jerks had tried coming on to her. Yeah, they had been buddies right from the beginning.

In fact, she'd been more than a buddy; she'd been one hell of a friend, and she'd pulled his ass out of a sling more than once. He could always count on her—it didn't matter if he needed a second when the teenagers of Bolton headed out to the stretch of highway they secretly used as a drag strip, or if it was riding point on a hell-for-leather horse drive, Devon never once let him down. She had run cover for him, she had bailed him out of a pile of trouble over the years, and she had been there for him when Gran died—and she had given him her virginity when she was sixteen years old. And other than Tanner, she had been the one constant in his life.

A recollection from that final blowout with his old man surfaced, and Chase experienced a flashback of the fury he had felt that night. It had been one ugly scene, with his mother in hysterics and his father in a rage. But in spite of his mother's last-ditch concessions and his father's threats, he had left anyway and gone to live at the Circle S with his bastard half brother.

His leaving had created one hell of a stir, but it was when his old man found out he was sleeping with Devon that the sauce really hit the fan. And that was when he realized just how much his parents disgusted him and that he hated what they stood for even more. But up to that point, it was just another big battle between him and his father. What finished it for good was when his old man had him arrested for auto theft. Since his truck had been registered in his father's name, the RCMP had no choice but to pick him up. Devon had been with him, and she was the one who went for Tanner, and it was Tanner who bailed him out of jail that time. But it was Bruce's lawyer who talked him out of pressing charges.

Chase knew he could never put up with his father's BS if he stuck around Bolton. And since he'd had a fair amount of success in the local rodeos, he had decided to go after his pro rodeo ticket. It took him a year, and the rest was history.

Almost history. Devon was still only sixteen when he went down the road, and she had just gone to live with Sam and Marj at Silver Springs. But when he left, he promised her he would be back for her.

And it was a promise he'd kept. During the first two years, when he was carving out a space for himself on the pro rodeo circuit, he'd spent as much time as he could at the Circle S, and as much of that time as he could with Devon. Life was good, he was racking up the points, and he thought he had the world by the tail. Or at least he did until Devon turned eighteen and graduated from high school, and he wanted to get married. It had never entered his head that she would say no. And he was such a self-centered, egotistical bastard that he wouldn't even listen to what she was trying to tell him, that she needed a place to belong. As far as he was concerned, it was all her fault, and when he hit the road that spring, he vowed he would never go back.

And he didn't. Not for four years. And he probably wouldn't have gone back then, except he'd grown up some, and he missed her like hell. He'd spent a fair amount of time with a half-breed bronc rider, and that had made him realize just what a lousy life she'd had as a kid. It finally sank in that she needed roots, respectable roots—and that the Silver Spring Training Stables had given her that. He'd felt pretty much like a first-class son of a bitch when he went to see her that time. He knew just how damned glad she was to see him; he could see it in her eyes. He beat himself up pretty good over that, over being so slow to figure things out and for hurting her the way he had. He had a buggered-up shoulder and one wrecked knee and was definitely out of commission as far as sitting a bronc was concerned, so he ended up spending a month with her in the little house provided for her at Silver Springs.

Chase rubbed his thumb against his bottom lip, smiling a little. It still amazed him when he thought back on it. That his staying hadn't been at all sexual. In fact, as weird as it seemed now, they had stayed clear of all that the whole time he was there. It was simply the resurrection of a very old and important friendship.

And he'd vowed he was going to keep it at that. Anything else was just too damned confusing. But then they'd had a chance meeting in the barns at a major rodeo and quarter horse show in Las Vegas. She had been on the verge of pneumonia and running a high fever. He'd arranged for a buddy to look after her horses, and he'd taken her to a hotel and put her to bed. Only somehow or other, he'd ended up in bed with her, in spite of his good intentions. It was a night he would be a long time forgetting. It had been one hell of a homecoming.

But that night had effectively screwed up the easygoing friendship they had reestablished the year before—and now he didn't know what they had. Whatever it was, she was in deep under his skin. There were more times than he wanted to count when he got drunk enough that he broke down and phoned her, needing to hear the sound of her voice like he needed his next breath. And all he knew for sure was that he went through a meaner-than-hell period every time he left her. But he knew why he went through that ugly period every time he walked out of her life. He had never quite forgiven her for saying no years before, and he had no doubt he would get the exact same answer now. And there was no way he could ever go back to Bolton. There was nothing left for him there, and he had no intention of getting suckered into taking over the McCall ranch. He would shoot himself first.

And besides, he liked what he was doing—heading down the road, hitting all the rodeos, running the business. It was a damned successful business that he and Ernie had built, and it was getting bigger every year.

Yeah, he liked his wandering ways, and he would be the first to admit that he had the road in his blood. But he had Devon Manyfeathers in his blood even worse, and knowing that she was on the road behind him, heading in the opposite direction, left a hole in his gut that a tank could drive through. Anger started to build in him, and he welcomed it. Nurtured it. Wanted it.

But then he remembered all the feelings he'd been hit with when she told him not to bother with any protection. He'd garnered a hell of a reputation years ago, and it had tended to stick with him. Granted, that kind of Russian roulette had never been his style, but she didn't know that. Yet in spite of all the water that had gone under the bridge between them, she still had that basic trust in him. Maybe that was one reason he'd never gone without protection with any other woman—because he wanted to make damned sure he would never bring anything back to her. Maybe that was the reason. Maybe not. But one thing he knew, she was the only one he'd ever got completely naked with, and when he slipped inside her with no barriers between them, like he had last night, there was no purer sensation, nothing that could ever equal it. And he could feel her around him now, the heavy pull of her spasms as—

Chase swore and slammed his elbow hard against the door, using the numbing pain to block out the memory of those heavy, thick and darkly erotic sensations, using anger as a mental block. He would have saved himself one hell of a pile of aggravation if he'd just stuck with the bottle of Jack Daniel's and the dingy motel room. Now he was going to have to go looking for a damned good fight.

*Chapter 3*

*February*
*Bolton, Alberta*

The fresh fall of snow covered the landscape, the stalks of dead range grass perforating the blanket of whiteness like golden quills. Hoarfrost glistened and sparkled in the bright sunlight, the long, thick crystals coating the bare branches of the shrubs and trees and sparkling like tinsel on the wire fences. The valley, bounded by the steep-cut banks of the Highwood River on one side and the razor-backed ridges of the Porcupine Hills on the other, opened up to a spectacular view of the Rocky Mountains to the west. Gray and imposing, their rugged peaks and crevices capped with snow, the jagged granite sentinels pierced the bright blue sky, the coniferous forests huddling around their bases like thick skirts.

Silver Valley was probably one of the prettiest places on earth, as far as Chase was concerned. And he'd been to a few. It was west of Bolton, where the rolling grassland was carved by deep gullies and dotted with copses of evergreens and aspen. It was so damned beautiful, and with the hoarfrost and fresh snow it looked like a Christmas card. He took a deep breath and felt something in his gut let go.

The hundred-percent UV screen in his sunglasses did little to filter out the brightness of sunlight refracted from the hoarfrost crystals, and he squinted slightly as he reached for the thermal coffee mug on the dash. At least the roads were decent, in spite of the heavy frost. Hauling a horse trailer on icy roads wasn't his idea of a good time, especially when some of the horses weren't his.

The road made a sweeping curve over a rise, and before him lay a piece of flat land, the cut banks along the southern boundary giving it a plateau effect. Beyond the trees, ranch buildings came into view, and sunlight glinted off a huge corrugated steel arena. His expression sobering, Chase braced his elbow on the window ledge and absently rubbed his thumb against his mouth, thinking about the last time he'd been here.

Nearing the approach to the long lane, he signaled for a left turn and slowed to a crawl, checking the side mirror as the big six-horse trailer tracked into the turn, the whole outfit rocking as it slid into a rut; he could feel the horses in the back shift. He kept his speed to a crawl as he drove across the cattle guard, and he checked the side-view mirror again. Once clear, he accelerated slightly, the bright sunlight bouncing off the snow and making the silver lettering on the midnight blue sign shimmer.

His mood reflective, he absently rubbed his thumb across his mouth again, his gut tightening. He wasn't exactly sure what he was doing here. Granted, he'd brought up three horses that Tanner had purchased when he was in Denver six weeks ago—but that didn't explain why he'd brought three of his own, as well. Nor did he know why he'd had Tanner make the arrangements for his animals instead of calling Sam himself. And he didn't know why his gut was suddenly in knots, or why he felt as if he was a hair away from disaster. All he knew was that for the last four and a half months, he'd had an itch that just wouldn't go away. Every time he went to sleep, he saw Devon the way she'd looked that last morning in Wyoming, when he rolled out of her life one more time. He knew he'd hurt her, but he hadn't known what to do about it then, and he sure as hell didn't know what to do about it now.

But in spite of knowing all that, he'd still cleared the deck so he could spend at least a couple of weeks here. He allowed himself a wry grin. And he also knew that if he didn't lay his eyes on her pretty damned quick, he was going to break out in a cold sweat.

He parked the rig in front of the big metal arena, then tossed his sunglasses on the dash. Settling his hat on his head, he grabbed his fleece-lined vest and got out of the truck, shrugging into the vest after he slammed the door. Two border collies came around the back of the truck, and he reached down and scratched their necks, grinning when one crouched at his feet, obviously hoping for a little action.

He straightened, sliding his hands into the pockets of the vest, looking around for changes. Various outbuildings and a long, low barn were situated a hundred yards below the arena, the space in between blocked into paddocks. Beyond that was the big house where Sam and Marj lived, along with more paddocks and pastureland. The little cedar house where Devon lived was north of the arena, tucked in a natural stand of spruce and aspen. Nothing much had changed, except that the trees were bigger and some of the corral fencing was new. Thinking about how some things remain the same, he headed for the side door into the arena.

Once inside, he had to wait for his eyes to adjust to the dim interior, the fiberglass panels along the arch of the roof letting in a faint tinted light. Only the center row of mercury vapor lights high above the arena area was on, and Chase grinned. Knowing Sam, he was surprised they were on at all.

Box stalls had been built all along one side of the structure, with a concrete alleyway between them and the actual arena. His hands in his pockets, he sauntered down the shed row, watching the two riders who were working a small herd of cows inside the four-foot-high cambered plank wall. Realizing he wasn't all that visible in the dim light, he rested his arms on the arena wall and watched a buckskin gelding perform, the horse's movements quick, sharp and highly tuned as he prevented the wheeling, running steer from returning to the herd. A good cutting horse was poetry in action as far as Chase was concerned, with the horse and rider as synchronized as man and animal could ever get. The horse's athletic ability had to be top caliber for it to work, and the animal had to have cow sense. When it really came together, it was show-stopping. And it made his pulse speed up every time he watched Devon put a horse through its paces.

But it wasn't just the highly trained, athletic ability of the horse that he appreciated. It was the woman's stillness, her grace, her oneness with her mount that made his pulse hit overdrive. She was something to see on a horse, especially one working like this one was. It was almost as though she were an extension of the gelding, her hands motionless, the hard, fast, twisting action of the horse barely shifting her in her seat. The lady could stick to a horse like lint, that was for damned sure. He allowed himself a small smile. And she looked mighty fine while she was doing it. He could see why she'd built the reputation she had over the past few years.

She worked the horse another fifteen minutes, then dismounted, handing the reins to another young woman, then taking the reins of the horse the other rider had been warming up. She was just about to mount when Chase stepped out of the shadows and started toward her.

He knew the instant she saw him. She froze, a whole host of expressions crossing her face, but when he saw her close her eyes and drag in a deep breath, he realized she'd never expected to see him there. What he wanted to do was vault the wall, grab her and give her a damned good shake, but instead he kept his hands in his pockets and gave her a warped grin. He could see her pull herself together; it took some effort, but she gave him a lopsided smile. "Well, look what slid into town. What happened, Slick? Did you just make a wrong turn, or are you here on purpose?"

It was all he could do to keep his hands in his pockets, but he knew that there would be at least two or three stable hands drifting around, and for what he had in mind, he didn't want an audience. He held her gaze and grinned at her. "Watch it, Manyfeathers. I've got six horses out there that are going to pay your wages for the next month. So I'd keep a civil tongue in my head if I were you."

Her smile became more real. "I'm always civil, McCall."

Resting his forearms on top of the wall, he stared at her. She had on blue jeans and tan suede shotgun chaps, and probably had long johns under that. He could see at least the tip of her white insulating underwear, two insulating mountain sweaters—one red, one purple—and a fleece-lined stone-washed jean jacket. Her deerskin gloves were darkened with age and use, and she had her hair stuffed under a navy blue corduroy ball cap with the Blue Jays logo on it. She had sawdust in her hair and a big smudge of dirt on her cheek, and by rights she should have looked like a bag lady. But not Devon. She looked like she had just walked out of some fashion magazine. He remembered how she was always cold in the mornings. And those long legs in tight chaps were enough to make a man forget his good intentions about keeping his hands to himself.

He raised his gaze and found her watching him give her the once-over, a look of mild rebuke in her eyes.

He gave her a lopsided grin and spoke, keeping his voice low. "Hell, Slash. You can't blame a man for looking."

She shook her head, a glimmer of dry amusement appearing. "You'd better take a deep breath, McCall. I think your brain took a trip south."

His grin deepened, and he decided it would be a good idea if he changed the subject. "So what do you want me to do with all this horseflesh? Unload it in your kitchen?"

She called to a young man, who came out of one of the box stalls, then gave him instructions for the horses before glancing at Chase as she swung into the saddle. "If you feel like doing a little turn back when you get them unloaded, come on back. I'll be working cutters all afternoon."

Holding her gaze, Chase nodded, something in her face registering with a cold twist. He saw the smile, but he also saw that she was trying very hard not to let him see how shaken she was by his arrival. Realizing that he hadn't done her any favors by showing up here, he gave her a terse nod, then closed down his expression. Giving him one last uncertain glance, she reined the horse around and headed toward the herd. Clenching his teeth in self-disgust, Chase turned. Just what in hell was he trying to prove, anyway? That he could still hurt her? That he was never really going to forgive her for a decision she'd made when she was eighteen years old? Or was he just trying to prove what a real bastard he was? He should never have looked her up in Wyoming, and he should never have come here. Sometime he was going to have to quit turning up in her life like a bad case of flu. Ignoring the rider moving into the herd, he headed toward the door, swearing to God he wasn't going to yank her around ever again.

He helped Luke, the kid she had given the orders to, get his stock settled in. He turned them out in one of the paddocks so they could get rid of the kinks from a long trailer haul, then he found Sam and spent an hour shooting the breeze with him. During the walk from the arena to the lower barn, he'd made up his mind that he was going to back off and quit crowding her. Maybe it was time to let the dust finally settle.

Determined to give her some space and hoping he had his head together enough to handle it, he returned to the arena when Sam left for town, deciding he would take her up on her offer of a little riding. It was the kind of thing they would have done years ago—before they'd screwed up their friendship.

As soon as she saw him, she got off the horse she was working, handing the reins over to Luke as she gave him a few instructions. She had taken off her coat, and she had arena dust all down one side. Chase grinned at her. "What happened to you? Some old bronc dump you?"

She gave him a sharp, censuring look as she came through the gate. "Some old bronc? It was that little bay filly you brought up—took real exception to the new blanket we tried to put on her." She pulled off her gloves and motioned to a box stall farther down. "Come here. I want to show you something."

He followed her into the dusky box stall, pulling the half door shut behind him. Talking softly to the little filly, she ran her hand down the animal's rump, then crouched. "Look here."

He crouched beside her as Devon indicated a nasty swelling on the horse's stifle. "It looks like she got kicked, but it's really hot. Like there's some fluid building up in the muscle. We could try hosing it down, but I think we should call the vet."

Chase frowned, shaking his head. "I'll be damned. I never noticed it when I loaded her, but that doesn't mean anything. It wouldn't be that easy to spot if you weren't looking for it. Or unless you were trying to get a blanket on her." He glanced at her. "Yeah. By all means, call the vet."

Devon rose, stroking the horse's back, something almost wary in her movements.

Giving her a long, assessing look, Chase stood up, noticing that she was looking everywhere but at him, and he experienced a hefty shot of guilty conscience. Determined to get their friendship on track, he caught her by the back of the neck and gave her a friendly little shake. "Hell, Manyfeathers. You mean you got taken down by *this* little filly? She hasn't got an ounce of mean in her."

Expecting some sort of smart comeback, Chase was caught completely off guard when Devon rested her arm on the horse's withers and covered her eyes with one hand. It was only then that he saw how badly her hand was shaking.

Calling himself every name in the book, he stared at the ceiling, trying to ignore the tight feeling in his chest. Why in hell had he come here? He heard her take a ragged breath—a breath that sounded too much like a sob for him to ignore, and with his resolve evaporating like smoke, he caught her wrist and turned her into his arms. Stripping the Blue Jays ball cap off her head and tossing it in the corner, he gathered her up in a fierce embrace. "Ah, Dev," he whispered gruffly. "Don't, darlin'. I should have known better than to come here."

Drawing a tremulous breath, she slid her arms under his open jacket and around his back. "Don't get a big head, McCall," she whispered, her face wet against his neck, her voice breaking. "It was your *horse* that tried to run me over."

Tucking her head tighter against him, he savored the silky disorder of her hair, a flicker of amusement surfacing. "I see. The famous horse trainer is all upset because one little filly dumped her." Sweeping her hair back, he cupped the side of her face and brushed a light kiss against her cheek. "Tell you what—just to even things up, I'll take her out and shoot her."

He got an unsteady laugh, and he hugged her tighter. Devon's voice was a little stronger when she responded. "That's right, McCall. Take it to the extreme."

He waited until he felt her begin to relax; then he eased his hold and lifted her face so he could see her eyes, his expression sobering. "Now that we've settled that," he said, his voice gentle, "why don't you tell me what this is really all about?"

Her black lashes matted, her mouth not quite steady, she looked at him, her eyes so dilated there was hardly any color. She stared at him a moment, then spoke, her voice husky. "Are you leaving right away?"

He debated about lying to her, but he couldn't quite do that to Devon. In spite of all that had happened between them, and even knowing that nothing could ever come of this, he gave her a small smile. "No. I was going to stick around for a while."

"For how long?"

"Two or three weeks."

Closing her eyes, she rested her forehead against his jaw, and he could feel her start to tremble all over again. "Where are you staying?"

*Ah, hell,* he thought. Catching a handful of hair, he tugged her head back, his expression dead sober as he looked square into her eyes. "Where do you want me to stay?"

He knew that was going to be hard for her to answer. Not because she would evade the truth, but because Devon had spent most of her life believing she didn't deserve anything. She didn't know how to ask for something she wanted. And it was at a time like this, when he put her on the spot, that her uncertainty showed.

She held his gaze for a moment, then wiped a smudge off his face, her voice unsteady. "I have space for a roommate, if you want."

Realizing that she was really struggling, he pulled her into a tight embrace and rested his head against hers. Not sure what they were getting themselves into, or how they would come out of it, he let his breath go. "Yeah," he answered, his voice rough. "I want."

He felt her catch an uneven breath, and he tightened his hold, experiencing a sudden thickness in his chest. Waiting for the contraction to ease, he slid his hand under her hair, molding the collar of her sweater around her neck, then spoke, allowing a trace of amusement into his voice. "We'd better back out of here, Slash. As I recall, the last time we got caught in a box stall, I ended up unloading about three hundred bales of hay for Sam."

She gave an unsteady laugh and stuck her hands in the back pockets of his jeans. "Caution from Chase McCall? I don't believe it."

He grinned and pulled her closer. This didn't feel a whole hell of a lot like caution.

They didn't finish chores until after five. It was starting to get dark when they walked up to Devon's house, the evening sky shot with shades of pinks and grays and blues, the snow-covered landscape tinged with pink from the setting sun. The snow squeaked beneath their feet, and their breath rose in white vapor, the cold air sharp and invigorating. This had always been Chase's favorite time of day, that last hour of daylight before it got dark, and he draped his arm around Devon's shoulders, their strides synchronized. That was another thing he liked about her—the way their strides matched. And he liked her silences. He could remember times when they were kids, when they wouldn't speak to one another for hours. Holding her against him, he opened the back door, kicking the snow off his boots before he entered. He could tell she was tired. Without saying anything, he took her coat when she peeled it off, then hung it and his own on the hooks along one wall of the big back hall.

She kicked off the hiking boots she'd put on to do evening chores and silently climbed the three stairs leading to the kitchen. Using the bootjack, he peeled off his own boots, then followed her in, knowing exactly where she was headed.

She'd stripped off her two sweaters and was already sprawled facedown on the sofa in the living room. She looked like a rag doll. He stood at the archway rolling up his sleeves, smiling at her predictability. She was like a slug first thing in the morning, and she had a power crash every night when she came in. Finished with his sleeves, he folded his arms and checked out the living room. He'd always liked this little house. It was all cedar, inside and out, and had a very basic design—a decent-size kitchen, the living room, two bedrooms and a bath. That was it. But it always seemed so snug, somehow, especially with a fire in the fireplace. And the view was without price. The house was set at an angle, and the front room faced southwest, with a view of the mountains that was phenomenal.

He assessed the changes since his last visit. She'd bought all new furniture since he'd been there. But then, that had been a couple of years ago. He eyed the black leather sofas. Thank God she hadn't gone for any of that awful flowered crap he hated.

The bedrooms and bathroom were directly behind the kitchen and living room, and he went down the stubby hallway and into the bathroom. When he came out, he checked out her bedroom. The old double bed was gone, replaced by a new queen-size. As unbelievable as it seemed now, though they hadn't made love when he'd spent that month with her years ago, they *had* slept together. He had kind of liked that old bed, in spite of the fact that it used to collapse without warning, most often in the middle of the night when they were both sound asleep. The first time it happened, he'd come off the floor like he'd been shot out of a rocket, and she'd ended up on her knees, tears in her eyes from laughing. He'd thought they would never get that wreck back together, but then, it wouldn't have taken them so long if she hadn't started laughing all over again every time she looked at him.

She was still flat on her face when he entered the living room, and he watched her for a minute. He wouldn't want to bet the farm on it, but he thought she was asleep, or damned close to it. He went out to the kitchen and opened the fridge, not quite sure what he would find. Devon's idea of cooking was to make a pot of stew, or cheese and macaroni, and she could build the best sandwiches he'd ever tasted. But as a cook, forget it. Still, she did keep a decent fridge. Which was good, because he'd gotten used to eating like a real person the last few years.

Whistling softly to himself, he assembled everything he needed for Mexican omelets and set to work. When supper was ready he carried two plates and two mugs of coffee into the living room and set them on the coffee table, then reached over and turned on a light.

She had her head turned toward him, her hair falling all over her face. He sat on the coffee table and watched her, his forearms across his thighs, his hands inches away from all that damned hair. There wasn't even a trace of motion in her closed eyes.

"I'm dreaming, aren't I?" she asked, not moving a muscle. "That's not real food I smell, is it?"

He grinned and hooked his thumb under the thick fan of her hair, collected it up and dragged it off her face. "You must be running on empty."

"Shut up, McCall." She opened her eyes and stared at him, then gave him a drowsy grin. "So, Betty Crocker, what have you whipped up for us tonight?"

He chuckled and stroked her cheek. "I've got a hot Mexican omelet that is guaranteed to rev your engines. I've got fried ham and hash browns. And I've got fresh brewed coffee."

Her eyes were still heavy with sleep. "Are you going to feed me?"

He grinned at her. "With your face stuck to the sofa? Of course I'm not going to feed you." He handed her a plate. "Up and at 'em, or I'll eat it myself."

With obvious reluctance, she slowly dragged herself into a sitting position, then yawned. She gave a little shiver, then looked from her plate to his. "How come yours is bigger than mine?"

He twisted around so she couldn't get at his food. "Because I made it, while you, on the other hand, did nothing."

"I bought the groceries."

He gave her a resigned sigh, took her plate and gave her his. "There. Satisfied?"

Her eyes alight, she leaned over and gave him a soft kiss. "Why don't we just dump everything back in the frying pan, and we'll both eat out of that?"

"What's your problem? Do you want both of them? Is that it?"

She leaned back and looked into his eyes, a sparkle of mischief in hers. "No. I just wanted to see if I could get you going."

Satisfied that she had, she settled on the sofa, drawing up her feet so she was sitting cross-legged; then she flipped her hair over her shoulder and dug into her supper. Sometimes he felt like strangling her. And sometimes he wanted to grab on to her and never let go. He managed a lopsided smile instead. "Did anyone ever tell you that you're a pain in the butt?"

She just smiled and chewed a mouthful of omelet, then closed her eyes in reverent appreciation. "Mmm, McCall. This is heaven."

He watched her savor her food for a moment, then started on his own, not sure if he was going to be able to swallow. He missed that—that little piece of cheekiness in her. She didn't do that anywhere else but here. It was as if this was the only place she felt secure enough to let that childlike part of herself out. It made him realize just what he'd asked of her so many years ago.

"What's the matter?" she asked softly.

Shoving aside the tight feeling in his chest, he looked up and gave her a half grin. "I was just thinking that this omelet could use a little more salsa."

"McCall," she said, her tone emphatic, "this omelet could strip varnish."

He held her gaze for a moment, then shook his head in amusement and went back to his meal. She was something else. They finished the rest of their supper in silence, and when he was done, Chase took his empty plate and hers to the kitchen and refilled their mugs. When he returned, he set both cups on the end table beside the sofa, then sat. Bracing his back against the arm, he propped his feet on the coffee table. He stretched his arm out toward her. "Come here," he said, his tone low and a little gruff. She hesitated a moment, then untangled her long legs and came toward him. He lifted her onto his lap, then slipped his arm around her and snuggled down with her. He handed her a mug of coffee, and she sighed and looked at him. "I should go have a shower."

He settled deeper in the sofa, taking her with him. He knew that he had maybe fifteen minutes before she would start to wake up, and he knew exactly what was going to happen when she did. And he wanted to just be able to hold her for a little while, to let that old familiar feeling fold in around them.

"Nah," he said softly, reaching back to hit the wall switch that would shut off the lamp. "Let's just sit here and watch the stars come out."

She didn't say anything. She twisted around and set her coffee on the end table, then snuggled down and slipped her arm around his back, resting her head on his shoulder. Her breath was warm against his neck, and he clenched his jaw and closed his eyes, the sensation setting off one hell of a ruckus inside him. Abruptly setting his coffee beside hers, he closed his eyes and tightened his arms around her. No matter where they were, holding her always felt like home.

It was later that night that Chase lay in bed with Devon asleep in his arms, listening to the coyotes howl in the distance. Her bedroom had one long window that went nearly to the floor, and he stared out it, the moonlight so bright that it made eerie shadows in the trees. He absently fondled her hair, thinking it would have been a perfect night for a ride—or for watching the stars. But they had made long, leisurely love instead, and then had watched the stars in the black night sky before she'd fallen asleep. He smiled. At least he assumed she was asleep. She hadn't said anything for the past half hour.

Shifting his head, he gazed at her, liking the feeling of her head on his shoulder, of her arm tucked around his chest. Her face was turned toward his, and he smoothed his thumb along her temple, then tucked his chin and brushed a kiss against her mouth, smiling a little when her lips parted.

He watched her a moment, then folded his arm under his head, lightly rubbing her arm, thinking about how things were with them. But he didn't kid himself, either. She had never once tracked him down, never once phoned him or sent him a letter, had never dropped in at his spread in Colorado. In fact, that had hurt pretty bad, when he found out from Tanner that she'd been down to a horse show and had been within sixty miles of his place and hadn't stopped. But then, she'd never gone with him, even for a couple of days, after he hit the rodeo circuit. It was as if she was scared of what would happen if she ever did.

He changed his mind. They weren't like two trains at all. It was as if they had suffered some kind of weird fate in the cosmos and they each had their own orbit—but every once in a while, those separate orbits would bring them together, and for a brief time they could share each other's light. Then they would both move on. He sometimes wondered what his life would have been like if she'd never moved to Bolton. The thought disturbed him more than he liked. Just knowing that she was living and breathing somewhere had kept him going more than once, and he could not imagine his life without her somewhere in it. He did not want to think what it would be like if he knew he would never see her again.

His throat got thick, and he closed his eyes, cradling her tighter against him. He wasn't going to think about it. Not tonight. Not while he had her safe in his arms.

## Chapter 4

Chase found out his first morning there that Sam and Devon had been running a man short since Christmas, and Devon didn't hesitate to put him to work. What she needed most, she told him, was an experienced rider who knew what he was doing with young horses. And they didn't come much more experienced than Chase. So he spent most of his time in the arena with her and Sam, working with the two- and three-year-olds that were there for training. By the fourth morning, he had muscles—damned sore muscles— that he hadn't even known existed before. Devon thought it was a big joke, especially when he groaned as he got out of bed, and all he got from her was a pat on the cheek and a "poor baby" in passing. It served him right. He'd been a cocky SOB, thinking he was in pretty good shape—but after five or six hours in the saddle three days in a row, he was bloody well finding out differently.

Chase glanced down the shed row, where four horses stood saddled. He and Devon had groomed and saddled all the horses they would be riding that morning, and then had tied some in their stalls until they were ready for them. Adjusting the saddle on the back of the horse he would be riding, he hooked the stirrup over the saddle horn, a small smile playing around the corner of his mouth. He was just damned glad she hadn't made him clean out stalls. Anne and Luke and old Jimmy, the barn boss, had been at it for two hours, and they still weren't done. He would have been flat on his face in no time. The smile deepened. No wonder Devon had the muscles she did—and could eat like a stevedore and never gain any weight. He tightened the cinch, then dropped the stirrup and ran his hand down the horse's neck. It was a three-year-old colt that had more cow sense than good manners, and the horse and Devon had got into a battle of wills two days earlier. It had been something to watch, and Chase was only beginning to realize just how good she was. All the clinics she was asked to give and the full stalls in the arena and lower barn attested to that. She had built something for herself here. Something she could take a whole lot of pride in—and her pride was something that had taken a hell of a battering when she'd been a kid, when her mother spent more time drunk than sober, and all they had to live on was welfare checks. Yeah, she'd built something worthwhile here, something that had given her back her pride.

"Just stalling, McCall, or are you going to need some help getting into the saddle this morning?"

Ducking under the horse's neck, he undid the halter shank, then looked up at her. She was on the other side of the boards, mounted on a pretty little Arab filly that the owners' daughter showed in a Western pleasure class. Now *that* horse had good manners. He rested his arm on the wall and grinned at her. "That kind of sass isn't going to get your supper cooked for you," he commented, not the least bit hesitant about stooping to blackmail. "So I'd be a tad less cocky if I were you."

Sam's voice interrupted from down the alleyway. "Now there's a case of the pot calling the kettle black. I sorta fig-

ured you wrote the book on cocky, son." They both turned
and watched the older man hurrying toward them in the
half-hitch gait of his. Chase knew that Sam had broken his
hip three or four years ago, and he could see from the way
the trainer walked that it was giving him considerable trouble this morning. Chase looked at him from beneath the
brim of his hat, allowing himself a wry grin. "Hell, Sam,
she doesn't need anyone to help her fight her battles for her
anymore. She does just fine on her own."

Sam chuckled and tipped his head in agreement. "Well,
you got me there, boy. Most of the time, she just ignores me
when I try to tell her anything."

He stopped directly in front of Chase, his worn mackinaw coat held together by mismatched buttons and one
safety pin, the fleece collar nearly worn bare. He was shorter
than Chase and only a little taller than Devon, with a barrel
chest and ruddy complexion. He'd been in the business a
long time—and, in Chase's opinion, was one of the best.

Sam pulled a red polka-dot hanky out of his back pocket
and wiped his red nose, then stuffed it away. He looked up
at Chase. "I was wondering if I could get you to give me a
hand."

Chase nodded. "Sure. Shoot."

"Well, we just had a load of bales roll in here a day early,
and Jimmy's gotta haul Jake Samson's horse back to him,
and I gotta take Marj to town for a doctor's appointment.
Devon's going to need Anne in here, so that just leaves
Luke, and we're probably looking at three hundred bales."

Chase stared at the older man, humor pulling at his
mouth, thinking that maybe, just maybe, he had this coming. He heard a muffled sound beside him and looked at
Devon, who had her hand plastered to her face, her shoulders shaking. He'd never known anyone who could laugh so
hard without making a sound. "You're going to pay for
this, Manyfeathers, and don't think you aren't." He
straightened and turned with the horse. "Just let me tie this
one back in his stall, and I'll be right out."

Sam nodded and fell into step with him, a twinkle appearing in his eyes. "As I recollect, it seems to me that you unloaded bales for me once before."

Chase cast Devon a damning look and cocked his finger at her. She blew him a kiss, then wiped the tears off her face. "Yeah," he responded dryly. "Three hundred."

By the time they finished unloading and stacking the bales, Chase found out exactly just how out of shape he was. It wasn't three hundred bales, it was only two hundred, but they had to weigh eighty pounds each, and Luke had the easy job of stacking them. Chase felt like he'd ripped his shoulders right out of their sockets. But other than that, he felt pretty damned good. Clean fresh air, the smell of clover and sweet hay, working up a good sweat, finding out Luke was okay. They covered the stack with a tarp, and Luke went to the lower barn to finish doing stalls, while Chase went into the arena. Devon was standing in the middle of the arena, watching Anne work a horse. Grinning, Chase approached the gate and took off his gloves, tucking them behind an electrical conduit. She turned to face him when he stepped through the gate, laughter suddenly sparkling in her eyes. Narrowing his eyes at her, he stripped off his jacket and dropped it, then sailed his hat toward the stalls. He shook out his arms, fixing her with a predatory smirk. "You're on your own, Manyfeathers. Sam's not here to pull your butt out of a sling, and you're going to pay for all that sass."

She started to laugh and back away. "Cut it out, Chase. You'll spook the horses."

"I'm not going to spook the horses," he said, coming after her. "But I am going to dump you in the sawdust bin, and I'm going to love every minute of it."

"No, you aren't."

He grinned and started to circle her. "Yeah, I am." He knew damn well how much she hated getting sawdust on her. They used a mix of it and shavings as bedding in the stalls, and as good as it was for that, it was a royal pain if you got it in your clothes and in your hair. Especially long, black hair.

He leered at her. "You're going down, Manyfeathers. And you're going down big time."

She put up her hand, trying a new tack. "Come on, Chase," she pleaded laughingly. "Don't. You know how I hate it."

"Down, lady. Down."

Realizing that he was backing her into a corner, she changed her tactics again and started taking off her own coat. Chase's grin broadened. He knew she wouldn't go down without a fight, and she would probably get in a few good licks in the process. But she was going headfirst into the sawdust or he was going to die trying. She balanced her weight like a wrestler and began circling away from him. He wanted to laugh. She knew damn well he wasn't going to fight fair. But then, she didn't fight fair, either. He expected her to go to the right. She went left and landed a solid tackle, dumping him in the mix of dirt and shavings on the arena floor. He managed to catch her leg, and he brought her down, then yanked off her hat. It took him a while, and she did put up one hell of a scrap, but after three or four aborted attempts, he finally managed to hoist her over his shoulder.

She was laughing and out of breath, but she was still trying to break loose as he carted her across the arena, his legs feeling a little shaky.

"Chase, damn it! Put me down." She tried to push away from his back, but he knew she couldn't see a thing for her hair. She tried to kick free, but he simply tightened his hold on her legs, giving her backside a smart smack. "Gotcha, Dev. Fair and square."

"Please, Chase," she pleaded, her voice breaking from laughter and exertion. "Come on—"

"Well, well, well, isn't this cozy? What happened, Chase? Did you forget the telephone number?"

Devon ceased her struggles, and Chase turned, steadying her as she slid down his chest. Securing her against him with an arm around her waist, he faced his brother, his expression hardening. He had hoped he could avoid the usual family scene. Exhaling a sigh of exasperation, he spoke, his voice devoid of any welcome. "Hello, Milt. Isn't this a little far out of your way for a social call?"

Milton McCall stared across the space at him, the collar of his pricey overcoat turned up, bitterness etched into his face. There had been bad blood between them for a long time—ever since Chase had taken off and left him to deal with the old man alone, ever since Milt had made the mistake of repeating his old man's words about Devon being a half-breed whore. Chase had slammed his brother's face into a wall for saying it, and he felt like slamming his face into a wall again now. He had nothing to say to his younger brother, but he knew Milt had a lot to say to him.

And in that respect, Chase couldn't really blame him. Milton had spent the last fifteen years busting a gut trying to get their old man's approval. It had almost become a disease with him, an obsession, and he resented Chase because he'd been able to say to hell with it and walk away. It was like when they were little and Milt would do everything to try to get some attention from his father—but their old man didn't operate that way. Bruce McCall didn't give his kids his attention. He withheld it. It was all part of maintaining control.

Milton stared at him, his face rigid, then swung his gaze to Devon. Chase felt her stiffen, and anger unfolded in him. He spoke, his tone abrupt. "What do you want, Milt?"

His brother turned his attention back to him, a look of distaste on his face. "Is there anywhere we can talk?"

Chase stared at him, the muscles in his face taut. He motioned to the door. "There are about two hundred acres outside that door. Take your pick." Turning so he blocked his brother's view of Devon, he dredged up a warped smile, then wiped a glob of sawdust off her cheek. "This shouldn't take long. We don't have a history of long, friendly conversations.''

She looked at him, worry darkening her eyes. ''Chase, don't—''

He gave her another warped smile and pressed his finger to her mouth. ''Shh. This is old garbage, darlin'. And we're going to have to deal with it sooner or later.''

She stared at him a moment, then finally managed a tight smile and nodded. Tipping her face up, he gave her a quick kiss, then turned and started across the arena toward his brother. He paused to sweep up his jacket, slapping it against his legs before putting it on. When he reached the gate, he pulled his gloves from behind the conduit, then silently took his hat when Milt handed it to him. Without glancing her way, he followed his brother outside into the bright cold sunlight.

Milt indicated the Mercedes parked in front of the arena. ''We may as well sit in there, where we'll be comfortable.''

Chase shoved his gloves in his pockets and looked at his brother. ''I'm not looking for comfort. I'm looking for short and to the point. So spit it out. You came out here for a reason, and it wasn't just to see if I was here or not.''

Milton turned to face him, a dull red climbing up his face. ''I think the least you could have done was let us know you were here.''

''So I've got bad manners. Sue me.''

Milton swore and turned away, then turned back. ''Okay. Forget consideration. Somewhere along the line, we have to decide what we're going to do about the ranch.''

Chase narrowed his eyes and stared at the horizon, trying to corral his anger. Damn it, when were they going to get the message? He shifted his head and looked at his brother, his expression fixed. ''I don't give a tinker's damn what happens to the ranch. I don't want it. I never did, and even if I did, you wouldn't get me on that place with a knife at my back. I'm not going to play Dad's damned games anymore.''

His brother took a step toward him, jabbing at him with his finger. "Well, you're going to have to play his games, because he has it in his head that you're going to come home and take it over. You're the eldest son. It's your responsibility."

Chase gave him a twisted smile. "You're forgetting something here, little bro. I'm not the eldest son. Tanner is. Now, if the old man wants to turn it over to him, that's just fine with me."

Milton clenched his fist, and Chase had no doubt his brother wanted to bury it in his face. "What is it with you and Eden? Both of you walk out of here as if it didn't matter a damn, as if you didn't have any responsibility to the family, and then, to make matters worse, you both align yourself with him!"

Choosing to ignore the reference to Tanner, Chase folded his arms, a small smile appearing. It did his heart good knowing that his sister had finally walked. Their old man had tried to run her life, as well. There had been a time when he'd thought she was going to knuckle under, but then she'd gone away to school, and Bruce had lost his influence over her, as well. Considering his brother, he made his voice a little less harsh when he spoke. "There you go. Why doesn't he turn the damned ranch over to Eden? She could run it as well as anyone."

A look of anger and frustration on his face, Milton shook his head and angrily stared off into space. Finally he looked at Chase, the resentment replaced by weariness. "Look. He hasn't been all that well this winter, and all he talks about is you coming back to take over. Couldn't you at least talk to him?"

"Not a chance. I can't talk to him, and you know it." He leveled his finger at his brother, his expression hardening. "And if you think he's ever going to give you any credit for handing your life over to him, you're in for one hell of a big surprise. He's never operated that way, and he never will. He doesn't want me running the Bar M. What he wants is me back under his thumb—where he can call all the shots. And like I said, I'm not playing his damned games anymore."

Milton's face reddened, the veins in his temples standing out. "That's an easy out, and you bloody well know it. You just don't want the responsibility!"

Anger building in him, Chase took a step toward his brother, his face rigid. "It's not the responsibility I don't want, Milt. It's his BS. Look at you. You don't want to run his damned ranch or manage his auction mart, and you can't convince me that you get off on his damned political connections. Yet Sam tells me there's a rumor going around that you're thinking about running in the next election. You aren't thinking about tackling something like that because you want it, you're doing it because that's what *he* wants." He paced across the path, then turned and jammed his hands in his pockets. "Look at yourself, Milt. For God's sake. Is this really what you want to be doing for the rest of your life? It had better be, because you can be damn sure nothing's going to change. You want to live your life in his back pocket, fine. You do it. But don't expect me to climb in there with you. I'm not going to be his toady for the rest of my life. I'd rather starve first."

Giving his brother one last furious look, Chase turned and started walking. Only he didn't turn to the arena. He headed for the lower barn instead. There was one rank, hardheaded stallion down there that needed a good hard workout in an open field—and he was going to give it to him.

Chase deliberately stayed away until he'd cooled down—until he could take a breath without wanting to lash out at something. This was one reason he'd stayed away for so many years. His old man—hell, his whole family—could still push him over the edge, and he didn't want to give them that kind of control ever again. And it had nothing to do with the kind of manipulating control his parents had over

Milt—it had to do with his own rage, and how his old man could provoke him into it. There had been too many times in the past when he'd lost it over something his old man had done or said—a couple of times when he might even have killed him if there hadn't been someone there to pull him off. And as long as his father could goad him into that kind of reaction, Chase didn't have control, and he knew it. And he would chop off his arm before he gave his father that kind of weapon.

By the time he got back to the ranch, he and the stud had pretty much come to terms with the issue of control. The bay was giving his head and taking commands with considerably more attention, and it almost made Chase smile the way he went into the barn without his usual ruckus. Maybe there was something to be said for hammering things out. It would be interesting to see how much of that lesson the stallion remembered tomorrow.

Dismounting in front of the empty stall, Chase flipped the reins over the rail. He stripped off the saddle and put it away, then led the horse into the big box stall and slid the bridle from his head, smoothing his hand down the animal's chest to make sure he was completely cooled down. Lifting the blanket off the half door, he put it on the bay, his expression turning thoughtful when he noticed the time. They would be starting chores in the arena in another half hour, but he wasn't going up to help. The last thing he needed right now was a bunch of people, especially one as chirpy as Anne. He would do the chores down here by himself instead.

The shadows were long and the clouds were tinged with gold when he finally went up to the house, the dogs trailing along behind him. Kicking the snow off his boots, he entered the back hall. Devon's coat and boots were there, and he could hear the shower running. His expression sober, he stripped off his outerwear, experiencing a twist of guilt for walking out on her the way he had. She had good reason to expect the worst when any of his family showed up, and she'd probably spent the afternoon wondering where he'd gone.

He washed in the kitchen sink, then started on supper. He had the steaks under the grill and potatoes frying and was in the living room checking out her CD collection when she finally came out of the bathroom. She had on a terry robe and a towel wrapped around her head, and he felt like an even bigger heel when he saw the relief in her eyes when she saw him.

Tying the belt on the robe, she stared at him, her gaze anxious. "Hi," she said softly, trying to smile. "I thought maybe I'd have to go looking for you."

He chose a CD and hit play, then went over to her, strains of muted flamenco guitar drifting out. Her collar was tucked inside her robe, and he straightened it, thinking just how many times she had gone looking for him when they'd been kids. She knew him better than anyone, knew how he felt about his old man. The collar straightened, he met her gaze, managing a small smile of his own. "And I thought I might have to go fishing for you. I thought you'd drowned in there."

"I took so long," she said, her tone pointed, "because I couldn't get the dirt from the arena out of my hair."

He gave her a warped grin. "Maybe next time you won't think two hundred bales are so funny."

She watched him, the anxiousness still in her eyes, and started to speak. He pressed his thumb against her mouth, then lifted her face and kissed her. "Supper's ready, Dev," he said quietly. "Let's leave it until after, all right?"

She nodded and met his gaze, then turned away. She came to the table in her housecoat and towel, and for some reason that made Chase feel a little less removed. But even so, he couldn't quite shake the introspective mood he'd been in all afternoon. They talked a little bit about the training program for a couple of the horses, but for the most part they ate in silence. As soon as he finished, he stacked his dishes in the sink and turned to leave the kitchen.

She looked at him, concern still darkening her eyes. Her voice was husky when she spoke. "Tanner called this afternoon. He wanted to know if you could make it over for supper tomorrow night. I told him I'd have you call him back."

Chase aligned two pot holders lying on the counter, then looked at her, his expression solemn. "Will you come with me?"

She stared at him for a moment, then nodded.

He knew he was leaving her hanging about what had happened that afternoon, but he didn't want to talk about it. At least, not yet. Knowing he was being unfair, he reached out and trailed his knuckles along her jaw. "I'm going to have a shower, okay?"

She nodded again, and he stared at her for a moment, then turned and left the room. He collected clean clothes, then headed into the bathroom. His mood somber, he undressed and tossed his clothes in the laundry hamper. He turned the water on full blast, then stepped in. He roughly soaped himself, then closed his eyes and let the water beat down on him, using the stinging spray to ease the tension left over from his brother's visit. If nothing else, today had reminded him why he'd based his operations in Colorado. It was as close as he could get to his old man without getting sucked in. Bracing both hands on the wall of the shower stall, he bent his head and made himself let go of the tension, focusing on the hammering spray and the heat. He had maybe three weeks here with Dev. Then he was going to have to go back. And he wasn't going to waste what little time he had with her on family crap. It hadn't been worth it eighteen years ago, and it sure in hell wasn't worth it now.

The hot water was starting to fade when he finally got out, and the room was full of steam. He made a cursory effort to dry himself, then pulled on a clean pair of jeans, not bothering to do up the snap. Avoiding his reflection in the fogged mirror, he reached for the can of shaving foam, his mood somber. He sometimes wondered if the BS was ever going to stop.

Devon was in the kitchen when he entered the living room, and she came to the doorway. "Finished?"

He nodded and draped the towel around his neck, then turned toward the sound system, absently rubbing a drop of water off his bare chest. He hit the replay control and set the liniment he was holding on the table, then used the end of the towel to dry his hair. He rolled his shoulder and smiled wryly, knowing he was going to wake up tomorrow and be forced to get acquainted with some more sore muscles. He heard Devon start the dishwasher; then the kitchen light went out, and he turned. She still had on her robe, but the towel around her hair was gone, and she had a thick-toothed comb in her hand.

He went to her and caught her wrist. "Come on," he said quietly.

Tossing a couple of cushions on the floor at his bare feet, he sat down on the sofa, then pulled her down in front of him. Settling her back between his thighs, he reached over and took the comb from her, then adjusted her head. Her hair was clean and shiny and slipped like strands of silk through his hands. It was so thick it was still damp, and he slowly eased out the tangles with his fingers. She drew up her knees and wrapped her arms around them, and he knew from the way she was sitting that she had her eyes closed. That was another thing he appreciated about her—she never pushed for explanations. She knew that he would talk to her as soon as he had things sorted out in his own head.

He worked out a thick tangle, then let her hair slide through his fingers. Finally he spoke, his voice husky. "Remember the time you shut the end of your braid in the truck door, and I tried to drive off?"

She gave a soft chuckle and tipped her head back, yielding to the tug of his fingers through her hair. "You mean the time you tried to scalp me?"

He ran his fingers up the back of her head, massaging her scalp. His voice was even huskier when he answered. "Scared the living hell out of me. I had the shakes for two weeks, thinking about what would have happened if I'd peeled out of there the way I usually did." He also remembered that was the first time he'd held her—really held her. Amusement tugged at his mouth. He could still remember how it had felt, having her plastered against him. He'd been sixteen and nothing but a walking hormone, and he'd thought he'd died and gone to heaven.

Her hair free of tangles, he started combing it, his mood softened by the memory. Hell, he would likely still be standing out in the middle of the street holding her if old Mrs. Brady hadn't come out on her front porch and taken a strip off him. Devon had been the best friend he ever had, and he didn't know what he would do if he ever lost that. His throat suddenly thick, he clenched his jaw and dragged the comb through the full length of her hair. He waited until the tightness eased, then spoke. "I'm sorry about today, Dev," he said, his voice gruff. "I shouldn't have taken off the way I did."

She shifted, hooking her arm around his upper leg, her touch reassuring as she caressed his calf. She didn't say anything; she didn't have to. He knew she understood, maybe even better than he did. Using both hands, he smoothed her hair into one thick fall. "Do you want me to braid it?"

Without speaking, she handed him a covered elastic. He took it and laid it on his thigh, then tipped her head back and began sectioning her hair, another flicker of humor working loose. "What's with the silent treatment? Or is that another one of your Indian tricks?"

She gave a soft, husky laugh. "What's the matter, Slick? Can't you handle a little silence?"

"I can handle it," he responded, his tone slightly amused. "It's my damn family I can't handle." His expression shutting down, he braided her hair in a five-strand weave he used in leather work, his thoughts turning inward. Every once in a while, he would catch himself thinking about what it would be like to move back here, but all it took was one confrontation like today's and he knew it would never work.

"Chase?"

He dragged his attention back, his mood grim. "What?"

"You're pulling my hair."

Exhaling sharply, he leaned over and tipped her head back, giving her a soft, upside-down kiss. "I'm sorry, babe," he whispered gruffly. "My mind took a hike." Feeling like a heel for a whole lot of reasons, he released her, his jaw set as he fixed the elastic around her braid. Who the hell knew? Maybe she wouldn't want him hanging around on a permanent basis.

The moment he let go, she turned, rising on her knees. Her expression solemn, she caught his face between her hands and stared at him, then she leaned into him and gave him a soft, comforting kiss. The feel of her hands against his face, the absolute comfort in her touch, made his throat cramp up, and he closed his eyes, experiencing such a surge of emotion that he was damned near upended by it. Opening his mouth against hers, he ran his hand up her back, urging her toward him. But she didn't yield. Instead she tightened her hold on his face and withdrew, then smoothed her hands down his shoulders and across his chest, her mouth moist and warm as she brushed her lips against one nipple. The jolt of sensation made him grit his teeth, and he sucked in his breath when she touched it with the tip of her tongue. Gripping her arm, he opened his eyes and looked down at her, his vision hazed with sensation as she continued with her slow, soft exploration.

Dragging her mouth lower, she slipped her fingers beneath his waistband and began easing down his zipper, her touch sending another jolt of sensation through him. Bracing himself for what was coming, he twisted his head to one side and straightened his hips to give her access, his face contorting in an agony of sensation, his whole body going rigid as she gently, slowly, softly freed him. Then she lowered her head, and he closed his eyes and ground his teeth together, her touch setting off a chain reaction that made him stiffen and groan. And with a blinding surge of sensation, he gave himself up to her moist, questing mouth. Nothing mattered. Nothing but her. Nothing but her.

# Chapter 5

His thumbs hooked in his belt, Chase sat slouched in the passenger seat, idly watching the thick, heavy snowflakes plaster themselves against the windshield, the intermittent swipe of the wipers clearing half circles of visibility.

He turned and looked at Devon, a flicker of amusement lifting the corner of his mouth as he watched her handle the high-powered truck. He'd always liked to watch her drive. She handled a vehicle with the kind of assurance and skill that most men couldn't match. He'd taught her the fine art of drag racing when she'd been fourteen years old, and he'd talked her into enrolling in a weekend training course at the speedway in Calgary the spring she turned seventeen. She had impressed the hell out of all of them, even a couple of professional drivers who'd been there. She had been as cool as ice and as quick as a cat, and he'd been so damned proud of her that he'd spent the whole weekend puffed up like a peacock. That had been the second year he'd been on the rodeo circuit.

Bracing his foot against the door ledge, he shifted his shoulders, then slid his hand down her thigh. She gave him a drilling look—the one she used when she was warning him to behave. He gave her leg a squeeze and grinned at her. "Do you want to pull over and check out this side of the truck?"

She shot him a slightly amused look. "No, I don't want to pull over. I told Kate we'd be there by six, and we're going to be there by six."

Resting his head against the back of the seat, he studied her profile. "So, have you seen this new niece of mine?"

She shook her head. "No. Tanner's brought the boys over for their riding lessons the last couple of weeks. He said that Kate didn't want to take the baby out when it was so cold and stormy."

His expression altering, Chase absently rubbed his thumb along her thigh as he stared out at the swirling snow. He finally spoke, his voice gruff. "I'm so damned glad that things worked out for him and Kate the way they did. He sure in hell deserved her, and those boys couldn't have found a better father if they'd special ordered him." He shook his head in amused disbelief. "Mark is so much like him you'd swear to God he was Tanner's kid, and everything Scotty says is peppered with 'my dad.' And I doubt if Tanner has ever raised his voice to either one of them."

Devon gave a soft laugh. "Well, little Allison isn't going to be quite so accommodating. He brought her with him the last time, and she was bound and determined she was going to climb the stairs to the loft. He told her no two or three times, but she just gave him that big smile and did it anyway. She's definitely not your run-of-the-mill two-year-old."

Chase watched the snowflakes splatter against the windshield, his expression thoughtful as he mulled over Devon's comments. He found her statement about a run-of-the-mill two-year-old oddly disturbing. Disquieted by his thoughts, he deliberately shifted his focus, watching the familiar landscape of Circle S land flash by. He'd spent a year on the ranch with Tanner. His hiring on at the Circle S had started out as a public act of defiance, to let everyone know exactly what he thought of his old man, but it had turned out to be one hell of a lot more than that. Tanner was eight years older, and Chase had looked up to him most of his life, but that had changed in the year he'd worked on the Circle S. They'd had a chance to become brothers, and Chase would always be grateful that Burt Shaw, Tanner's partner and originally the sole owner of the Circle S, had seen fit to take on another son of Bruce McCall's. That had been eighteen years ago, and Burt was now in his eighties and nearly crippled from a stroke, but he'd been more of a father to Chase in that one year than Bruce had been in the previous eighteen. He was family. And going to the Circle S was like going home.

"You got quiet all of a sudden."

He glanced at Devon and studied her profile, wondering what his old man thought when he met Devon the first time and realized she was part Indian. He wondered if he was human enough that it might have kicked off a few flashbacks about Tanner's mother. It had for his own mother, but who could tell with his old man? Rubbing his hand down her thigh, he spoke, his tone quiet. "I was just thinking about that year I spent out here. I sometimes wonder where I would have ended up if it hadn't been for Burt and Tanner."

She cast him a dry look, then turned her attention back to the road. "You need to ask?"

Amused by the dryness in her tone, he caught the inside of her thigh. "Don't be a wiseass, Manyfeathers. There's more than one road to redemption."

"Then I think you'd better get yourself a good map, McCall."

He grinned and ran his hand higher, deliberately provoking her. "Seems to me you're the one who's doing the driving here, Slash." She gave him a censuring glance, amusement lurking around her mouth; then she very deliberately removed his hand from her leg. "Yes, I am," she responded, her tone eloquent. "And don't you forget it."

Chase chuckled and caught her by the back of the neck, giving her a companionable squeeze. Lord, but she was a piece of work.

Supper at the McCall house wasn't even remotely similar to the formal dinners that Chase had had to suffer through as a kid. Mealtime at the Circle S was congenial, relaxed and sometimes as uncontrolled as a wild horse race, but above all else, it was first and foremost a family gathering—a large, noisy family gathering. Besides Tanner, Kate and their four kids, there was eighty-year-old Burt Shaw and his longtime sidekick and Circle S cook, Cyrus Brewster, who had been the foreman on the Bar M when Chase had been small. Including Chase and Devon, it came to ten, but no one seemed to notice. It frankly amused the hell out of Chase to watch Tanner deal with four kids, especially two-year-old Allison. She definitely had a mind of her own, and with her black curly hair, her daddy's big hazel eyes and a grin that could melt stone, she was something to be reckoned with. She and her father had a go-around over her vegetables. Tanner had given her a stern look, and Miss Allison had narrowed her eyes and stared right back, and Chase had nearly laughed. And he'd thought Devon was a piece of sass. There was a brief staring match; then Tanner had said her name in a tone that no man in his right mind would challenge, and Miss Allison gave her dad a disgruntled look, then dug in and ate every one of the offending vegetables.

Chase also noticed that his brother had considerably more laugh lines around his eyes than he used to have, and that realization gave him a constricted feeling in his chest. If anyone deserved some happiness, it was Tanner. His life had been pretty bleak until Kate and her two boys had shown up. But now all that had changed. Now his brother had a family, with two new daughters of his own. Yeah, Tanner's life had come up all aces. Chase grinned to himself. His brother also had a damned full house.

Kate had left the table partway through the meal to feed the baby, and Chase's attention shifted as she entered the kitchen carrying his new niece. Her eyes widening with alarm, Allison immediately scrambled from her high chair into her father's lap, taking his face between her pudgy hands. "Me, Daddy. Me."

His eyes twinkling, Tanner draped his arm around his small daughter and gazed into her worried little face. "Don't you want to hold Casey?"

Allison shook her head and tightened her hold on his face. "No Casey. Me, Daddy."

Kate rolled her eyes and met Tanner's gaze, exchanging an amused look with him. Shaking her head again, Kate shifted her attention and addressed her small daughter. "How about if you and Daddy take Casey so I can finish my supper? Then someone else can hold her."

Allison thought about that, then turned and settled herself in her father's lap and reached for the baby. "Okay."

Kate handed the baby to Tanner, and the newest McCall scrunched up her face and gave a big stretch, and Allison chuckled and patted her sister's tummy. Resting his arms on the table, Chase watched his brother and his two small daughters, a smile hovering around his mouth. Who would have thought it—Tanner McCall and a lap full of babies.

"Who wants dessert?"

Cyrus smoothed down his white drooping mustache and looked up at Kate, a twinkle gleaming in his wily old eyes. "Well, now, Miz Kate. That sounds jest fine. Especially if it's a wedge from one of them fine pies I saw coolin' on the counter when I came in."

Burt snorted and gave Cyrus a cranky look. "Don't think you're going to weasel more'n one piece outta her. You can make your own damn pies."

The twinkle in Cyrus's eyes intensified as he glanced at his old friend. "Now, Burt. No need to get your tail in twist. I can settle for one piece. I jest ain't said how big it's going to be."

Responding to a glance from his mother, Mark slid from his chair and removed the plate from in front of Burt, then helped the old man straighten the towel tucked in the front of his shirt. Leaning back in his chair and folding his arms, Chase watched the boy and the old man, watched Mark whisper something and Burt's sly wink. Chase had been around the Circle S enough to know that Burt and the boys were thicker than thieves. He also knew that Cyrus was inclined to egg the three of them on, then stand back and watch the fireworks. Chase suspected it was one big conspiracy. He also suspected that Tanner and Kate knew all about it. He wondered if Scotty and Mark knew how lucky they were.

The baby started to squirm in Tanner's arms, and he bent his head and murmured something to Allison. She turned and looked at Chase, her gaze steady and unblinking. Restraining a smile, he watched her size him up; then she gave a single nod and scrambled off her father's knee. She came around the table and pushed between Chase and Cyrus, slapping him on the thigh. "You. Unca Chase." She opened her eyes wide and lifted her arms to be picked up. Amused by her presumption, he slid his chair back and picked her up, setting her against his cocked knee. She folded her hands like an angel, batted her eyes and gifted him with a sweet, disarming smile.

Checking his amusement, he straightened the strap of her overalls. "So, princess. What's up?"

She gave him an eloquent shrug and turned her hands palms up. "Nuffin."

He wanted to laugh. "Nuffin, huh? What do you think of your new sister?"

She turned and pointed at the baby. "Casey."

Looping his hands around her chubby bottom, he rocked back in his chair. Her eyes widened, and a bright sparkle appeared. She leaned forward and pushed his chest, obviously wanting him to rock back farther. Chase grinned. The kid was going to be a daredevil, that was for damned sure. He rocked back farther, and Allison's eyes lit up like the Fourth of July.

Kate spoke from across the table. "For heaven's sake, don't encourage her, Chase. She's bad enough as it is."

He straightened his chair and gave his small niece a wink, and she grinned at him and tried to wink back. Chase chuckled. If this kid didn't give Tanner a few gray hairs, nothing would. The baby started fussing in earnest, and Tanner got up from the table and took her into the living room, Casey's tiny form snuggled up against his shoulder. Chase could hear Tanner talking to his small daughter as he walked her back and forth, her head against his shoulder as he rubbed her back. A funny sensation settled around Chase's heart, and he looked away, schooling his face into a blank expression. Yeah, Tanner's life had come up aces, all right. He had it all. But that wasn't what had given Chase a kick in the chest. It was the level of commitment he felt every time he came here. Tanner and Kate's commitment to each other, to their family, to their way of life. It was a commitment that would last a lifetime, and it left a big hole in the middle of his gut. A very big hole.

As soon as supper was over, Cyrus and Burt headed into the newly added family room to watch a hockey game, and Chase and Tanner went into the living room, taking the two little ones with them. Tanner continued to walk the floor with the baby, and Chase settled into one of the easy chairs with Allison, sinking down into a comfortable slouch as she plopped her picture books on his chest. The sounds from the kitchen followed them, and he caught himself listening for Devon's husky voice as she and Kate and the boys cleared away the meal. He wondered if she ever felt as if she was missing out on something.

Disconnecting from that thought, he rested his head against the chair back, and Allison snuggled down in the crook of his arm, then opened one book. She began pointing to pictures, and Chase realized he was supposed to identify whatever she was pointing at. Her wide-eyed persistence got a smile out of him, but he couldn't shake the disquieting feeling that had hit him with such a wallop. Funny how he was seeing things differently all of a sudden. Funny how damned much it hurt.

As if realizing that her uncle had zero attention span, Allison gave up on him and began softly jabbering at each of the pictures, and Chase slouched lower, rubbing his chin against her soft, dark curls. He wasn't sure how well he was doing with this uncle thing, but she seemed content to cuddle up with him, and he was at least keeping her out of action and corralled in one place—something that he suspected was no small feat.

Allison eventually got quiet and started making soft humming sounds and pulling at her eyelashes, and Chase shifted his arm, nudging her head against his shoulder. He flattened her curls, kind of liking the feel of her weight against him. Shifting the baby to the other shoulder, Tanner glanced at Allison, then gave him a warped grin. "I'll be damned. She's almost asleep, and it's only seven-thirty." He repositioned Casey's head, then looked at Chase, the glint in his eyes intensifying. "How would you like a job? The benefits are good, and the pay's not bad."

Chase managed a drowsy half smile. "I dunno. I think I'd be wise to stick with wrangling wild broncs."

The laugh lines around Tanner's eyes deepened. "You should know. Cyrus says she's exactly like you were at that age."

Chase shook his head and chuckled. "Nah. She's cuter and smells better than I did."

Devon came into the living room, a large wet spot on the front of her emerald green T-shirt. Chase didn't know why, but that wet spot did unnerving things to his insides. There was something so domestic about it, and for some reason it made him want things that were out of reach. Not wanting anyone to read his face, he tipped his head and glanced at his small niece, a smile appearing when he saw how hard she was fighting sleep.

Tanner's voice broke the quiet. "Devon, would you mind taking this one for a bit? I'd like to get small stuff upstairs to bed before she falls asleep. She gets really owly if we have to wake her to get her ready for bed."

Chase looked up, a funny sensation settling heavily in his stomach as he watched Tanner transfer his now-quiet daughter to Devon's outstretched hands. He tore his eyes away from her, his expression tightening as he slid his hand under Allison's bottom, then lifted her up so Tanner could take her. He watched his brother and his niece disappear up the stairs, then propped his feet on the footstool and folded his arms, his expression shuttered as he watched Devon with the tiny baby. Humming softly, she gently cradled the baby against her, her long slender fingers cupping the infant's dark head as she began pacing the floor with her. It was one of those moments—one of those unforgettable instances— that would stick in his memory for the rest of his life. The aching gentleness in Devon's expression, the helplessness of the tiny form snuggled protectively against her breast, the straight black hair poking through her splayed fingers. Black hair exactly like Devon's. So alike that the baby could be hers.

Tightening his jaw against the jolt of awareness, Chase dragged his eyes away, the sudden thickness in his chest crowding his breath. She looked so right holding that baby—as though it was as natural to her as breathing. She was thirty-three years old, and her biological clock was ticking. But in all the years he'd known her, he could not remember her ever making one reference to having kids of her own. He wondered if it was because of her poverty-stricken childhood. Or if it was because she had laid those hopes and dreams aside.

Resting his loosely linked hands across his chest, he shifted his gaze to her, the hollow sensation in his gut spreading when he saw her brush a kiss against the baby's temple, then smile softly and snuggle the tiny, black-haired head against her cheek. He felt as if he'd suddenly been blindsided, and he jerked his gaze away, a sudden rush of anger surging through him. He didn't have to wonder any longer. His answer was right there on her face. And he suddenly realized that in spite of all the things they had shared, complete honesty wasn't one of them. Thrusting himself out of the chair, he turned away from her and headed to the kitchen. Never, in all the years he'd known her, had he been as furious with her as he was right then.

By the time they left for home, Chase's anger had settled into a lump in the pit of his stomach, setting off one hell of a headache. He'd suffered from migraine headaches when he was a kid—blinding, mind-splitting headaches so bad that it felt as if his skull would explode if he so much as moved his head. He couldn't remember the last time he'd had one, but by the time they got to Devon's, he was cooking up a beauty. And by the time he got into the house, he knew he was going to be in worse shape if he didn't lie down soon. Fighting against the nausea boiling in his stomach, he stripped off his coat and boots, then went up the darkened stairs to the kitchen, praying to God she wouldn't turn on the light. She didn't.

The yard light down by the arena faintly illuminated the kitchen, and Chase headed straight for the living room. Gritting his teeth against the sickening jolt of pressure in his skull, he stretched out on his back on the living room floor, then rested his arms across his eyes. Remaining absolutely motionless, he waited for the nausea to ease, trying to release the grinding tension in his jaw. Years without one, and one run-in with Milt, one night at his brother's, one run-in with reality, and he felt as if someone was trying to drive a tank through his head—which put him right back where he'd been eighteen years ago. Sometimes he wondered if he would get so bent out of shape if he could just have one good knock-down-drag-out fight with his old man. That might do one hell of a lot to clear away the garbage that just kept sitting there festering.

There was a soundless movement beside him, and Devon very gently slid her hand under his head. "Here," she said softly. "Let's get a pillow under your neck." Carefully cradling his head against her thigh, she fixed the pillow, then gently lowered his head, making sure there was a secure roll under his neck. The excruciating pressure in his head eased, and he was finally able to unclench his teeth. Letting go of that grating, brittle tension left him feeling cold and shaky. As if tuned in to his every need, Devon drew a lightweight comforter over him, her touch infinitely gentle as she tucked the blanket around his shoulders. His throat closed up, and he had to shut his eyes against the sudden surge of emotion. He'd forgotten how many times she'd nursed him through one of these in the past.

She gently brushed his hair from his forehead, her voice husky with concern when she asked, "Would you like an ice pack?"

He opened his eyes and looked at her, her profile blurred in the semidarkness of the room. Warmed by the pressure of her thigh against his ribs, he caught her hand and pressed it against his chest. "No. This is good."

Devon laced her fingers through his, and Chase tightened his hold, then closed his eyes and began stroking her palm with his thumb. The anger he had experienced at Tanner's was gone, replaced by a haunting ache that sat squarely in the middle of his chest. He wondered how many more times their separate orbits would come into alignment before one of them got knocked off kilter. The heaviness in his chest expanded, and he clenched his jaw against it, then reached up and caught Devon by the back of the neck and pulled her down beside him. Her braid was like a rope of silk beneath his forearm as he cradled her head against his shoulder, then began stroking her upper arm. In spite of the shape he was in, he couldn't get the image of Devon holding that baby out of his mind. He wished like hell he could stop feeling as if they were living on borrowed time.

A nasty storm front blew in the following day, driving in gray skies, flurries and blowing snow and, by afternoon, near-blizzard conditions. The weather suited Chase's mood perfectly. His head felt as if he'd just come off a nine-day drunk, and his mood wasn't much better. In an effort to spare everyone, he spent most of the morning by himself in the lower barn, taking care of a bunch of small repairs that had piled up. He had just finished replacing all the belts on the oat crusher and was fixing to check out a gash on one stallion's hind leg when Sam came into the barn, the snow and cold swirling in around him as he came through the side door. He slammed the door behind him, then stomped the snow off his feet, his plaid wool hat yanked down on his head, the earflaps covering his ears. He looked cold and slightly harried. Pushing back his hat, he stripped off his gloves and wiped the end of his nose. "Damn, but it's cold out there. We're going to have to keep an eye on all the water troughs—make sure the heaters are all turned up, or we're going to have nothing but blocks of ice out there."

Securing the stallion to the heavy metal ring outside the stall, Chase acknowledged Sam's comment with a single nod, then crouched down and started unwinding the wrap on the horse's back leg. Sam watched him for a moment, then went into the tack room, and Chase heard him rummaging around. A few moments later he came out with two snaffle bits and a set of reins in his hand. He closed the door behind him, pulling out a blue handkerchief and wiping his nose again as he watched Chase inspect the gash. "How's it looking?"

Chase tested the area around the wound for swelling, then reached for the jar of ointment and unscrewed the lid. "Looks good. You should be able to start working him tomorrow." Chase applied the ointment to a dressing and stretched it over the nearly healed gash, then began wrap-

ping the leg. Sam continued to watch him, and Chase
glanced up at the older man, his attention sharpening when
he saw the somber, preoccupied expression on the trainer's
face. Chase stared at him for a moment, then went back to
wrapping the stud's leg. "Something on your mind, Sam?"
he said quietly.

Sam shot him a startled look, then frowned and glanced
down, his expression solemn as he fingered the reins. "I
dunno. I've been pondering things lately. Maybe it's time I
hung up my chaps and got out of this business."

Chase glanced at him, recognizing the somberness in the
older man. He finished the final wrap and pressed the Vel-
cro grip into place. "Marj having a bad day?" he asked, his
tone deliberately offhand.

Sam exhaled heavily and gave a terse nod. "Yeah. She
could hardly make it out of bed this morning, and I could
tell her hands are paining her plenty." He shook his head,
then stuck the reins and bits in the pocket of his mackinaw.

Chase studied him for a moment, then replaced the lid on
the jar of ointment and set it in the veterinary kit. "How
was she on the cruise?"

Sam heaved another heavy sigh. "She was good. Real
good. She really enjoyed herself."

Picking up the kit, Chase stood up, keeping his tone even
when he responded. "You could always spend the worst of
the winters down south."

Sam shook his head and heaved another sigh. "You can't
run a business like this part-time, boy. And Devon can't
keep it going on her own." He rubbed the back of his hand,
then took his gloves out of his pocket and pulled them on.
He slapped the stallion on the rump, then turned toward the
door. "Come on up to the arena for a cup of coffee when
you get him squared away. No sense in working yourself
blind on a day like today."

His gaze somber, Chase rested the first aid kit against his
thigh and stared after Sam as he went out into the blizzard,
a whirl of snow and bitter cold sweeping in before he closed

the door. Chase stood there for a moment; then he turned and swore, slamming the kit onto the lid of the feed bin. Damn it, why in hell did life have to be so bloody complicated?

A feeling of being crowded, of being boxed in, moved in on Chase, and he didn't like it one bit. And the storm only made it worse. By late afternoon he was beginning to feel like a trapped cat, and he finally headed down to Devon's basement, assembled her set of weights and put himself through a workout that had sweat pouring off him. But it didn't release the pressure in his chest. Ten years ago—maybe even five—he would have gone looking for a fight, but he'd finally got it through his head that that was a less than honorable way of dumping his ugly attitude off on some poor unsuspecting bastard. And it didn't solve a damned thing. He liked to think he'd grown up some since those barroom brawling days—but the prowly way he was feeling, he wasn't so sure.

He had supper almost ready when Devon came in, and he knew by the uncertain expression in her eyes that she had picked up on his edginess. He turned the heat down under the spaghetti sauce and dumped the spaghetti into the boiling water, then leaned against the counter and folded his arms, watching her as she pulled her thermal sweaters over her head. The hair that had worked loose from her braid fanned out in a corona of static electricity, and he suddenly remembered what it felt like to have the silky weight slithering across his chest and down his thighs. He clenched his jaw against the heated rush of physical response, knowing that after the way he'd been acting, she deserved more than a quick fix.

He wasn't sure *how* to fix things, but he knew it wasn't going to be by asking her about her day. He watched her as she untangled her arms and tossed the sweaters on a chair, aware that she was wary about meeting his gaze. If he'd learned one thing in the past few years, it was the value of getting right down to the bottom line. And by the stark look in her eyes, he knew this was not the time to waltz. He spoke, his voice quiet. "I'm not going to cut out without telling you."

Her gaze swung sharply to meet his, the fluorescent lights in the kitchen washing the color out of her face. She stared at him for a moment, then looked away, suddenly intent on separating her sweaters and folding them.

Hooking his thumbs in the front pockets of his jeans, Chase watched her, his expression solemn. He didn't say anything for a moment; then he spoke again, his tone slightly husky. "Come here, Dev."

He saw her swallow hard, then she met his gaze, her eyes dark and haunted. He shifted, widening his stance, then reached out his hand. "Come on," he urged gruffly.

She set the sweaters aside, and drawing a deep, unsteady breath, she crossed the room, her body stiff with tension when she slipped her arms around his waist and turned her face against his neck. Drawing her hips against his, Chase exhaled heavily and drew her fully against him, resting his jaw against her head as he began slowly massaging the small of her back. Devon tightened her arms around him, and Chase could detect a light quivering in her, as though she had been braced for pain that hadn't materialized. Shifting his hold, he cradled her head firmly against him and brushed a gentling kiss against her temple, his expression disquieted. He didn't know what in hell was going to happen to them. And if he'd realized anything during the past few days, it was that they couldn't go on like this. He'd been jerking her around for too many years, and time was running out for her. They were either going to have to get it together, or he was going to have to cut her loose once and for all. And maybe he was just being a selfish bastard—maybe he'd dug in his heels so deep over his old man, he couldn't see the forest for the trees.

He gave her a reassuring hug and pressed his mouth against her hair. Shifting his hold, he turned slightly, keeping her against him as he checked to make sure the spaghetti wasn't one big lump of starch, then rubbed her shoulders. "Supper's going to be ready pretty quick here," he said gruffly. "Did you want to have a shower first?"

Devon exhaled heavily and reluctantly eased back in his embrace. Avoiding his gaze, she nodded. "Yes, I think I'd better."

Hooking his knuckles under her chin, Chase lifted her face and made her look at him, the heavy feeling in his gut intensifying when he saw the bleak expression in her eyes. He held her gaze for a moment, then tightened his hold on her jaw and brushed a soft kiss against her mouth. "Life's a bitch, isn't it?" he whispered huskily.

Devon gave a shaky laugh and looked up at him, the look in her eyes not quite so stark. "You just figured that out, did you?"

He held her gaze, the corner of his mouth lifting a little. "I never said I was quick."

She wiped his bottom lip with her thumb, the humor in her eyes lightening her expression. "Hang in there, Slick," she answered, her tone amused. "You've just found the road to enlightenment."

He grinned and gave her another quick kiss, then turned her around and gave her a push toward the bathroom. "You've got ten minutes, Manyfeathers. Then this kitchen is shutting down."

Leaning against the counter, he watched her cross the kitchen, appreciating the rear view, appreciating the lazy, loose-hipped way she moved. He wondered what she would look like pregnant. Caught square in the gut by that random thought, he clenched his jaw and turned back to the stove, wishing he could punch somebody. He knew what was building inside him, and he didn't like it one damned bit. It was like recognizing the shadow of something hovering motionless in very deep water, something still and silent and dangerous. He had enough of his old man in him to recognize it for what it was, and if he ever let it get away from him, he knew it was the kind of thing that could get ugly and mean. It was a kind of cold, quiet rage that could eat away at a man until it corroded a hole in him.

That shadow was there in him, shimmering deep below the surface, and he could still clearly remember the first time he had experienced that ugly little clutch in his gut. It had been right after he and his old man tangled the final time. And he had felt the first stirrings of it three times after that. Once when Devon turned him down flat when he asked her to marry him; once two years ago, when she had slipped away in the middle of the night without so much as a good-bye; and he had felt it again last night, hovering deep beneath the surface, when he watched Devon cuddle his tiny niece with all that untapped maternal warmth.

Folding his arms, he stared at the floor, his expression taut. That piece of his old man had disgusted him like nothing else had, and Chase had vowed a long time ago that he would never let it get away from him. And after that time with his old man, he'd sworn he would walk away and never come back before he would expose Devon to that side of himself.

Dragging his hand across his face, Chase straightened and turned to the pots bubbling on the stove. Hell, maybe it was just the storm that was eating away at him, making him edgy. He'd never liked having to stay inside for any length of time, and with the exceptions of a couple of trips to the barn and back, he'd been locked up inside all day. And twenty-four hours was just about his limit.

They ended up eating supper in the living room, sitting on the floor in front of the fire. Devon was quiet, almost as if she were walking on eggs. He knew she was doing her damnedest to accommodate him, and that made him feel like some kind of heel. She'd always been like that, he realized. Even when she was just a kid, she would bend over backward to keep the peace, to try to accommodate his bad moods. Devon had never been big on confrontations, and given the choice, he knew she would still skirt one if at all possible. It was a quirk of hers that he had abused in his youth, before he really understood why she was like that. He knew it was all tied up with vulnerability and self-doubt and a nearly disabling insecurity that came from the kind of humiliation that left deep and indelible scars. She would fight with him over some things; his flirting with danger, the way he used to act up in school or his chippy attitude. But she would never confront him where she risked any kind of emotional exposure, where her personal insecurity was on the line. It was just too big a risk. He understood it, but he didn't like it. He didn't want that kind of power. And he didn't like what it stood for.

"Would you like some more?"

Shifting his gaze from the dancing flames, he glanced at his plate, then at Devon. He shook his head. "No, I'm fine."

She stood up and reached for his empty plate, and Chase saw the misery in her eyes. He reached out and caught her wrist, taking her plate from her and setting it on top of his. Pushing the plates aside, he exerted a steady pressure on her arm. "Come here."

She gave him a forced smile and tried to pull free. "I'll go get us some coffee first."

He tightened his hold. "I don't want coffee. I want you to sit."

Her smile was a little more genuine the second time around. "What you want isn't always what you get, Slick."

He knew what she was doing, and he wanted to shake her. He didn't argue with her. He simply caught her behind the knees and gave her arm a sharp tug, tumbling her across him. Before she had time to get untangled, he shifted her legs, then locked her up in a tight embrace. "No coffee. No back talk," he said, his voice suddenly gruff. "Just shut up and let me hold you."

She remained rigid in his arms for an instant, then the tension went out of her, and she slid one arm around his back and pressed her face against his neck. As soon as she wrapped both arms around him, he let go of her. She hadn't shampooed her hair when she'd had her shower, and he stripped the elastic off her braid, then started loosening her hair. But the lingering scent of herbal shampoo wafted free as he slipped his fingers through the silky strands, and Chase leaned his head against the sofa and closed his eyes, a sudden tightness in his chest. It wasn't just the weather that was closing in on him. It was hard, cold reality. After last night, he knew they could not keep marking time like this. Something was going to have to give. He hoped like hell it wouldn't be his heart.

## Chapter 6

The storm had blown itself out by the following morning. Chase wished he could say the same for the grim feelings he had taken to bed the previous night. He had awakened in the middle of the night, his heart pounding, his chest tight as a drum, and for one awful moment he hadn't known where he was. Then Devon had stirred beside him, and the relief had been so intense he'd had to grit his teeth against it.

He had left her bed shortly after that and spent the rest of the night staring out the living room window, watching the storm settle into a still, winter night, the snow blown smooth and unblemished, the emptiness making him keenly aware of his aloneness.

He had been unable to face her in the morning. He just felt too raw, too naked, to deal with anyone, and especially Devon. He needed some hard labor to get rid of the edginess, and he needed some time alone to get his head together; then maybe he would be fit to be around, but sure in hell not before.

He had fed all the horses and completely stripped two stalls before Jimmy, Luke and Anne showed up, and he had two horses worked and was just warming up a third when Devon entered the arena. He could tell by the way Luke and Anne exchanged looks that they weren't sure what was going on, and he could also tell by the way Sam checked the clock over the tack room door that Devon was rarely, if ever, late. Chase experienced a flicker of amusement. She looked like hell. She still had the imprint of the quilt on her face, her hair looked as if it had been braided by a blind drunk, and her top sweater was on inside out.

Reining his mount around, he rode across the arena, giving a quiet whoa when he reached the wall. Letting the reins go slack, he leaned forward and rested his arms on the saddle horn, taunting her with a grin. "Nice of you to join us, Manyfeathers. We were beginning to wonder if you'd run off with the feed salesman."

She gave him a foul look and opened the gate. "Can it, Slick. I'm in no mood for this."

He watched her come toward him, his grin deepening. "Hey, how were we to know? You could have the hots for the feed salesman for all we know."

She glared at him. "I know it's a strain, McCall, but try to elevate your mind above your belt buckle." She reached him and pulled the reins out of his hand. "I'll take her."

Amused by her irritability, Chase continued to watch her, wanting to pick on her in the worst way. "Do you always wear your clothes inside out, or is this a new fashion statement?"

"It's a fashion statement," she snapped. She collected the reins, then gave him another annoyed look. "Now get off."

He continued to watch her, wondering how high she was going to blow. He gave her an insolent grin. "No."

Her gaze swiveled to his face, then her eyes narrowed. She didn't say anything; she just glared at him. Without a shred of warning, she grabbed his leg and shoved his foot out of the stirrup, then hooked her shoulder under his leg and gave him the old heave-ho. He was lying flat on his back on the arena floor before he ever knew what hit him. Turning the horse out of the way, she bent over him, giving him a sweet, malicious smile. "Don't mess with me today, Slick. I'm in a bad mood."

Chase thought about upending her and carting her off to the sawdust bin, but there was something so cute and smug about the look on her face that he decided to give her this one. He stacked his hands under his head and gave her a lazy grin, his voice deliberately husky when he said, "Hey, baby. Nice legs."

She gave him another vile look, then collected the reins and swung into the saddle. Turning the horse so it was parallel to his body, she looked down at him. "You'd better pick yourself up, McCall, or you're going to get trampled. Jimmy is bringing in the herd."

"This is a hell of a way to treat a volunteer, you know."

He caught the glint of amusement in her eyes, and the corner of her mouth lifted, but she managed to keep from smiling. "That's just how I like you, Slick," she said, her voice as smooth as satin. "Spread out and flat on your back."

Her response tickled him no end, and he grinned at her, liking her sass. "Why, Miss Manyfeathers," he said, his tone a lazy drawl, "I do believe you're a loose woman."

She cocked one eyebrow, giving him a dry look. "I don't know, McCall. I'm up here, and you're down there. Maybe you need to redefine 'loose.'"

He was still lying there flat on his back, grinning like a fool and watching her ride away, when Sam slammed in through the side door, his earflaps at right angles to his head. Shivering from the cold, he stopped at the open gate and stared at him. "What are you doing on the ground, boy? Are you grabbing a nap, or did some little filly dump you?"

Deciding he was getting cold lying on the ground, Chase got up and dusted the mixture of loam and shavings off his jeans, then picked up his hat and dusted it off against his leg. He settled it low on his head, then gave the older man a rueful look. "Hell, Sam. No wonder you can't get good help out here. Your head trainer just dumped me out of the saddle."

Sam chuckled and shook his head. "Not that you had it coming or anything." He looked across the arena to where Devon was working with the filly, then he glanced at Chase, his expression turning sober. He spoke, his voice modulated so Devon wouldn't hear. "Your mama's outside, Chase. I tried to get her to wait at the house with Marj, but she has her mind set on speaking to you pronto." He glanced at Devon again, then turned to Chase. "I figured it was best if she didn't talk to you in here."

Chase stared at the trainer, then he swore and looked away. First Milt, and now his mother. When in hell were they going to get the message? He swept his gloves up from the arena floor and smacked them against his leg, anger flaring in him. He wanted to talk to his mother about as much as he wanted all his teeth knocked out. He jammed the gloves in the back pocket of his jeans, then met the older man's gaze. "Thanks for stalling her, Sam. She has no business coming out here."

Sam tipped his head, his expression thoughtful. "She's your mama, boy. That counts for something."

Chase could have debated the point, but he let it go. What he had to say to his mother was best said in private.

He found her standing by her car, staring off across the pasture, her fur hat covering her hair, the collar of her mink coat pulled up around her ears. The beautiful, elegant Ellie McCall had changed very little in the years since he'd seen her last, still beautiful and aloof, still elegant, still someone he had no desire to talk to. He flipped up his collar, then slid his hands into the back pockets of his jeans. "You wanted to talk to me?"

She turned, her mouth compressing into a hard line. She had aged well. Her hair had turned a perfect silver, and the lines in her face did not detract from her stately good looks. Yeah, she had aged well, but she hadn't aged softly.

Sliding her hands into the pockets of her full-length coat, she met his gaze dead on. "Is there some place where we can talk?"

He gave her an insolent smile. "We're fresh out of drawing rooms, Ma. But there's a nice barn down the hill."

Ellie McCall gave him an annoyed look, her mouth compressing even more. Chase knew she hated it when he called her "Ma." She had lectured him long and hard about it when he was a kid, saying that it was a crass and common form of address. He hadn't been able to see what the big deal was back then, and he couldn't see what the big deal was now. Besides which, he didn't care much.

She waved her hand toward the house. "What about there?"

Chase slung his weight on one hip, his smile just a little nasty. "That's Devon's—you remember Devon, don't you, Ma?" Realizing that he had reverted to childhood tactics, he turned and rested his hand on the hitching post, forcing cold, cleansing air into his lungs. Man, she could get him going almost as bad as his old man. Determined to keep it together, he turned and faced her. He stared at her, then spoke, his tone flat with resignation. "What do you want? Or did Dad send you out here?"

She brushed her fingers along the chrome on the car door, then looked at him, her expression stiffly composed. "I'd rather not stand out here discussing family business. Could we at least sit in the car?"

Chase looked at the brand-new Lincoln, the sidewalls of the tires still unmarked. He didn't have to check it out to know it was top of the line and fully loaded—after all, the McCalls had an image to maintain. Recognizing the undercurrent of bitterness in that thought, Chase looked at his mother, his expression flat. "I'll meet you down at the lower barn." Snapping his fingers at the dogs who had bounded out from behind the arena, he turned and started down the path.

The barn was empty except for the cats. The stall doors stood open, the horses either turned out or up at the arena, the chitter of sparrows in the rafters the only sound. He picked up a hoof pick and curry comb that had been left on a sack of alfalfa pellets, then entered the heated tack room. Tossing the hoof pick and curry comb in the proper bin, Chase stripped a saddle blanket off one of the chairs and draped it over a saddle, dust rising in motes in the sunlight coming through the narrow window. He heard the crunch of snow as the car pulled up outside, and he braced his hands on the workbench and bent his head, trying to let go of the tension, trying to disconnect. He did not want to get sucked into the same old crap. All he would get out of it was another headache and a knot in his gut.

He heard the outside door open, then footsteps on the concrete. He straightened and started sorting through the leather scraps and hardware that cluttered the workbench. She came through the door, the scent of her perfume at odds with the smell of leather and saddle soap.

Chase cast her a quick, expressionless glance, motioning to the chair by the door. "Have a seat."

She glanced at the chair but remained standing. She abruptly stripped off her kid leather gloves, her voice quivering with emotion when she spoke. "I'm very disappointed in you, Chase. You could at least have called. Your father was very upset when he found out you were here."

Chase tossed some rivets in the appropriate can, then gave her a bitter smile, his tone caustic. "So what's new? That's pretty much the story of our lives, isn't it?"

Her gloves gripped in her hand, she stared at him, tight compression lines around her mouth, then she released a long breath and glanced around the room. There was a silence, then she finally spoke, her tone less brittle, more entreating. "I realize you've got some hard feelings about your father, but I'd hoped you could set those aside under the circumstances.''

Chase glanced at her, his face devoid of any expression. "And just what circumstances are those?"

She ran her fingers along the back of the chair, then looked at him, her expression fixed. "He hasn't been well. And he wants you to come home and take over the ranch. You owe him some consideration, Chase. At least give him the courtesy of coming in and talking to him."

He tossed several buckles into another can, then swept some leather scraps into a garbage can. He didn't say anything for a moment; then he responded, his voice flat. "I don't owe him a damned thing. And he doesn't want me running the ranch. He wants me back under his thumb, just like Milt." He turned, bracing his hand on the surface of the workbench, his expression unyielding. "I'm not playing his damned games anymore, and you can tell him that for me. As far as I'm concerned, he blew it eighteen years ago. I don't care what he wants or what he does. He can stuff it, for all I care."

His mother's face went white, and he could feel the indignation in her. "How can you say that? That ranch has been in the family for generations—there's a responsibility that goes along with that kind of heritage. You're his eldest son. It's up to you to assume it."

Something clicked in Chase's mind, and something cold and deadly started to unfold in his gut. He stared at his mother, his eyes narrowed, his gaze unwavering. He finally spoke, his tone deadly quiet. "This isn't about me at all, is it? This is about what happens if the old man dies."

His mother stared at him; then her gaze shifted away, and she began straightening the cuff of one glove. Chase continued to watch, disgust knotting his gut. "So what's he put in his will, Ma? Is there a clause in there stipulating different terms if I'm running the ranch?"

She continued to fidget with her gloves, her profile taut in the bright light reflecting off the snow outside. Chase turned his head away in distaste, the muscles in his jaw rigid. God, but it made him sick. He waited until he got his fury under control, then he turned back to her. "This is really about Tanner, isn't it? You're afraid he's going to contest the will when Dad dies." He paused, his eyes narrowing in speculation. "Or maybe the old man included him in the will, and you think that if I take over the Bar M before the old man dies, he'll turn the deed over to me. And if he does that, that finishes any chances of Tanner getting his hands on the big McCall heritage." It was clear by her refusal to meet his gaze that he was close, if not dead-on, and Chase made a derisive sound and straightened. "That would just be too much, wouldn't it? If a half-breed McCall got his hands on the McCall heritage?" Clenching his jaw, he turned, bracing one arm on the shelving adjacent to the workbench as he stared out the window, anger welling up in him. The whole thing made him sick. Turning his head, he looked at his mother, giving her a bitter smile. "You thought you had all your bases covered, didn't you? Except once I got my hands on the ranch, there would be nothing stopping me from turning it over to Tanner. But you never even considered that possibility, did you?"

He mother shot him a startled look, and Chase gave her another cold, twisted smile. "So, Mother. Do you still want me to pay a visit?"

She stared at him, her face pale, then she began yanking on her gloves, her actions jerky and agitated. "You don't think of anyone else but yourself, do you, Chase? And you don't care what people think. Have you ever once considered that he might not be your father's son? She was nothing but a little tramp. She was a trick rider, for heaven's sake. That should tell you something. Who's to say he wasn't someone else's?"

Discovering a whole new level of disgust, Chase leaned against the workbench and folded his arms, shaking his head in unbelief. "You just never give it a rest, do you? First of all, I didn't give a damn what people thought back then, and I don't give a damn what they think now. Secondly, everyone knows, including my father, whose kid Tanner is— all you have to do is look at him and it's pretty bloody obvious." Anger began to flicker through him, and he straightened and took a step toward her, pointing his finger at her. "You'd better remember that Tanner is just as much my brother as Milt. And I don't give a damn if his mother was a trick rider or a brain surgeon. Dad's the one who was at fault, not her. And the fact that you let Dad take that little six-year old kid—his own son, for God's sake—and dump him with a pair of twisted, abusive sickos doesn't say a whole hell of lot for you, either, Ellinore."

Flustered and angry over his charge, Ellie fussed with the cuff of her glove, then met his gaze, her eyes snapping with righteous indignation. "That's a totally unfounded accusation, Chase. I had nothing to do with the boy's placement. And if his mother hadn't killed herself, there wouldn't have been any need to find a home for him."

Chase shook his head and snorted with disgust. "That's it, Mom. Whatever you do, don't get your hands dirty, and be sure and excuse yourself and Dad from any responsibility. Hell, why not? He was just a little half-breed kid no one cared a damn about. What difference did it make?"

His mother started to tremble, her indignation turning to something else. She gripped the back of the chair, a fevered glaze in her eyes. "How dare you stand there and pass judgment on us! No matter what we did, it was never quite good enough, and now you don't even have the decency to talk to your father."

His hands on his hips, Chase stared at her. "You want to talk about decency? Fine. As I recall, he was the one who had me charged with grand theft auto."

Dark spots appeared in her cheeks, and she gripped the chair with both hands. "You were ruining your life, for heaven's sake! He didn't want you to make the same mistakes he had, and he could see what Devon was like. God, they lived in a hovel. Her mother was the town drunk, and they lived from one welfare check to another. It was clear to everyone what she was after, and she had no scruples about how she got it. If she got pregnant, she knew you'd marry her, and they'd both be set for life." Her chin came up and she stared at him, her expression tight with defiance. "So your father did what he had to when he found out you were sleeping with her. No McCall money, no McCall respectability, no Devon Manyfeathers."

His face like granite, Chase kicked the chair out of the way, a cold, deadly fury sweeping through him. "Well, you can go back and tell him that his little plan backfired. Because he ended up with no son, either. I don't want a damned thing to do with him, I don't want anything to do with the ranch, and I sure in hell don't want to be drawn back into the bosom of the family." He took a step closer, his expression cold, his smile pure venom. "And you can also tell him his little plan backfired twice, because I'm still sleeping with her."

She grabbed his arm, her eyes frantic. "You cannot just turn your back on your—"

Chase snatched his arm away and took a step backward. "Just watch me." Picking up the chair, he slammed it down in front of the workbench and started toward the door.

She followed him, her voice shrill with desperation. "Don't you see what you're doing? You're throwing everything away over some piece of trash, just like your father nearly did!"

Chase stopped dead in his tracks, then turned on his heel and stared at her, his rage cold, dark and deadly. "Don't you ever, ever make that mistake again, Ma. Because if you bad-mouth Devon, you'll see a side of me you won't like very much. And," he added, his voice even more deadly, "don't you ever compare me to my old man. He has the morals of an alley cat and the principles of a snake. You can tell him for me that I don't want his kind of respectability, and I sure as hell don't want his money. I wouldn't touch the Bar M if I had a gun at my head."

He snatched up two halters and lead shanks that were hooked on a nail by one of the stalls, then turned toward the back door of the barn, knowing he had to get the hell out before he totally lost it. He was going to get the horses Sam wanted worked today, he was going to take them up to the arena and then he was going to find a stack of bales to move. But a sudden wave of reaction surged through him, and he slammed the latch on the door, rage born of frustration roiling in his gut. He was going to need one hell of lot more than a stack of bales to work his way through this one.

The horses were in the pen just behind the barn. Sunlight glinted off the wind-polished drifts, and the snow squeaked beneath his feet as he crossed to the corral, the moisture in the animals' breath vaporizing into clouds of tiny ice crystals. Looping the shank around the bay filly's neck, he slipped on the halter, his actions swift and automatic. He tried to shut down the anger churning through him, tried to disconnect from the ugly encounter with his mother, but this time it wasn't going to be that easy. This time the anger was different. This time he felt as if it could suffocate him.

"Do you need a hand?"

Avoiding making eye contact with Devon, he pulled the filly's forelock free of the halter and straightened the nose band. "No. I can manage."

Ground tying the filly, he crossed to the sorrel and went through the process again. Then, collecting both leads in one hand, he started toward her. Devon slid the metal crossbar back and swung open the gate, holding it open as he led the horses through. He started up the path toward the arena, the two horses following along behind him, the two dogs romping belly deep in the drifts beside him. His jaw set, all expression erased from his face, he put one foot in front of the other, feeling as if there was a big hand jammed in his chest.

"Chase?"

Devon appeared at his side, and he changed the shanks to the other hand. "What?"

She looked at him, her eyes dark with concern. But she didn't ask. She wouldn't say anything unless he did. She never had.

He glanced over to where the dogs were chasing each other through the snow beside her, a mirthless smile appearing. "I had a visit from my mother."

"What happened?"

Chase stopped and stared off across the distance; then, clenching his jaw, he met her gaze. "Nothing happened, Devon. Not one damned thing."

The sun behind her created a corona of light around her head, the cherry red collar of her thermal top bright above the neck of her fleece-lined jacket. Her braid was caught under her jacket, and her head was bare, her hair shining like black satin in the sunlight. She was standing with her hands jammed in her pockets, her eyes dark and anxious as she watched him, and Chase's chest tightened even more. It was all so familiar, as if she had stood before him like that a thousand times. He swallowed hard and looked away.

"She wanted me to talk to my old man," he answered, his tone expressionless. "Apparently he's got it into his head that I'm going to take over the Bar M."

Her could feel her watching him, judging his response, waiting for more, but he didn't elaborate. How could he elaborate on disgust?

She hunched her shoulders against the cold and huddled deeper in the warmth of her coat. "There was more to it than that, wasn't there?"

He looked at her, a flash of anger coursing through him. "Leave it, Devon," he commanded curtly. "It was the same old garbage. She also tried to inject some good old guilt, but I'm not buying it. And I'm not going to talk about it, either."

She stared up at him, her gaze dark and assessing, then she looked away, not a trace of expression on her face. She motioned toward the horses. "I can take these two up if you want."

He exhaled sharply and shook his head. "No. I've got em."

She hesitated, then turned and started toward the arena. "All right, then."

Chase watched her walk away, then bent his head and swore. Damn it. He didn't want her mixed up in this mess. He had never wanted her dragged into the crap with his family, never wanted her exposed to their kind of bigotry. And even back then, he'd made damned sure she never got dragged into it. But neither had she ever shown any kind of reaction. She would listen, and she would ask a few questions, but she never made any kind of comment. She had always remained removed from it all. He suddenly realized that he had never challenged her aloofness, never questioned her lack of reaction. But for some reason, all that had suddenly changed. He didn't want her to turn her back and walk away. He didn't want her standing outside the circle, damn it. He wanted some kind of reaction from her. Something. Anything. Something to indicate she gave a damn. Just one bloody damn.

A jolt of adrenaline and anger swept through him with pure, energizing force, and he stopped, suddenly so damn furious that he could barely see straight. Damn it all to hell, this time he wasn't going to let her pull that stunt. Enough was enough. It was time they laid some cards on the table; to hell with this not talking crap. They had skirted too many problems and avoided serious confrontations for too long. He started after her, his temper at the boiling point as he yelled at her, "Stop right there, damn it!"

She turned, her eyes wide, her expression sharp and questioning.

He closed the distance between them, the snow practically melting in his wake. He walked right up to her, anger surging in him. "You plant your butt, Devon. You're not going to pull that damned stunt this time around."

She frowned, looking at him as if he'd lost his mind. "What are you talking about, McCall?"

He gave a sharp command to the horses, then glared at her, wanting to shake her. "I'm talking about you walking away as soon as anything starts to get a little dicey. I'm talking about how you clam up and don't say one bloody word about things like this. And I'm talking about how you keep holding out on me, Manyfeathers. Or don't you give a damn?"

Her expression startled, she stared at him, alarm flickering in her eyes; then she turned as if to walk away. Dropping the lead lines, he grabbed her arm and wheeled her around, his irritation skyrocketing. He caught her by the jaw and forced her to look at him, something dark and painful breaking loose in him when he saw how pale her face had gone, when he saw the fear in her eyes. "Damn it, don't do this to us, Dev," he commanded roughly. "I'm tired of these games we keep playing with each other, and I'm tired of not knowing where the hell I stand with you." His temper crested, and he dropped his hand and looked away, a thick ache unfolding in his chest. Hell, where did he go from here?

Inhaling deeply, he finally shifted his gaze and looked at her, his stomach dropping like a rock when he saw the stark, distressed expression in her eyes. He stared at her, then exhaled heavily, his anger settling into a heavy, resigned feeling. "Do you know," he said, his tone softening a little, "that I'm not even sure if you know why I left eighteen years ago? It hit me last night at Tanner's that I don't even know if you want kids. In fact, it's just hit me how little I do know about you." He held her gaze for a moment longer, then he looked down and crushed a clump of ice with his boot, his voice quiet and very subdued when he continued. "You were always there when I needed to blow off steam or when my old man was leaning on me. But you never came to me if something was bugging you. You never let me get close enough to find out how you felt about anything." He looked at her, his expression somber, the cramp in his chest getting worse. "I didn't realize that until this time around. And I gotta tell you, it hurts like hell."

She stared at him, her eyes dark and fixed, then she swallowed hard and abruptly turned her head, her expression starkly contained. Chase watched her for a moment; then looked down, his expression grim as he raked the splinters of ice into a pile with his foot. He didn't say anything for a moment, then he lifted his head and looked at her, his face devoid of any expression. "You shut me out, Dev. You always have. And who the hell knows? Maybe you always will."

Her hands jammed deep in her pockets, she hunched her shoulders against the cold, her face averted, but Chase saw the glimmer of tears in her eyes. He looked away, experiencing a feeling that was a mix of guilt and anger. Damn it, she was doing it again. Closing up. Pulling into herself. His anger grew, and he turned and caught the two horses, then roughly looped the ropes over her arm. His expression grim, he started walking toward the lower barn. He had taken half a dozen steps when she called out his name.

He turned, the torment in her dark eyes kicking off another twist of guilt, and he pushed back his jacket and hooked his thumb in the waistband of his jeans, fixing his gaze on the horizon. Damn it, why did they keep doing this to each other?

She spoke, her voice trembling, an edge of anxiety in her tone. "Why did she come here?"

He swiveled his gaze to look at her, his jaw taut. He stared at her, eighteen years of frustration boiling up in him, eighteen years of resentment finally surfacing. Nothing would change. Not a damned thing. He gave her one final disgusted look, then turned, his voice flat when he snapped, "Don't expect me back for supper."

If Chase had ever wondered what he'd really been dodging for all those years, he sure as hell found out over the next three days. At one point in his life he would have gone on a five-day drunk, but he knew from experience that didn't solve a thing. So instead he headed for Tanner's line camp in the foothills and put himself through some of the worst body abuse and hard physical labor he'd ever heaped on himself. The dead of winter was hardly a good time to stockpile firewood, but he did it, and he did it with nothing more than an ax, a handsaw and a lariat to drag the felled trees out of the bush. He worked until his clothes were frozen with sweat, until his shoulders felt like someone was operating on them with red-hot pokers, until his muscles were quivering from sheer physical exhaustion. But the hard work didn't cut it. There was only one way to deal with the rage of emotions. And that was to face them and take them apart, piece by piece, until he got to what was hidden underneath.

Something had happened on that narrow trail by the barn. It was as if he'd come flying out of a chute, half expecting to hit a brick wall, but finding a thirty-foot drop instead. And for the first time in his life, he'd been forced to stand back and take a second look. Admittedly, for the first eighteen hours at the line camp, he'd wallowed in anger, blaming her for the mess they'd made of their lives. But as he worked through that explosive buildup of anger and resentment, he started connecting with other feelings, and he began to see things from a different angle. He realized that he hadn't always been totally honest. He had accused her of withdrawing, but he was just as much to blame. He'd never really been totally frank with her. Yeah, she knew how bad the situation was with his old man, but he hadn't really explained all his reasons for pulling the pin eighteen years ago. He'd just been so sure she would pack her bags and go down the road with him when she turned eighteen that he hadn't given it much thought.

It had been years later, after he'd grown up a bit, that he'd been able to see things from her point of view. But he saw now that that wasn't the only mistake he'd made. He had allowed her to withdraw when things got a little rough.

Yeah, he had wanted to shelter her from the redneck bigotry that existed in a small community like Bolton, and he sure in hell never told her about all the fights he'd gotten into over her. Maybe that had been a big mistake. Maybe he should have stood beside her instead of in front of her. Maybe if he'd forced her into a few confrontations back then, maybe, just maybe, they wouldn't be in the mess they were in right now.

But after three days of hard labor and a whole lot of soul-searching, all Chase really had to show for it was a pile of firewood, one buggered-up shoulder and a bunch of blisters. He certainly hadn't come up with any answers, and he was beginning to feel like a dog chasing its tail. And he hurt like hell inside. He felt as if someone had punched a hole in his gut, and nothing he did eased the heavy, hollow feeling. He didn't know what he would do if he ever lost her for good.

By the evening of the third day, he was so damned exhausted his mind finally shut down. He was lying on his bedroll in front of the fire in the old stone fireplace, ice packs made out of snow and one of his ripped T-shirts packed around his shoulder, his arms folded across his eyes, that awful, lonely feeling climbing up his throat. There was nothing more lonely than wind sighing through the fir trees and moaning around the small cabin. He clenched his jaw, willing the tightness to go away. Maybe it was a chinook blowing in.

The crunch of snow outside the door brought his head around, and he riveted his gaze on the door, his body primed for action, but before he had time to react, the door swung open. A cold draft rolled across the floor as Tanner McCall stepped in. Chase stared at his brother for a moment, then turned his head and rested his bad arm across his chest and draped the other over his eyes. His tone was curt when he spoke. "You're a little far from home, aren't you?"

Tanner shut the door, and Chase heard him pull off his gloves. "That depends." There was the sound of Tanner wiping his feet, then the sound of a chair being moved from the battered old table. Chase heard his brother set the chair down facing him. There was a brief pause, then Tanner spoke, his voice quiet. "Devon showed up early this morning. She was pretty worried—wondered if we knew where you were."

Clenching his jaw against the sudden thickness in his throat, Chase remained silent. There was the rustle of clothing, then Tanner spoke again, his tone offhand. "I thought maybe you might have holed up at the Bar M somewhere. Then I remembered how you used to come here the year you were with me. Figured I'd check it out."

"I'm not eighteen, for God's sake. I can take care of myself."

There was a mixture of amusement and patience in Tanner's voice when he responded. "I don't intend to wipe your nose, Chase. I just thought you might want to talk."

Chase made no response, not sure why Tanner's appearance made him feel like he was ten years old again and trying not to bawl.

"That's a nice pile of wood you got out there. Too bad it's not summer. You could have rebuilt all the corrals and fixed all the fences."

Giving in to a flicker of humor, Chase lifted one finger in a rude gesture, and Tanner chuckled. There was a short pause, and then Tanner spoke again, his tone mild. "I take it you screwed up your shoulder again. Or have you been doing a little bronc busting up here, as well?"

His dry tone wrung a smile out of Chase, who shifted his arm and looked at his brother. "What's the big deal? Can't a man just lie around feeling sorry for himself?"

Hooking his ankle across his knee, Tanner folded his arms and rocked back in his chair, a smile lurking around his mouth. "Is that what you're doing? Feeling sorry for yourself?"

Chase held his brother's gaze for a moment, then closed his eyes and exhaled heavily. "I don't know what the hell I'm doing."

There was a long pause; then Tanner spoke again, his voice quiet. "She was pretty upset, Chase. I got the feeling she thought she'd done something wrong, and you'd taken off."

The muscles in his jaw flexing, Chase shifted his arm onto his forehead, noting that the ice packs had helped, but his shoulder still felt as if someone had tried to rip his arm off. He stared at the dancing flames for several moments, his expression somber; then he let go another long sigh. "I was pretty damned stupid when I was twenty-one."

"I don't know. I always figured you had things pretty well sorted out by then."

Chase turned his gaze to his brother, surprised by the response. "I was a screwup, and you and I both know it."

Tanner flicked some dried dirt off his jeans, his expression thoughtful. "You had pretty much worked through the serious stuff," he said quietly. "And you were putting things back together. That takes some doing for anybody." Hooking one thumb in his belt loop, he lifted his gaze and looked at Chase. "You weren't a screwup—just a kid with problems."

Chase turned his head and stared at the fire, his voice gruff. "I don't know what in hell to do, Tanner."

There was another pause, then Tanner spoke. "Maybe," he said softly, "you're saying that to the wrong person."

# Chapter 7

The headlights glanced off the side of the arena, the swath of light glistening in the hoarfrost that had settled on the trees and drifts of snow. He parked by the side door, not bothering to plug in the block heater, and started up the path to the darkened house. The two dogs appeared out of the shadows and ran along the path ahead of him; then one turned and came back to him, ears alert, tail wagging. A flicker of humor lifted the corner of Chase's mouth, and he paused and scratched the border collie behind the ears. There was something to be said for a dog's life. And he wished he knew what he was going to say to Devon.

He'd considered half a dozen options on the drive back from the line camp, but nothing seemed to stick. He knew what needed to be said, he knew what *he* needed to say, but tonight was the wrong time. All he knew for sure was that before he got into anything heavy, he had to tell her how sorry he was for walking out on her the way he had. He had made too many exits like that over the years, and he knew if he ever made another one, it would be for good.

The interior of the house was wrapped in silence, but the small fluorescent light was on over the sink, casting the kitchen in a faint luminescence. With a knot in his gut the size of his fist, Chase entered the half-darkened room and set his boots by the heat vent by the door, the silence like a weight around him. The tension that had been riding him since he left the line camp let go in a rush, and he rested his hands on his hips and wearily tipped his head back, three days of exhaustion piling in on him. Hell, what had he expected? That she would be waiting up for him?

"Chase?"

He straightened and looked into the gloom in the living room, his heart missing a beat when he saw a shimmer of white rise from the sofa. He watched her, a sudden ache jamming up his throat. He spoke, his voice gruff. "Hi."

Her arms folded tightly in front of her, she stepped into the archway, and he realized she had been sleeping in one of his shirts. The tightness in his throat made his jaw ache.

She tried to smile, the worry in her eyes evident in the half-light. "Hi," she said, her voice soft. "I was getting worried about you."

One hand still on his hip, he looked away, trying to handle the sudden stinging in his eyes. God, but she could turn him inside out. Finally managing to get a shaky breath past the lump in his throat, he looked at her, aware of how she was huddled in the warmth of her own arms, aware of the dark uncertainty in her eyes. That uncertainty stripped him to the quick, and he walked across the shadowed kitchen toward her. "Come here," he whispered gruffly.

With a choked sound, she came into his arms, and he gathered her up in a tight embrace, roughly tucking her face against the curve of his neck. Chase felt her take a deep, tremulous breath, then she pressed her face tighter against him as she slid her arms around his waist. He could feel her trembling, as if she'd had a bad scare, and he pressed a kiss to her temple, then slid his fingers along her scalp, cradling her head in his firm grip. The heavy, silky weight of her hair tangled around his fingers, the loose fall like satin down her back, and Chase closed his eyes and hugged her hard, a swell of emotion making his chest tighten. Lord, but she filled up that hole in him.

He felt her take another tremulous breath, and he smoothed one hand across her hips and up her back, molding her tightly against him. Easing in a tight breath of his own, he brushed a kiss against her ear, then spoke, his voice gruff and uneven. "I'm sorry I cut out like I did." He tucked his head down against hers and drew her hips flush against him. "And I'm sorry I acted like such a damned jerk."

A tremor coursed through her, and Devon dragged her arms free and slipped them around his neck, the shift intimately and fully aligning her body against his. Chase drew an unsteady breath and angled her head back, making a low, indistinguishable sound as he covered her mouth in a kiss that was raw with regret, governed by the need to comfort and reassure. Devon went still. Then, with a soft exhalation, she clutched at him and yielded to his deep, comforting kiss. Chase slid his hand along her jaw, his callused fingers snagging in the long silky strands of her hair as he altered the angle of her head. She moved against him, and Chase shuddered and tightened his hold, a fever of emotion sluicing through him, wishing, ah, God, wishing he could draw her right inside him and keep her there forever.

Dragging his mouth away, he trailed a string of kisses down her neck, then caught her head again and gave her another hot, wet kiss. His breathing ragged, he tightened his hold on her face and drew back, holding her against his chest. He held her like that, his hand cupping the back of her neck, until his breathing evened out; then he turned, tucking her against him as he headed for the bedroom.

She was shaking like a leaf by the time they made it to the bedroom, and he paused by the bed and drew her into a fierce embrace. Roughly pressing his face against the curve of her neck, he held on to her like she was his next breath, trying to get a grip on the wild clamor rising up inside him. Forcing her head against him, he gritted his teeth and tipped his own head back, taking several deep breaths; then somehow he got her panties and his clothes off without letting her go. Somehow he managed to tear open the small foil packet and sheath himself.

He was shaking nearly as badly as she was when he lifted her onto the bed, then followed her down, ripping open the snaps of the shirt she wore before dragging her beneath him. He felt as if his heart would explode, as if his lungs would seize up, if he didn't get inside her, if he didn't get as close to her as he could possibly get. She made a small, desperate sound and drew up her knees, urging him forward with urgent hands, and Chase clenched his jaw and closed his eyes, burying himself deep inside her. God, so deep. So tight and deep.

He locked his arms around her, a shudder coursing through him, and he ground his teeth together, the sensory onslaught nearly ripping him apart. It wasn't the sex; it was the physical connection, as if being inside her fused them into one united whole. Braced against the mind-shattering sensation, Chase remained rigid in her arms, waiting for the heated, electrifying rush to ease. Releasing a shaky sigh, he braced his weight on his forearms and bracketed her face in his hands, his heart trapped in his chest as he covered her mouth in a slow, wet, softly searching kiss.

Devon sobbed into his mouth, her hands clutching at him, and she lifted her hips, rolling her pelvis hard against him. Chase roughly slid his hand under her head and locked his other arm around her buttocks, working his mouth hungrily against hers as he lifted her higher, then rolled his hips against hers. Devon made a choked sound, and Chase drank it in, his mind blurring with a red haze when Devon countered his thrust, her body moving convulsively beneath him. Aware of how desperately she needed this kind of comfort, Chase dragged his mouth away and gritted his teeth, a fine sheen of sweat dampening his skin as he moved against her, trying to give her the maximum contact, trying to exert the right amount of pressure where she needed it most, trying to hang on until she came apart in his arms. She made another wild sound, and her counterthrusts turned desperate and erratic, and Chase tightened his hold. His senses on overdrive, he roughly buried his face against her neck and thrust into her, fighting to go the distance, the red haze governing him.

Devon arched stiffly beneath him, and Chase's face contorted with an agony of pleasure as her body convulsed around him, pulling, pulling at him. Then, with a ragged groan, he went rigid in her arms and let go, emptying himself deep inside her. Holding on to her with convulsive strength, he held her head against him, her face wet against his neck. Feeling as if he had been turned inside out, he pressed his mouth against her temple and closed his eyes, his pulse choppy and erratic, the feelings in his chest almost too much to handle. God, but she filled him up—made him feel indestructible.

He drew a deep, shaky breath and pressed another kiss on the corner of her mouth, his touch slow and comforting as he softly stroked the angle of her jaw with his thumb. Realizing that her hair was caught under her, hampering her movements, he braced his weight on one arm and hip, lifting her with him, then dragged it out from under her. He spread it on the pillow, releasing the fragrance of wild roses, and inhaled deeply, letting the satiny length slither through his fingers. Taking another deep breath, he bracketed her face with his hands, shifting his weight so his hips again settled between her thighs. Realizing that she needed something to ease the emotional rawness, he tipped her head back and brushed a light kiss against her mouth, letting a touch of humor surface. "You could be in big trouble here, Slash," he murmured against her mouth, taking another slow, savoring taste. "I don't think I'm gonna be able to haul ass for at least an hour."

He felt her smile against his mouth; then she tightened her arms around his back and slid one hand back and forth across his shoulders. "Sticking in the saddle, are you, McCall?"

Chase grinned, loving her smart mouth. "Hell, woman. I'm after a championship ride and a silver belt buckle."

She poked him in the ribs, and he jumped and grabbed her wrist, trapping her hand above her head. The faint light from the yard lit the room, and he could see the smile in her eyes. His thumb on her pulse, he caressed her wrist, his voice gravelly when he spoke. "You wanna wrestle, Manyfeathers? Or are you just fooling around?"

She gave him a wry smile, idly massaging the base of his spine. "I never fool around, McCall."

Continuing to stroke her wrist, he lowered his head and slowly moistened her bottom lip, then he took her mouth again, taking great care to do it well. He released a soft sigh, and she slid her free hand up his torso, finally cupping the back of his head. He deepened the kiss, and Devon yielded fully to his questing tongue. Finally Chase let go of her wrist and slid his arm under her, holding her with infinite care. After a long, satisfying kiss, he reluctantly drew away, gazing down at her as he caressed her bottom lip with his thumb. He stroked her face, tracing her high cheekbones, the arch of her eyebrows; then he gave her another quick kiss, braced himself and abruptly withdrew from her moist warmth. She jackknifed against him, and he held her head against his shoulder until she caught her breath, then he rolled onto his back, taking her with him. He stripped off the protection and dropped it on the pile of clothes beside the bed, then drew her against him. Snuggling her head against his shoulder, he drew her long, muscled leg between his. Cradling her hips against him, he ran his hand up her naked back, then tucked his head and kissed her brow. "We need to talk, Dev," he said, his tone husky.

She went still in his arms, then she turned her face against his neck and tightened her arm around his waist. Pressing another kiss against her hair, he began slowly stroking his hand up and down her back. His expression somber, he considered all he wanted to say to her; then he spoke, his voice very quiet. "Do you remember when I started skipping school to go out to Nordstrom's to ride broncs, and you got so ticked off at me?"

Devon stirred and shifted her head, then he felt her eyelashes against his skin when she opened her eyes. "Yes," she whispered. "I remember."

Staring into the darkness, he let his hand rest on the swell of her hip, giving her a small, prompting squeeze. "Do you remember what we fought about?"

There was an odd hesitation, and he was aware of an unusual stillness in her. Finally she answered. "About you taking stupid, reckless chances."

His expression thoughtful with recollection, Chase absently stroked the rise of her hip with his thumb as he considered her response. Finally he spoke. "For me, it had nothing to do with taking chances, Dev," he said, his tone rough. "It was about dealing with disgust. It was about a kid hating everything his old man stood for." One corner of Chase's mouth lifted in a humorless smile. "It was about mutiny."

Devon lay still in his arms for a split second; then she rose up on one elbow and looked down at him, her hair creating a waterfall of inky blackness around her shoulders. She stared at him, the faint light from outside washing across her face and revealing the confusion in her expression. A glimmer of alarm appeared in her eyes. "What's this really about, Chase?" she whispered unevenly.

He stared up at her for a moment, then shifted his focus. Avoiding her gaze, he painstakingly hooked his thumb under a thick swatch of hair and drew it back, tucking it carefully behind her. "This is about the things we never talked about," he answered quietly. "About the things we—about the things *I* should have said to you and didn't." Finally he met her gaze, his expression somber. Screwing up his courage, he took the step that he knew could change everything. "Do you know *why* I went down the road, Devon?"

She gazed at him, her eyes wide with uncertainty, then she looked away. She lightly ran her fingertips along his collarbone, lingering at the joint of an old break—one he'd gotten when one of Nordstrom's range-wild horses piled him into a corral fence. Her gaze averted, she continued to stroke his collarbone, and Chase waited, sensing her struggle. Her hair was draped around her face, and she lifted it. Chase waited for her to answer, knowing this was critical. Lingering on the old heal mark, she finally answered, trying to be offhand. "I expect it had something to do with the male warrior thing."

Feeling disappointed and a little bit angry, Chase grasped her face and jerked her head up, forcing her to look at him. "Don't," he ordered sharply. "Just don't, okay? I want you to talk to me."

She stared at him, then she swallowed hard and looked away. He brought her head around, his gaze demanding and intent. "Please, Devon. I need you to talk to me."

She held his gaze for a moment, then she bent her head and started rubbing her thumb back and forth across the lump in the collarbone again, her touch not quite steady. She swallowed, then took a deep, unsteady breath. "I don't know why. I guess I thought you didn't want to be anchored in one spot—that you did it to spite your father. I tried not to think about it."

For some reason Chase felt as if he'd just been let out of a dark, tight space, and he closed his eyes and hugged her hard, feeling as if he could take his first deep breath in days. He pressed a kiss against her brow, then hugged her again. His chest expanding with a deep, uneven breath, he spoke, his voice gruff. "No, babe, you got it wrong. It wasn't about spite. It was about my fight for independence. I left because I didn't want to be in my old man's back pocket. I didn't want him calling the shots and telling me how to run my life. And I sure as hell didn't want his damned money.

He would have buried me alive if I stuck around here, and I knew it. I had to get out—had to make it on my own.'' Cupping his hand against the angle of her jaw, he stroked her ear and brushed another soft kiss against her forehead. Smoothing down some wisps of hair, Chase rested his head against hers, a solemn, reflective expression appearing. He stared off into the darkness, then inhaled and spoke, gently caressing her ear. ''I left for a lot of reasons, babe,'' he said quietly. ''I left because I didn't want anything to do with my old man, but there was more to it than that.'' His throat suddenly closed up on him, and he tightened his hold on her face, hugging her head against the curve of his shoulder. He had to wait for the tightness to ease, then he spoke, his voice husky with emotion. ''There was also you.''

Her head came up, and she stared at him, a stunned expression on her face. ''Me?''

A warped smile appearing, he tucked some loose hair behind her ear. ''Yeah,'' he said, his voice husky. ''You.'' She stared at him, and Chase ran his thumb down her cheek, a tight feeling unfolding in his chest. ''You were only sixteen, Dev.''

''But—''

He pressed his thumb against her mouth, trying his damnedest to maintain the trace of a smile. ''I knew I was leaning on you pretty hard, and I knew how much you wanted to finish school.'' The tightness in his chest expanding, he shifted his gaze to her mouth as he drew his thumb along her lower lip. Clearing his throat, he stroked the corner of her mouth. ''I knew I wasn't going to be able to leave you alone, and I was afraid if I stuck around, you'd end up pregnant. And I was afraid if I hung around much longer, people would figure out what was going on and there'd be talk.'' He shifted his thumb to the fullest part of her mouth, his expression sobering. ''You were too young for that kind of crap, Dev,'' he said, his voice gruff. ''And I saw how the people around here treated Tanner because of my old man. I didn't want the same thing to happen to you.''

He looked up, something painful happening around his heart when he saw the glimmer of tears in her eyes. Sliding his hand along her jaw until his fingers were buried in her hair, he drew her head down, the fullness in his chest making his throat cramp. He took her mouth in a soft, comforting kiss. Wrapping his fingers around the back of her head, he held her still as he softly, slowly brushed his mouth back and forth across hers, tormenting her, tormenting himself. "You were so young," he whispered unevenly against her mouth. "And all I could think about was getting you alone, getting inside you. I would have got you pregnant for sure."

Releasing her pent-up breath in a rush, Devon slid her arms around his neck and moved on top of him. Closing his eyes against the onslaught of sensation, Chase turned his face against her and wrapped her in a hard, enveloping embrace, wondering how in hell he would ever manage without her. Grasping a handful of hair, he clenched his jaw and turned his head against hers, something raw and wild breaking loose inside him. Inhaling raggedly, he clutched her against him. A tremor coursed through her, and she drew her knees up and pulled out of his hold, her hair cascading around her face as she rose above him. Realizing what was happening, realizing what she intended, he snatched her hand away. She twisted her wrist free, then drew his hand to her mouth, placing a hot, wet kiss against his palm. Lacing her fingers through his, she caught his other hand and repeated the hot, erotic caress, then forced his hands down by his head. Another tremor shuddered through her, and she rose up, then lowered her weight upon him, taking him deep inside her. Naked. Unprotected. Deep, deep inside her.

Breaking out in a cold sweat, Chase clenched his jaw against the sharp, electrifying surge of feeling, his shoulders coming off the bed as she moved once, twice against him. His heartbeat a frenzy in his chest, his pulse thick and heavy, he tightened his fingers through hers in a white-knuckle grip, turning his head against the pillow.

"Dev... honey. Ah... God. I can't... you've gotta stop, babe."

Bending over him, she stroked the palms of his hands with her thumbs, her breasts grazing his chest. "No," she whispered brokenly. "No." Another shudder coursed through her, and she tightened her hold on his hands, her breath catching as she flexed her hips, her hot, wet tightness gripping him, stroking him, drawing him closer and closer.

An agony of sensation shot through him, and he rolled his head again, the cords of his neck taut, and he sucked in a breath through clenched teeth. God, he wanted to let go, wanted to ride out the hard, swelling need. But Devon. This was Devon.

Then she moved again, taking him ever deeper inside her, and he went under, the fever claiming him. He groaned and flexed beneath her, driving inside her. He couldn't stop.

Trailers of a dream faded in his mind when Chase surfaced from sleep, half-conscious of a numbing weight on his arm. He shifted and stirred, a jolt of pain shooting through his shoulder, and he drowsily licked his lips and opened his eyes. The room was still dark, and Devon was sound asleep, her head resting in the hollow of his shoulder, but he knew from his internal clock that it was early morning. He waited for the mental fog to clear a little, then he carefully drew her head onto his chest and flexed his hand against the pins-and-needles sensation. Scrubbing his face to rid himself of the last vestiges of sleep, he tucked his head and brushed a soft, lingering kiss against her forehead, smiling a little when she made a soft sound and turned her face toward his warmth. If only things could be that simple.

Brushing back the wisps of hair clinging to her face, he kissed her again, then cautiously rolled his throbbing shoulder. Easing the tightness, he leaned forward and stuffed two pillows behind his shoulders, settling himself into a more comfortable position before resting his still-tingling arm along her hip. He stared into the darkness, thinking about what had happened last night. He had received something from her that he had never expected. An emotional gift. And he wouldn't be sorry if she ended up pregnant because of it.

But what left his gut in a knot was that she had lost it the way she had. Devon never lost it. Until the other day, he had never seen her cry. She never got flustered, she never panicked, and she sure as hell never went over the edge. There was a coolness, a kind of control in her, that he had always admired. Maybe it was because he was such a damned hothead that he admired that evenness in her. Yeah, he'd seen her uncertain and a whole lot vulnerable, but he'd never seen her really lose it—not like she had last night. And he wondered what it meant. For the first time in five years, he would have chewed nails for a cigarette.

Releasing a heavy sigh, he gazed at her, his expression solemn. Even in the faint light from outside, he could see the shadows under her eyes, and he wondered if she'd had as little sleep during the past three days as he had. It was pretty obvious he'd shaken her up. A small, wry smile appeared. Of course he'd given himself a good shake in the process. He lightly brushed his thumb along her high cheekbone, then tucked a loose piece of hair behind her ear. Remembering that galvanizing instant when she had taken him deep inside her, Chase tipped his head back and closed his eyes, fighting the urge to draw her up against him. He waited for the thick, heavy surge to ease a little, then took a deep, steadying breath and glanced at the clock on the bedside table. Five o'clock. Maybe it was time to stack a few thousand bales.

She stirred when he eased away from her, and he leaned over and brushed a light kiss against her temple. "It's okay, darlin'," he whispered gruffly. "Go back to sleep." He lifted her hair off her face, then drew the comforter over her shoulders. He waited until he was sure she was asleep, then eased his weight from the bed. Making as little noise as possible, he collected a set of clean clothes and the alarm clock, then went to the window and closed the blind. It was Saturday, and they never worked customers' horses on the weekend. They could manage fine without her. He listened for any change in her breathing, then left the room, closing the door soundlessly behind him.

His expression somber, he went into the bathroom, avoiding his reflection in the mirror over the sink as he turned on the taps. That fragile look in her face bothered the hell out of him. He had never seen her like that before. He'd seen her withdraw, and he'd seen her wounded and as wary as a wild deer, but he had never seen her look so fragile, so bloody breakable, before. It made him uneasy. It was almost as if some inner defense had been stripped away, leaving her exposed. He wasn't sure how she would handle that exposure. After all, Devon Manyfeathers had spent her whole life keeping her guard up. He didn't know how she would react if someone ever brought it down.

It was midmorning when Devon finally showed up at the arena, and it only took one look at her face to know that something serious had happened. She almost pulled off that cool, kind of removed, slightly amused demeanor, but there was something about her that made Chase's gaze narrow. She met his glance when she first came in, and the hollowness in her eyes made his gut clench. It was grief he saw— deep, gut-wrenching grief. That glimpse stunned him, and he stood in the alleyway, his hand resting on the rump of the horse he was saddling, feeling like someone had just kicked his feet out from under him. Grief?

Without thinking, he went after her. Grabbing her arm from behind, he hauled her into an empty stall and into the corner where no could see them, then caught her by the back of the head and forced her pale face into the curve of his neck. The bill of her Blue Jays hat was in the way, and he peeled it off and tossed it aside, then wrapped her in a tight embrace. He didn't say anything; he just held her tight. It took a while, but finally the rigidness left her body, and she drew a deep, uneven breath and slid her arms around his chest.

He pressed a kiss against her neck, then snuggled her closer into his warmth. He knew better than to ask her what was wrong. Dev was like a filly that was head shy and real skittish—he didn't want to do anything that would make her pull back. Resting his jaw against her head, he rubbed his hand against her firmly muscled hips. "This is a hell of job I got here, Manyfeathers. I work long hours, I don't get paid, and it's cold as hell. The least you could do is show a little appreciation."

She gave a shaky laugh and slid her bare hands into the back pockets of his jeans. "Just what did you have in mind?"

He mimicked her hold, then leaned back and grinned at her. "Hell, I don't know. How about a lesson in French kissing? I figure with a little practice I could get pretty good at it."

She watched him, giving him a slightly scandalized look. "The only lesson I'm going to be giving is one on reining, McCall," she responded dryly. "And I suggest you give it a try yourself. The Nordstrom kids are going to be here any time for their riding lesson."

He brought his head up, his tone one of surprise. "Keith Nordstrom's kids?"

A wry smile lifted one corner of her mouth. "None other."

"I thought he and Lisa had moved to Lethbridge."

Devon gave a little shrug. "They did, but they only stayed a couple of years—until he got the farm dealership up and running. They moved back here last fall."

"Well, hell. I didn't know that." Chase pinched her bottom and grinned. "So if I'm not going to get my lesson, what are we doing in here?"

She gave him a slow, lazy smile, the shadows gone from her eyes. "I don't know. But you've got your hands pretty deep in my pockets, Slick."

He chuckled, then leaned down and gave her a quick, hard kiss. "You like it."

She smiled against his mouth. "Quit fishing, McCall."

Chase grinned and gave her bottom another little squeeze, thinking about her lesson. He knew that because of the work load, Devon had stopped giving lessons to the kids in the district several years ago, and in fact, that was why Sam had hired Anne. He wondered if she was giving this one. "Are you giving this lesson?"

She nodded. "I fill in for Anne on her day off."

He gave her a wicked grin. "Does that mean that Anne fills in for you on your day off?"

Devon gave him a pithy look. "You wish."

Keith Nordstrom and Chase went back a long way. They had been nearly inseparable all through school, and they had raised more hell, got into more scrapes and set the town on its ear more times than anyone could count. Keith's father had a farm implement dealership in town, but he also owned a ranch just east of Bolton. He also had the darnedest horses that walked on four legs. They were part draft horse, part thoroughbred, with a little bit of quarter horse thrown in. Running loose in a corral, they were as tame as sheep, as docile as milk cows and as friendly as retriever pups, but the minute you dropped a saddle on them, all hell broke loose. Then they turned into the wildest, snorting, bucking, crow-hopping broncs that ever drew breath, and every one of them made it a personal mission to dump any man who tried to get on him. They loved to buck. From the time he and Keith were big enough to do up the rigging, they spent hours trying to stick on them—to ride out the eight-second horn. They spent all their free time out there, and when Devon came on the scene, they used to take her along to keep time. Chase had no idea how many hours the three of them had spent in that old corral, but it had been a few. And when he decided to hit the rodeo circuit when he turned nineteen, Keith had packed up his saddle, his spurs and his harmonica and gone with him.

They were on the road together eight years. Then Keith met Lisa at a rodeo in Oklahoma. By then, Chase had enough silver belt buckles, trophies and broken bones to last him a lifetime. Keith packed up his considerable winnings, his new wife and his harmonica and went to Bolton to settle down; Chase packed up his belt buckles, trophies and mended bones and bought a spread in Colorado. As soon as he was settled, he bought all the stock Hal Nordstrom would sell him, took those horses and used them as the foundation for the best string of bucking broncs the pro circuit had ever seen. His broncs had won more championships and money than he had, and they were worth a small fortune, but the most amazing part was that the breeding stayed true. Any of the horses from Nordstrom stock still had the same easy dispositions until the chute crew dropped a saddle on their backs or tightened the flank straps. Then they turned into the wildest broncs ever to come out of a chute. Those horses had taught Chase more about bronc riding than a lifetime of riding clinics could have, and now they made him a damned good living. It made him grin just thinking about it.

Chase was doing some light work on one of his horses when Keith and his two girls showed up. Checking the horse to a walk, he rode over to the wall and reined in. He grinned when he saw the silver saddle bronc belt buckle from the Calgary Stampede. They had been tied going into the final round, and it had taken three rides, one right after another, to break the tie. The crowd had loved it. On the last round, Keith drew a horse full of spit and vinegar; Chase drew one who was a little short on try. Keith took the top money by a single point; Chase took one hell of a fall when his horse went down just after the horn sounded. They'd been so hammered up and beat down and hung over the next day, they could barely pull on their boots. It had been a dumb stunt, considering they had always split their winnings, anyway. But Keith had got the engraved silver buckle.

Letting the reins go slack, he hunched over and folded his arms on the saddle horn. "Glad to see you taking such good care of that buckle, Nordstrom. Even if your belly's starting to hang over it a little."

Keith's head swiveled around, his eyes widening with surprise; then a huge grin creased his face. "Well, I'll be damned. What are you doing here, McCall? Getting some riding lessons?"

Amusement kicking at the corner of his mouth, Chase nudged the horse against the wall, stepped out of the saddle onto the fence and swung down to the ground. He grinned and took Keith's outstretched hand. "I didn't know you were back in town or I'd have stopped by before now."

Keith slapped him on the shoulder, his eyes glinting with mischief. "You'd better get a bucket for your butt, old buddy. When Lisa finds out you've been hiding your face out here, she's going to come after you with a gun."

Chase rested his shoulder against the cambered wall and hooked his thumb over the front buckle of his chaps, fighting a grin. Lisa Nordstrom was probably the sweetest, best-natured woman Chase had ever met, and the thought of her going after anything with a gun was worth smiling about. He gazed at Keith from under the brim of his hat. "Right."

Keith chuckled, then turned. His two daughters were feeding carrots to a couple of horses down at the far end of the shed row. He called to them. "Hey, Marcy, Beth. Come see who's here."

The two girls looked toward their father, stared, then threw their carrots in a stall and came hightailing it down the alleyway. "Uncle Chase! Uncle Chase! What are you *doing* here?"

Chase straightened and stepped away from the wall, grinning at the two of them as he braced for the onslaught. They hit him going ninety miles an hour, and he caught one in each arm and hoisted them up. Marcy was nine, Beth was seven, and Chase was godfather to both of them. He hadn't seen them in two years, when Keith and Lisa had brought them down for a visit.

Nearly strangled by a clutch of arms and double hugs, he hiked them higher and grinned at them. "So how are my best girls?"

Beth planted a big kiss on his cheek, smiling from ear to ear. "We're doing fine." She stuck out her foot. "See my new boots?"

Settling them on the top of the wall, he checked out their boots. "Hey! Red ropers. Pretty classy."

Marcy gave him another hug, her bright blue eyes sparkling. "Boy, is Mom going to be surprised!"

Devon came up the shed row, swinging a bridle, and Beth turned to look at her. "Guess what, Devon? My Uncle Chase is here."

Devon smiled, shooting Chase an amused look. "Just can't keep away from the girls, can you, McCall?"

Keith chuckled and hooked his arm on the gate. "Hell, Devon. Don't worry about these two. They're just playing him for a fool."

The glimmer of amusement intensified, and she responded, her tone pointed, "Well, that shouldn't be too hard."

Chase gave her a long, level look and a menacing smile. That crack was going to get her a trip to the sawdust bin.

Devon didn't look too worried.

Chase took a particular interest in watching his goddaughters' riding lesson. Devon was not only an excellent trainer, but she was an excellent teacher, as well. He thought again about her having kids of her own.

Keith put one foot on the bottom rail of the metal gate and hooked his arms over the top, his gaze fixed on his two girls. "You're looking pretty serious there, old buddy. I got a couple of ears that aren't doing anything right now."

Bracing one arm on the upright by the gate, Chase watched Marcy do a decent stop, his expression somber.

"I'm afraid your ears aren't going to do me a hell of a lot of good this time around."

Keith rolled the straw he was chewing to the other side of his mouth and laced his hands together, watching Devon; then he cast a glance at Chase. "As I recall, my ears weren't much help last time around, either."

Chase managed a warped smile. "Hell, Nordstrom. The only thing your ears are good for is keeping your hat from slipping down over your eyes."

The other man chuckled and shifted his stance, resting his other foot on the gate rail. He watched his girls for a moment, then spoke, his tone casual. "I hear Sam's thinking about selling this place."

Chase shrugged. "He's mentioned it. I can't see him doing it, though."

Keith didn't say anything for a minute, then he spat the straw out of his mouth, turning his head to look at Chase. There was a sharp glint of amusement in his eyes. "You're damned boring today, McCall."

That got another warped half smile out of Chase. "You wouldn't know boring if you stepped in it, Nordstrom."

Chuckling, Keith straightened. "Tell you what. Why don't you and Dev come on in for supper tonight? We'll drink a little beer, shoot a little pool, and then I'll let you look at all my pretty silver belt buckles."

Chase grinned and shot his buddy a quick look. "I dunno. Sounds pretty damned boring."

There was a sly tone in Keith's voice when he answered. "Lisa's making chicken and dumplings."

Laughing, Chase slapped his old rodeo buddy on the back. "We'll be there."

Later that night, Chase lay staring into the darkness, one arm folded under his head. In a peculiar sort of way, it had been like stepping into the past, the evening at the Nordstroms'. Devon had been a little hesitant about going—not reluctant, just hesitant—and it made Chase remember one time when he had taken her out to the Nordstrom ranch with him. She'd been about thirteen—a mature, shy thirteen who looked more like sixteen—and Mrs. Nordstrom had invited them in for lemonade.

She had been so shy and hesitant that day. Suddenly his buddy, his pal, had turned into this shy, hesitant young girl who sneaked her hand into his and hung on to him like glue. She had touched some very deep, very territorial and protective feelings in him that day, and that was when their relationship had shifted. She was still his friend, his soul mate, his nearly constant companion, but from that point on, he was always acutely aware that Devon Manyfeathers was a beautiful, sensual young woman. And it sure as hell inflated his young, cocky male ego the way she ignored all the other young studs. Keith was different, though. She had let him get closer than anybody else, but even back then, Chase knew she allowed it only because of him.

It had taken Chase a long time to figure out that Devon was reserved and wary by nature. At first he'd thought it was because of her alcoholic mother and their impoverished situation, but he'd finally realized that she would have been that way no matter what. It was simply a part of who she was. And he'd seen one side of her tonight at the Nordstroms', that shy, hesitant part that he hadn't seen for a very long time, not since she was thirteen. It made him realize just how damned vulnerable she was. Staring into the darkness, he wished he was smarter, wiser. He thought again that she was like a head-shy, skittish young filly right now, and his gut instinct told him not to rush her.

He would back off and give her a little time. Maybe all he had to do was wait her out, and she would eventually take a step forward. And then again, maybe he was just whistling in the dark.

# Chapter 8

During the next week, Chase did back off. He didn't push her, he didn't try to get her talking, and he never asked her why she got that bruised, haunted look in her eyes. And he didn't ask her why he kept seeing traces of the hesitancy that had surfaced the night they went to Keith's and Lisa's, either. He knew she was wrestling with deep-seated emotions, and he knew she was more vulnerable than he'd ever seen her, but she had to make the next move. It was as if she was stranded on a high, narrow ledge. No matter what he did or said, it didn't matter a damn unless she let go and took that first step. He didn't care how big a step it was, or how she took it. He just knew nothing would change unless she did.

There were times when he felt as if he was an inch away from climbing out of his skin, and then there were times when she seemed so damned fragile that he would get her alone somewhere and just hold her. And every time he did it, she would huddle in his arms, almost as if she was cold and hurting. Nights were different. At night, she didn't want comforting or gentleness. There was a kind of wildness in her, an urgency, and she pushed him to the limit, pushed him until he finally lost it. And then the fire in her would consume him, and he would need her so damned bad and be so desperate to get inside her that there was no room for patience, for gentleness, for comfort.

He'd never had such blinding climaxes. And he'd never felt so emptied afterward. Or so hollow. He had never, ever used her to satisfy his own needs, but he felt as if he was using her now, and it bothered the hell out of him. He probably would have had it out with her, except that afterward, when they lay spent and trembling in each other's arms, she seemed to need him more than ever. She would hold on to him, her whole body trembling, and even in her sleep, she stayed close.

There were a dozen times when he came close to asking her what was wrong, but he didn't. He needed her to take that first step by herself. She had to let go of whatever handhold she was hanging on to and come to him. She had to; it wouldn't be worth anything if he forced her into it.

By Friday, Chase felt as if he were a trapped cat. Feeling as if he were an inch away from shaking somebody, he used Tanner as an excuse and took off in the afternoon. He helped Tanner move the cows that were due to drop their first calves closer to the ranch, then helped him get the calving barn set up. It was after eleven when he finally got back to Silver Springs, and Devon was already in bed, asleep. Chase had a shower and crawled in beside her, hoping she wouldn't wake up. She didn't, but the moment he stretched out beside her, she turned to him. He gathered her up and drew her head onto his chest, a heavy tightness unfolding in him. In spite of everything, that one unconscious act affected him like little else had. He snuggled her head closer and shut his eyes, his throat so full he could barely swallow. God, but he valued that. Her instinctive trust.

He awoke hours later from a disjointed, confusing dream, his heart racing and his lungs tight. For an instant he didn't know where he was. Oddly enough, it was the empty space beside him that registered first, and he scrubbed his face and tried to rid himself of the last dregs of sleep. Finally fully awake and realizing that Devon was gone, he threw back the covers and sat up, reaching for his jeans.

He found her in the living room, standing in front of the big picture window, her arms folded tightly in front of her. The yard light reflected off the snow outside, casting her in an eerie glow, the long black fall of her hair standing out starkly against the thigh-length white terry robe.

Resting his shoulder against the door frame, he folded his arms across his bare chest, his expression thoughtful as he watched her. He studied her for a moment, then spoke, his voice quiet. "Something on your mind, Slash?"

He could tell by the way her body stiffened before she turned that she hadn't heard him come in. She stared at him, then gave a little shrug. "No. I just couldn't sleep."

He continued to watch her, trying to read her face in the faint light, deciding he had no choice but to confront her. "Come on, Dev," he said, quietly chastising her lie. "Don't pull that with me. I know something's on your mind."

She stared at him for several moments, then she rubbed her upper arms and looked away. Finally she spoke, her voice soft and uneven. "Was it really because of your father that you wouldn't have anything to do with the ranch?"

Recognizing the significance of her question, realizing she was searching for verification, he watched her from the doorway. "Yeah. That was the real reason. I knew he'd try to keep his hands on the reins, and I wasn't prepared to spend the rest of my life fighting with him."

Rubbing her arms again, she turned to the window, her body tense. There was a long pause, then she spoke again, her voice so soft he could barely hear it. "I didn't know that."

It was all Chase could do to remain where he was. "Why did you think I took off?"

She shook her head, then slipped her hands up the sleeves of her robe. Chase waited, his belly in a knot. It took her a while, but she finally answered. "I thought it was because you were restless." She hesitated, then continued, a touch of wry humor in her tone, "I thought you wanted to see the world."

The knots in Chase's gut suddenly let go, and he dragged his hand down his face. For the first time, he sensed they were really headed somewhere. Massaging his eyes, he eased in a deep breath, then looked at her. "I *was* restless," he said huskily. "But if I wanted to see the world, I would have joined the Navy."

Devon turned and slid her hands into her pockets, and even in the shadowed room, he could see the hint of a smile. "You would have made a hell of a sailor, McCall. Except I don't think they would have liked your spurs."

He returned the smile, but he watched her like a hawk. "It took you a while to finish school, Slash, but I never forgot that you were here. And I never forgot where my roots were."

She looked at him, her eyes dark with doubts. "But you moved your roots, Chase. You didn't come back."

Straightening, Chase closed the distance between them, never taking his eyes off her. "Would that have made a difference? Would you have married me if I'd stayed, Devon?"

Framed in the faint illumination from the window, she stared at him, her expression stricken. It was also the first time she'd ever let him see her insecurity, and the knot in his gut eased a little more. She had taken that first step, and he couldn't ask for more, at least not right then. Not wanting to push her any further, he closed the distance, giving her a reassuring smile as he framed her face with his hands. "It's okay, darlin'," he whispered softly. "The answer isn't important. At least you listened to the question." He held her gaze for a moment, then lifted her face and gave her a slow, comforting kiss. He heard her breath catch, and she gripped his wrists.

Tightening his hold, he moved his mouth ever so softly against hers, the clean scent of her filling his senses. Releasing an unsteady sigh, he gathered her up in a secure embrace, tucking her head against the curve of his neck. He didn't say anything, he just closed his eyes and drew her deeper into his embrace, his chest tightening. You could walk around the world, if you did it one small step at a time.

He waited until he felt the stiffness leave her body, then he eased his hold. Hooking his arm around her neck, he drew her against him and turned toward the bedroom. Without him letting go of her, they negotiated the doorway into the hall, then went into the bedroom. Pausing by the bed, he lifted her head and gave her another quick kiss, then reached down and undid the belt of her robe.

He stripped off his jeans, then slid into the bed beside her, gathering her up in another snug embrace. Devon started to stroke him, but he caught her hand and lifted it to his mouth, then held it immobile against his chest. He waited until she relaxed in his arms, then he adjusted his hold. For some reason, it was suddenly important that they connect with the past. Resting his jaw against her head, he began fingering her hair. "Do you remember the time we went out to the ranch and rode up to that little box canyon south of the creek?"

She didn't say anything for the longest time; then he felt her smile. "You mean the time we got caught in that thunderstorm, and you thought you lost your wallet, and we spent an hour looking for it?"

He nodded and stroked her temple. "Yeah. That time."

"And by the time we got back to the truck it was dark, and we found the wallet on the dash, but the keys were gone?"

He smiled and stared into the darkness, remembering. "And we built a fire in the old bunkhouse to get warm and dry out our clothes, but you wouldn't stay the night because you were afraid the foreman would tell Dad if he found out."

She laughed softly and adjusted her head on his shoulder. "What I remember is that you were pretty ticked off, McCall."

"I *was* ticked. I was the one who had to go wake old Pete up so we could borrow his truck."

There was a brief pause, one that was underscored with reminiscence; then she spoke, her voice soft. "We played poker for matches, and you told me about the time you spent two days watching the herd of wild horses up in the high country."

"God, but old Pete was mad when I woke him up to borrow his truck. I spent four days fencing to work that one off."

Another recollection filtered through the others, a very special recollection, and he smiled a little, the details still crystal clear in his mind. He tightened his arm around her hip in an attention-getting hug. "Dev?"

"Hmm?"

He smoothed the thick fall of hair from her face. "Did you ever have any regrets about making love that first time?"

She shook her head. "No. Never."

"You were so damned young."

Her voice was laced with amusement when she responded. "Yes, I was. And you were such a sweet talker, McCall. I didn't stand a chance against all that virility and charm."

Chase grinned and gave her hip a little pinch. "I wasn't charming, Manyfeathers. I was a desperate man."

"Yes," she said, her tone dry. "I remember."

He gave her another little pinch, and she caught his hand, dragging his arm around her waist. He drew her closer, absently rubbing his stubbled chin against her hair. "I also remember the first time I came back after I left." He drew her even closer, brushing a soft, sensual kiss against her ear. "Remember?"

A shiver coursed through her, and she turned her head toward his caress, her voice weak and breathless when she responded. "Yes. I remember."

He'd never forget it. He had been gone four months, and he had been on the road for eighteen hours. It was one in the morning when he hit town, but he had headed straight to her house anyway. He had parked around the block, then walked down the back alley and ended up climbing in her bedroom window. He'd been running so high in overdrive, and she had been so damned glad to see him, they never even made it to her bed. It had been one hell of a homecoming. The memory turned his pulse thick and heavy, and he closed his eyes and trailed his mouth across her ear and down her neck, his breathing suddenly erratic. Devon whispered his name and moved into his arms, and on a deep, slow kiss, the darkness closed in around them. And nothing else mattered. Nothing.

Chase stood at the kitchen counter clad only in his jeans, unshaven, half-awake and feeling as cranky as a junkyard dog. It was cold, it was dark, and the fact that he hadn't got much more than three hours sleep the night before didn't help his mood. The darkness outside the window infused the still house with a nighttime silence, and the loud hum of the fridge irritated him even more. He must be getting old; he didn't function worth a damn on three hours of sleep. It was getting to the point that if it was dark outside, his body figured it should be in bed.

Thinking about the times when he and Keith had regularly driven all night to make a rodeo the following day, Chase scooped coffee into the basket, tossing in a little extra. He was going to need a whole transfusion of caffeine or he would be planting his face in the arena floor by ten o'clock.

Sliding the basket into the coffeemaker, he set the carafe on the element and flicked the switch. If he hung around here much longer, he was going to get a coffeemaker with a damned timer—this early-morning routine was a pain in the butt.

The jangle of the phone echoed shrilly in the silent house, and Chase snatched it up before the second ring. He glanced at the clock. What idiot would get on the phone at six o'clock in the morning?

The call was from Colorado, and the idiot was his partner.

"What the hell are you doing, Ernie? Or are you just trying to tick me off?"

There was a gravelly chuckle, and Ernie Bowman responded, "Hell, Chase. The day's half gone. You must be keeping banker's hours up there."

Chase leaned against the counter and crossed his legs, a flicker of amusement surfacing. "What the hell do you know about banker's hours?"

There was another gruff chuckle. "Not a damned thing. I just rolled in from Tulsa, so I thought I'd better give you a shout before I sack out here."

"So how was Tulsa?"

Ernie brought him up to date on what was happening as far as their rough stock contracts were going, and Chase found an empty envelope in a stack of papers on the counter and made notes. He finished writing out the schedule Ernie passed on, the receiver tucked against his shoulder.

Ernie gave him some other information, then paused, and Chase heard him take a deep drag on a cigarette before he continued. "So that's about it as far as the business is concerned. When are you coming home?"

Chase finished writing down the dates, a small smile appearing. Ernie was an old bulldogger, and he still liked to take the bull by the horns. Shifting the receiver to the other ear, Chase got a mug out of the cupboard and poured himself a cup of coffee. "Why do you want to know?"

There was a brief pause; then Ernie responded, his tone sheepish. "Ah, well, I heard that George Bruce is thinking about shortening his string some, and it's rumored around that he's going to retire Count Dracula. I thought if you got down here and twisted his arm just right, you might be able to get him for us."

His expression sobering, Chase set the carafe on the element, a disturbing sensation settling in his gut. Count Dracula was a fourteen-year-old stallion and one of the top buckers on the pro circuit. He was a big hammer-headed dun with the right kind of heart, and they'd had their eye on him for a long time. He might be retiring from the pro circuit, but they didn't want him for that; he was exactly the kind of stud they were looking for for their breeding program. That program was as critical and as carefully designed as the breeding program for top-stakes Thoroughbreds. They were breeding winners, and that was the foundation of their continued success. And with Count Dracula, they would breed a few more.

But it wasn't the news about the horse that hauled him up short. It was the shot of hard, cold reality that went with it. When he left, he'd told Ernie two or three weeks. His time was running out.

"You there, Chase?"

Chase exhaled heavily. "Yeah. I'm here." He considered his options, then let out another sigh. "Tell you what. I'll give George a call from here and see if we can work out a deal. I'll let you know what's going on."

"Sounds good. Talk to you later."

Chase hung up the phone, then stood staring at it for a minute, experiencing a flicker of anger. Not wanting to analyze its source, he picked up his mug and went to stand in front of the window by the table, staring out into the quiet barnyard as he took a sip. The wind had come up in the night, and there were streamers of snowdrifts in the lane. Luke would have to plow it again.

"I thought I heard the phone ring."

Without turning, he answered her. "You did. It was Ernie."

He heard the scrape of a chair, then the sound of her getting a mug out of the cupboard. "Is there a problem?"

"No. He just called to tell me about a stud we want for the breeding program." Chase finished off his coffee without looking at her, then set the empty mug on the counter. "I guess I'd better get a move on."

"Would you like some pancakes?"

Chase looked at her, his expression unsmiling. She was watching him, an air of uncertainty in her body posture. There was an anxious, questioning look in her eyes, but he knew that with all that had been going on between them, she would never ask whether something was wrong. She was too afraid he would tell her.

He managed a small smile. "Real pancakes?"

She gave a shrug, and he caught a trace of amusement in her eyes. "That depends on what you call real pancakes, McCall."

"I'm talking blueberries, buttermilk and whole-wheat flour."

"I'm talking pancake mix. Take it or leave it."

He studied her, wondering how far he could push it. Her expression said not far. He relented with a wry grin. "I guess I'll take it."

She smiled, but it didn't go as far as her eyes, and she stared at him with an odd kind of hesitancy. The silence stretched between them, and just for an instant he thought she was going to make a reference to what had happened the night before. But the moment passed, and he could feel her withdrawal from across the room. She abruptly turned away, her voice impassive when she spoke. "Do you want bacon?"

What Chase wanted was to shake her. He picked up the envelope with the information on it, his expression hardening. "No. I don't want bacon." Pushing the chair out of the way, he strode out of the room. What he wanted was to get the hell out of the house before he said something he would regret.

Breakfast was eaten in a strained silence, and as soon as he finished, Chase headed to the isolation of the lower barn. He didn't want to see anyone, he didn't want to talk to anyone, and he sure as hell didn't want to get on a horse in the mood he was in. The phone call from Ernie had yanked him up short, but her sudden withdrawal in the kitchen had stopped him dead in his tracks. He felt as if he were standing in the middle of no-man's-land.

Chase had the horses fed and the stalls cleaned out and was fixing the big push broom they used to sweep the concrete alleyway when Sam showed up. The older man stood in the doorway to the tack room, his arms folded as he watched Chase wrap the thread on the handle with a thin strip of duct tape. He didn't say anything for a moment, then spoke. "Your pa's lawyer called. Said he wanted to talk to you."

Using far more torque than necessary, Chase screwed the handle on the broom. "Well, I don't want to talk to him."

"Seems it's important."

Chase threw the roll of duct tape into the wooden toolbox, then rose. Resting his hand on the broom, he looked at Sam, his expression harsh. "When it comes to my old man, it's always important."

Sam gave him a level gaze. "Maybe you should talk to him, boy. Sometimes things aren't what they seem."

Chase stared at the trainer, then looked away and exhaled heavily. He looked down the row of box stalls, the dusky quiet perforated by the sound of chickadees outside. He considered Sam's comment, then let go another exasperated sigh. "Maybe you're right."

"He said he'd call back in fifteen minutes. You can take it in the house, if you want."

Chase picked up the broom, balancing the weight in his hand. He shook his head. "No. I've got to go into town anyway. If he does call back, tell him I'll stop by."

Sam nodded, scratching his jaw. "You planning on going soon?"

"As soon as I finish here."

"Would you mind stopping by the vet's? We're running low on bute."

Coster Feldman had been Bruce McCall's lawyer for as long as Chase could remember. He was polished, smooth and politically well connected, and Chase didn't trust him as far as he could chuck him. His was in the first law office that had been built in Bolton, somewhere around the turn of the century, and Coster had spent a small fortune restoring it to its original state. The waiting room was furnished with early 1900s furniture—several chairs and a walnut parson's bench—and in the corner by the window sat a huge fern that looked like it had been there ever since the office opened. A dark oak spindled railing with a gate separated the waiting room from the office area, and Chase's expression softened. He had a sudden mental flashback of his sister, Eden, swinging on that gate, her butt in the air, singing to herself.

He touched the wood, then his expression altered, and he pushed the gate open. The secretary looked up from the computer, and Chase shifted his weight onto one leg. "Chase McCall. I'm here to see Mr. Feldman."

Chase had half expected the attorney to pull one of his power plays and keep him waiting, but the secretary rose immediately and ushered him toward the back office. The speed of his reception set off a dozen warning bells, and Chase experienced the same rush he always got just before a chute gate swung open and fourteen hundred pounds of horseflesh bunched beneath him.

His black Stetson in his hand, he stepped into the darkly paneled office, his expression shuttered. Coster rose immediately and smiled a politician's smile, his string tie and Western-cut jacket somehow artificial. He looked as if he had just come off someone's campaign trail—or was ready to hit one. Like maybe his brother Milt's.

"Chase! It's damned good to see you. Welcome back."

Chase braced his feet in a gunslinger's stance, his jaw set at a determined angle. "Coster."

"Sit down, my boy. Sit down! I'll have Carla bring us coffee."

Chase remained standing. He stared at the other man, his expression set. "I won't be staying long enough for coffee."

The smile faltered just for an instant. "Well, now, why don't you have a seat anyway and we'll talk—"

"We don't have anything to talk about. Whatever my old man's up to, he can forget it. I don't want anything to do with him."

A voice came from behind him. "Still as bullheaded as ever, I see."

Chase turned, the muscles in his gut hardening. He faced his father for the first time in eighteen years. One corner of his mouth lifted in a cold, sardonic smile. "And you still like to operate behind a man's back."

His hand curling around an ivory-handled cane, Bruce McCall rose, his huge frame hunched with age, his eyes still as piercing as a hawk's. His hair was completely white, and his face was leaner and etched with years of hard dealing, but he still had the same aura of power. He stepped forward, a calculating glint in his eyes. "It's time to bury the hatchet, boy. You've made your point."

Chase almost smiled. "Glad to hear it."

Bruce McCall waved his hand at Coster in an impatient gesture. "Go on. Go on. Tell him the deal."

The lawyer shuffled through some papers on his desk. "We have the deed to the ranch here, and your father is prepared to sign it over to you, lock, stock and barrel. All you have to do is agree to a couple of terms that—"

Chase cut him off, his tone flat. "I don't want it. Give it to Milt or Eden, or better yet, give it to Tanner."

Coster Feldman made a conciliatory gesture. "Now, Chase. We're talking about ten thousand acres of prime land."

"I don't care if we're talking about the whole damned province. I'd rather get in bed with a snake than do business with my old man."

Bruce McCall stepped forward, his face mottled with rage. "Now just a damned minute! You aren't going to stand there spouting that kind of crap. That ranch is worth a fortune, and you aren't going to turn your back on it. You'll take it or I'll—"

Chase met his father's gaze, a bitter smile appearing. "Or you'll what? Disinherit me? Charge me with theft again? Turn your back on me like you did Tanner? Screw up my life like you did Milt's? Force me to leave home like you did Eden? What, old man? What will you do to me?"

Coster Feldman stepped between the two men, raising his hand. "Now, Chase. There's no need to get hot under the collar. Like your father said, it's time to let bygones be bygones."

His fury controlled, Chase turned his gaze to the other man, another bitter smile appearing. "So just what are the terms, Coster? And just how many strings are attached?"

The lawyer's gaze flicked to the senior McCall; then he glanced at Chase, a nervous tic appearing at the corner of his eye. He offered a placating smile. "Now, Chase. Let's be reasonable. The Bar M has always been passed on to the eldest son. Besides, neither Milt or Eden would be... appropriate."

There was something in the lawyer's tone that caught Chase's attention, and he paused, trying to figure out what it was. An artificialness...no, more like an evasiveness. His eyes narrowed, his gaze assessing, Chase studied the attorney, and a tiny piece fell into place. He smiled a dangerous smile. "But I'm not the eldest son, Coster. Or have you forgotten that?"

The attorney gave him another politician's smile and backpedaled. "Eldest *legitimate* son."

Chase folded his arms and rocked back on his heels, considering the man's response. His tone was ominously quiet when he spoke. "But I don't think that would really wash in court, do you, Coster? Or is that what this is about?" Reading the answer in the other man's evasive gaze, Chase looked at his father. He stared at him, his gaze cold and unyielding, a sneer in his tone when he spoke. "You might have disowned him, but I won't. And neither will Eden." He leveled his finger at his father, his voice ominously quiet. "He's my brother. And you'd better never forget that. Ever."

Settling his hat on his head, he gave them one last, drilling stare, then turned and left, pulling the door closed behind him.

Chase didn't let go of his rage until he cleared town; then he used speed and recklessness and the rush of danger-induced adrenaline to override the fury that threatened to explode with every turn of the wheel. With anger eating away at him, he swore savagely, so damned mad he could barely see straight. Someday he was going to get to the bottom of this mess, but not now. Now he had to clear his system or he would end up going back to town and beating the hell out of his father and his damn lawyer. One hell of a pillar of the community, his old man. It would be laughable, if it weren't so sick and twisted. Chase clenched his jaw, and the speedometer climbed. All he wanted to do was outrun the suffocating weight of pure, hot rage.

Chase parked his truck by the Circle S cook house, then leaned back in his seat and stared out the window. He wasn't too sure what he was doing here, but he knew he was in no shape to go to Devon's. It had taken two hundred miles of hard driving before he was able to let go of some of the anger that had clawed through him. He should never have gone to see Coster. He'd known as soon as Sam told him the lawyer had called that his old man was up to something, but he'd taken the bait anyway. And once he'd cooled off a little, he realized that a good chunk of his anger was directed squarely at himself. He should have bloody well known better. His father would go to his grave trying to yank his strings.

The driver's-side door opened, and Cyrus Brewster stuck his head in. "Are you goin' to jest sit here staring, or are you goin' to haul your scrawny butt in for some pie and coffee?"

Cyrus was in his late sixties, short and lean, with snapping eyes, a sweeping white mustache and a droll perspective that Chase had always appreciated. He had been the foreman of his father's ranch when Chase was small. Chase had idolized him then, and he knew that Tanner's kids idolized him now.

Resting one arm on the steering wheel, Chase gave the cook a warped smile. "It's nice to know I've graduated from milk and cookies, old man."

The cook studied him, a twinkle appearing in his eyes. "Sounds like maybe you haven't. Got a bean up your nose, boy? Or are you jest looking for a dog to kick?"

Chase stared at the older man, then grinned and shook his head. Tossing his sunglasses on the dash, he climbed out of the truck. One of Tanner's border collies bounded up, and he leaned down and scratched the dog's neck. "Nah. I think the dogs are safe." His grin deepened. "I hope I can say the same for your pie and coffee."

The cook house smelled of baking bread and the cookies cooling on the counter. One thing, Tanner never had to worry about his hired hands going hungry with Cyrus in the kitchen. Chase dropped his hat on the old trunk situated by the door, then pulled out a chair from the table and sat down. He watched the older man select a pie from the glassed-in dessert rack and slide it onto the counter. Cyrus had been one of the best cowpokes in the district in his day—dead steady on a horse, dead accurate with a rope and probably possessed of more horse sense than all the other Circle S hands put together. But he'd turned in his saddle and spurs for a stove and ladles when a horse went over backward with him fifteen years ago, damaging Cyrus's back and hips. He'd been ramrodding the Circle S cook house ever since, and Chase still had to bite back a smile every time he saw the old cowboy throw together a meal. Somehow or other, he still made it look as if he was out on the open range roping steers.

Cyrus returned to the table with two steaming mugs of coffee and two large servings of blueberry pie, the eating utensils stuck in his shirt pocket. He set everything down, then dumped the cutlery on the table and pulled out a chair.

He took the sugar bowl off the lazy Susan in the middle of the table, stirred a spoonful into his coffee, then set the container back. Cutting a piece of his pie with the side of his fork, he spoke, his tone offhand. "I expect by the set of your chin that you've been to see your pa."

Chase looked up, his gaze riveted on the older man, then a small, wry smile appeared. He shouldn't be surprised. Cyrus had always had an uncanny ability to read his mind. He stared at the cook for an instant, then cut into his own pie.

There was a short silence; then Cyrus spoke again, the same casual tone in his voice. "Expect he's made another stab at getting you back up here, with your feet planted in McCall ground."

Avoiding the cook's wily gaze, Chase washed the pie down with a swig of coffee, then set his mug down. He rubbed his thumb against the top of the handle, then spoke, his voice devoid of any expression. "That's about it."

"So what are you going to do, boy?"

"I wouldn't take that ranch if it was buried in gold."

Cyrus tipped his head in silent acknowledgment, and nothing more was said until both plates were empty. Then the old man stirred his coffee and slid the spoon onto his plate. "I imagine that stuck in his craw some."

His arms on the table, Chase hunched over, absently twisting his coffee mug in the ring of moisture. Finally he looked at the older man, his gaze solemn and unwavering. "I'd like to know why you left the Bar M, Cyrus."

Cyrus stared at him; then he, too, pushed his plate aside and leaned his arms on the table. Chase could tell by his solemn expression that he was considering his answer. The old man finally spoke, his voice gruff. "I can't tell you that, boy. It wouldn't be fitting."

Chase studied him, his face unsmiling. "It had something to do with Tanner, didn't it?"

The cook released a heavy sigh, then nodded once. "Yep. It did. But that's between me and him, Chase. It's not something to go digging around in."

Chase watched him for a moment, then looked down, rubbing his thumbnail against the rough surface of the cup. He knew that Tanner had been fourteen when Burt Shaw took him in. If both Burt and Cyrus wouldn't talk about it, it had to be bad. His gut tightened just thinking about it. He took another drink of coffee, then spoke, his voice even. "I don't want anything to do with that ranch, Cy. Just on principle, if nothing else."

A glint of amusement twinkled in Cyrus's eyes. "Well, now. If you had as much common sense as you did principle, you'd be a rich man."

The corner of Chase's mouth lifted a little. "Yeah. Well."

Cyrus made a big deal out of wiping some blueberry filling off the table, his tone just a little too offhand when he asked, "How's things goin' at Sam's?"

Chase turned his head and looked at the other man, not fooled by the innocent expression on Cyrus's face. The corner of his mouth lifted a little higher. "Things are going fine."

The cook moved all the items on the lazy Susan and wiped off a scattering of sugar. "So how long are you stickin' around?"

Chase stared at the other man for a moment, then looked at the table, his expression fixed and sober. "I don't know," he answered, his tone subdued.

There was a long pause, the hum from the clock on the wall the only sound breaking the silence. Finally Cyrus spoke, his voice gruff. "There's more on your mind than your pa's finagling, ain't there?"

His elbows resting on the table, Chase stared at the space in front of him. He considered the other man's question for several moments, then released a long sigh. "Yeah. There is."

The old man's voice was gruff with recollection. "Sometimes life is a whole lot like a poker game, boy. Sometimes you get dealt a hand you don't like or ain't even expectin'. But them's the cards you got, and you've gotta either fold 'em, play 'em or lay 'em. It ain't always easy to figure out what's the smart thing to do." He paused, then spoke again, a trace of humor in his voice. "And sometimes you gotta take the chance that's either goin' to make you or break you."

Chase looked at Cyrus, a heavy feeling settling in his gut. He could see the sorrow in the other man's face, and he knew the cook was thinking about the wife he'd lost thirty years before. He remembered the grief he'd seen in Devon's eyes.

Cyrus spoke again, his voice rough with emotion, his tone gruff with kindness and solemn counsel. "And sometimes you just gotta bite the bullet and get out of the game. You've been marking time for a lot of years now, and maybe it's time to get on with your life."

Chase swallowed hard and looked away, his jaw clenched tight against the sudden ache in his throat. The old man was right. He either had to lay his cards on the table or get out of the game. They couldn't go on the way they were. He had known it ever since he'd walked out on his father.

## Chapter 9

Chase lay on the leather sofa in Devon's living room, his hands under his head, watching the clouds through the picture window as they moved across the sky. A chinook had blown in that afternoon, and the weather had turned balmy and mild, the sky-wide chinook arch tinged with pink from the setting sun. He listened to the sound of the shower, his attention fixed on the moving clouds, his mind drifting. Sometimes he wondered if his life would have been less complicated if he'd been more like his old man.

The shower shut off, and Chase came out of his reverie. He'd come in while she was in the bathroom, and he wasn't sure how to play that first face-to-face confrontation. He wondered how many of his decisions had dramatically altered the course of his life. The decision to leave Bolton certainly had, but he wondered about others. He wondered what would have happened if he'd stayed. In fact, he'd been doing some heavy-duty wondering since he'd talked to Cyrus.

He heard the bathroom door open and he heard her go into the bedroom. A few moments later she entered the living room, her wet hair hanging down her back, darkening the fabric of her deep red sweat suit. Chase smiled a little, remembering the very first time he'd seen her. She had been wearing red then, too, only her hair had hung down to her hips. Now it hung to her shoulder blades. She had looked aloof and exotic, with her almond-shaped eyes and high cheekbones, and he remembered how the sight of her had stopped him cold—as if he recognized her from another time. He could clearly remember thinking she was someone special. That was one sentiment that hadn't changed in over twenty years. He still thought she was special, and he couldn't imagine what his life would have been like without her in it.

His throat suddenly tight, he spoke, his voice husky. "Hi. I was beginning to think you'd drowned in there."

She turned, her eyes widening with that startled doe look of hers, then she gave him a lopsided smile. "I hope you weren't planning on a hot shower."

He watched her, a peculiar soft feeling filling up his chest. His hands still under his head, he returned her smile. "And I hope you weren't expecting me to make supper."

She didn't miss the implication, and she stared at him, a glimmer of humor appearing in her eyes. A smile lurking around her mouth, she sauntered over to the sofa in that loose-hipped way of hers and knelt down on the floor beside him. Bracing one hand on his chest, she leaned over and gave him a soft, moist and deliberately provocative kiss. "It only takes twenty minutes for the water to heat up," she whispered huskily.

She so seldom used female persuasion to get her way that it caught Chase by surprise, and he laughed against her mouth. "You'd do anything for a meal, wouldn't you?"

She softly brushed her mouth against his, the warmth and moistness of the kiss making his pulse erratic. She licked his bottom lip slowly—very slowly. "You bet."

Opening his mouth beneath hers, Chase raised his head just enough to deepen the kiss, resolutely keeping his hands beneath his head. He wondered just how far she was prepared to take this little bit of seduction. She changed the angle of her head, perfecting the seal of her mouth against his; then she smoothed her hand down his chest, undoing the snaps on his shirt with little flicks of her thumb. Holding his head immobile with her other hand, she deepened the kiss and pulled his shirt out of his waistband, then lightly dragged her thumbnail across his nipple. Chase jerked, her touch sending a sharp current of sensation through him, and his heart went into overdrive when she lightly rolled the hardened nub under her fingers.

He wanted to grab her and drag her on top of him, but her seduction was too sweet, too rare, too arousing, to let go. With a wild flurry of excitement building in him, Chase tightened his muscles against her tormenting touch, yielding his mouth to hers as she deepened the kiss. Just as she stroked the inside of his bottom lip with her tongue, she trailed her fingernail down the hard ridge of flesh beneath his fly, and the dual sensations nearly put Chase through the roof. His breathing turned heavy, and it took every once of control he had to remain still and unmoving beneath her lightly exploring hands and mouth. She stroked the full length of his hard, thick arousal again, and Chase sucked in a ragged breath, releasing a guttural sound against her mouth when she trailed her nails between his legs and down the sensitive base.

Working her mouth slowly against his, she shifted slightly, then used both hands to undo his belt. Chase lifted his hips off the sofa, and she pulled the belt free of the loops and dropped it on the floor, then slid her long fingers beneath his waistband. Her intimate touch electrified him, and he lifted his head and drew her tongue deeply into his mouth, the pulsating hardness in his groin nearly exploding as she carefully drew his zipper down. With the same slow care, she freed him, and Chase abruptly ceased to breathe. Unable to remain passive one second longer, he caught her by the back of the head and ground his mouth hungrily against hers, heat searing through him as she lightly smoothed her thumb over the moist, slick tip of his arousal.

Grasping her face between his hands, Chase gazed at her, his breathing labored. Her eyes dark and heavy-lidded, her full, sensual mouth swollen from the urgency of his kiss, she was the temptress, the vixen, his ultimate fantasy. His hands circling her neck, he stroked the line of her jaw with his thumbs, her pulse frantic beneath the heels of his hands. He wanted her naked on top of him, he wanted to be buried so deep inside her that he would become part of her, and he wanted to let go of the heat that had him hard and erect. But this was as far as he could go. The box of condoms was in the drawer in the bedside table, and right then, he wasn't sure he could stand up long enough to get it.

Still wishing she was naked on top of him, he drew her face down and covered her swollen mouth with a soft, comforting kiss. "I like the way you negotiate, Slash," he whispered gruffly against her mouth. "But a critical piece of equipment is still in the bedroom."

He felt her take a deep, unsteady breath; then she kissed both his eyes closed. "Don't move," she whispered. She pulled free of his hold, and Chase clenched his teeth against the sharp sense of separation, the ache in him growing heavier. Resting one arm over his eyes, he tried not to think, not to feel. He was at the point where a single touch could set him off, and the thought of sinking deep inside her was enough to send him over the edge.

He heard her. Then there was the brush of her damp hair spilling against his chest when she leaned over and gave him a soft, seeking kiss. Chase let his breath go in a shaky rush and took her face between his hands, moving her head in counterpoint to his as he took control and thoroughly explored her mouth. She let him take what he wanted; then, with an unsteady sigh, she drew back. He realized that she had taken off her sweat suit and wore only her short robe, and Chase brushed his knuckles against the swell of her breasts. He heard her breath catch, and she moved her hand down his torso.

Chase clenched his teeth and sucked in a deep breath when she took his hard, pulsating flesh in her hand, stroking him with the lightest of touches. Her gaze locked on his, she stroked him again, and Chase's face contorted at the sharp, intense pleasure that ricocheted through him. Devon cupped him in both hands, her eyes dilating, her pulse quickening, and Chase rose up on one elbow and caught her behind the head, pulling her toward him. She resisted. Moistening her lips, she held his gaze for an instant longer, then looked down. His heart hammering like a wild thing in his chest, Chase watched her as she put the condom in place, then slowly began to roll it down, her touch soft and unsteady. Chase thought his heart was going to come right through his chest as he watched her carefully sheath him, and he gritted his teeth, need and want and a fever of desire reaching a flash point. The instant she had the protection in place, he caught her by the back of the neck and rolled, carrying her to the floor beneath him. Urgently finding her mouth with his, he drew up her knees and roughly settled himself in the cradle of her thighs. Emitting a low groan, he entered her, his awareness shattering into a sunburst of sensation. Then he slipped into a space where there was nothing except him and Devon—and driving urgency.

It took Chase a long time to come down after the earth-shaking climax. And it took him a long time before he could relax his urgent hold on her. But finally he was able to collect enough strength to ease back a little. The first two things that filtered through his consciousness were how fiercely Devon was hanging on to him, and that she was trembling in his arms. Shifting his hold on her, he lifted her hair out of the way, then protectively cradled her face against his chest, his hand cupped at the base of her neck. He brushed a kiss against her hair, then rubbed his thumb along her heated skin. "Hey," he whispered unevenly. "Are you okay?"

She nodded once, hugging him even tighter. Chase smiled a little, then kissed her again, a huge lump of tenderness jamming up in his chest. He held on to her for a moment longer, then tried to shift his weight, but she gripped him. "No."

Lifting a thick strand of hair from her damp neck, he tipped his head and kissed her shoulder. "The floor's cold, darlin', and I've got you jammed right up against the sofa."

Her chest rising on a deep, unsteady breath, she loosened her hold and cupped the back of his head. "I don't care."

Chase chuckled. "Well, I do. You'll get slivers in your butt from this wood floor." Not to mention the fact that their protection wouldn't be worth spit in a few more minutes.

Devon tightened her hold and shook her head. Not particularly hot on the idea himself, Chase grinned and hugged her, then shifted his hold. "Hang on, then, darlin'. We're going to turn this act around."

It took a bit of effort and some undignified grunting, but he finally shifted their positions so he was sitting on the floor, his back against the sofa, with Devon straddling him. She was still hanging on to him with her face buried against his neck, but he could feel her smiling. He rubbed one hand across her bare hips, nestling her closer. "What?" he queried softly.

She turned her head, kissing him just below his ear. "That was pretty slick, Slick," she answered, her voice husky.

Settling into a more comfortable position, he slid his hand under her robe and up her back. He rested his head against hers, a soft smile surfacing. "You like that, huh?"

"Uh-huh."

"How come I had to do all the work?"

She lazily stroked the back of his neck. "Because it was your idea."

His smile deepened, and he stroked her hip again. He held her for a few more minutes, then kissed the curve of her jaw. "You better lift up, babe," he whispered against her skin. She remained unmoving, and Chase tightened his hold on her, experiencing a rush of tenderness. He could stay like this forever, buried deep inside her, her body soft and pliant against his. And he would be happier than hell if he got her pregnant. But his conscience wouldn't let go.

He smoothed his hand across her firmly muscled back, then gave her a little squeeze. "Come on, babe," he said gruffly. "We're going to be in big trouble here if we stay like this."

She released a long sigh, then reluctantly stirred and braced her weight on her knees. Loath to do it, Chase tightened his hold on her and withdrew, pressing a kiss against her neck when she drew a sharp breath. He gave her a minute to adjust; then he shifted his hips under her. Closing his eyes, he slowly rubbed her back, a deep, tranquilizing contentment spreading through him. He didn't want to think about anything right now. Not about his father, not about Ernie, not about what he was faced with. He just wanted to try to get his fill of holding her.

Chase smiled to himself when, moments later, he felt her go slack in his arms, and her breathing became slow and even. He reached behind him and snagged the Mexican blanket from the far end of the sofa, then wrapped it around her. His throat suddenly tight, he gathered her damp hair and pulled it free, then tightened his arm around her back. Taking a deep, uneven breath, he rested his head against hers, wishing he knew how to say all the things that needed to be said.

Twilight slowly infiltrated the room, and the western horizon slowly sucked the color from the sky, leaving the mountains a ragged purple silhouette. With Devon asleep in his arms, Chase watched the changing landscape, his back growing stiff. One leg was developing a serious cramp, and he shifted slightly, trying to ease the strain.

Her breath feathered against his neck, and she spoke, her voice thick with sleep. "So, Slick. Does that get me supper or not?"

Smiling at her quirk of coming awake without any warning, Chase turned his head and kissed her temple. His tone gruff, he responded, "I'll have to think about that."

Devon stirred in his arms, turning her head so their mouths connected. "I'll give you a back rub," she negotiated, her tone still husky with sleep.

Chase closed his eyes and tightened his hold, a knot of raw emotion climbing up his throat. He waited for the aching contraction to ease, then he spoke the words he hadn't risked speaking for a very long time. "Do you know how much I love you, Manyfeathers?"

She went stock-still in his arms, then she lifted her head and looked at him, her eyes wide, her expression transfixed by a host of emotions. Chase took her face between his hands, his expression strained as he held her gaze. "Marry me, Dev. I want us to get married and have some kids and make a home. I want to stop this craziness."

Devon stared at him, unmoving, unbelieving, uncertain. Tightening his hold on her face, he took a deep, unsteady breath and gave her a little shake, then spoke, his voice catching. "Marry me."

She stared at him for an instant; then her eyes filled with tears, and she hugged him like there was no tomorrow. His throat closed up completely, and Chase shut his eyes and turned his face against her, hugging her back. Maybe there was still room for miracles. Maybe.

Trying his damnedest to get rid of the big lump in his throat, he ran his hand up her spine. "You gotta know I love you, Slash. You've been my girl since you were eleven years old."

She made a sound that was somewhere between laughter and tears, and she hugged him even harder. "I've missed you so much. So damned much."

Wrapping his arms right around her torso, he totally enveloped her and turned his face against the soft skin of her neck. Feeling lighter than he could ever remember feeling, he gave her a tight squeeze and whispered against her skin, "Do you know how bad I wanted to get you pregnant?"

Devon gave a shaky laugh and tipped her head against his. "Then why do we have half a drugstore in the bedroom?"

He grinned and kissed the tight cord in her neck. "Because I'm a nice guy, Manyfeathers."

She moved her hips slowly and sensually against him. "Yes," she whispered huskily. "You are."

Liking her double-barreled answer a whole lot, Chase chuckled and dropped his arms around her hips. "And here I thought you just wanted me to make supper. Now you're trying to stir up something else."

Laughing softly, Devon lifted her head and looked at him, her gaze bright with laughter and love. "You're disgusting."

Chase gazed at her, loving the sparkle in her eyes, loving her. His expression altering, he reached up and slowly dragged a thick tendril of hair over her shoulders, his touch soft and seductive. "Tell me you love me, Dev," he murmured. "It's been a long time, and I need to hear you say the words."

She stared at him, her expression altering. He knew he was asking her to do something that had never been easy for her. In all the time they'd spent together, for all they'd meant to each other, she had only said those words three times. And now he was asking her to say them again. Hooking his knuckles under her chin, he lifted her face and coaxed her with a gentle smile, his touch slow and provoking. "Say it," he commanded softly.

She tried to swallow; then tears appeared, and she looked at him, her heart in her eyes. She drew a shaky breath, then spoke, her gaze steady and unguarded. "I love you, Chase," she whispered unevenly. "You're my spirit." With tears glistening in her long lashes, she touched his face with infinite gentleness, then leaned forward and kissed him, whispering against his mouth. "You know I love you."

His throat thick and his chest chock-full of emotion, Chase caught her by the back of her head, his fingers tangling in her hair as he opened his mouth beneath hers, taking all that she offered. She gave him what he wanted; then she pressed her hand against his face and eased away. "Let's go to bed," she whispered.

It was going on eight o'clock by the time they made it to the kitchen for supper. Devon had put the red sweat suit back on, and she looked mussed and thoroughly sated and as soft as velvet. She sat on one of the kitchen chairs, her knees drawn up and her arms locked around them, watching him as he made omelets. Chase whistled while he efficiently whipped up the meal. Flipping the omelets, he turned down the heat on the burner, then glanced at her, amusement flickering through him. She looked like a pampered and lazy cat, sitting there with her chin propped on her upraised knees, her black hair a wild tangle around her face, just waiting for him to feed her. "You're taking a lot for granted, aren't you?"

She gave him her half-asleep attention. "What do you mean?"

He checked the omelets, then leaned against the counter and folded his arms. "I mean that you expect me to feed you."

She watched him, that same sleepy, satisfied look on her face. He caught a glint of amusement in her eyes, and her mouth lifted a little. "You're the one who learned to cook, Slick. So don't blame me."

He watched her, liking the way she held his gaze, liking the intimacy of the smile in her eyes. "You're a piece of work, you know that?"

She didn't say anything; she just continued to give him that drowsy smile. He wondered if she had any idea what a hell of a mess her hair was in. She'd had it combed when she first came out of the bathroom, but now it looked as if it had been styled with an eggbeater and dried in a wind tunnel. It was hard not to notice. But then, her hair wasn't all he'd noticed. He had also noticed that she hadn't actually said yes to his marriage proposal. He remembered one old mare he had. Wouldn't go through a gate—she would balk and throw a fit every time. She was a top bucker on the circuit, but she hated corrals, and as far as that old rodeo queen was concerned, every gate led to one. When Chase finally won a battle and got her to go through one leading to the pasture, the old mare had stood there, quivering and confused. It was as though it had finally sunk in that there was all that freedom on the other side. Devon was a lot like that old mare; all he had to do was get her through the gate.

"Why are you smiling?"

He continued to watch her, his amusement deepening. He wondered what she would do if he told her. "I was just thinking how you balk at gates, Manyfeathers. That's all."

"I don't know what you're talking about, McCall."

"I know you don't." He turned to the stove and switched off the burner. He would deal with her gates later. "Put your feet on the floor, Slash. Supper's ready."

They ended up eating their supper in front of the fire in the living room, sitting on the floor, shoulder to shoulder, with their backs braced on the sofa. They talked about the horses Devon had worked that day, they talked about training, but they didn't talk about them. Chase didn't mind marking time; he knew how Devon shied away from openness. He'd got her to say she loved him. Now all he had to do was get her to say yes.

He polished off his omelet and set his plate aside, then took a long swig of beer. Resting the bottle on his thigh, he glanced at Devon. He smiled when he saw the thoughtful frown on her face and the way she was pushing the remaining food around on her plate. She clearly had something on her mind.

Chase drained the bottle and set it aside, then drew up one leg and rested his arm across his knee. And waited.

It was as though his stillness had telegraphed itself to her, and Devon abruptly put her fork down and slid her plate onto the coffee table, as if she was getting rid of the evidence of her nervousness. Chase could tell she was wrestling with something, and he simply waited her out.

Her expression strained, she rubbed away a mark on the leg of her sweat suit. Finally she spoke. "Sam told me that your dad's lawyer called and that you went into town to see him."

"I did."

She shot him a quick glance, then averted her gaze, again picking at the mark on her pants. "What happened?"

His arm still draped across his upraised knee, Chase continued to watch her. It was the second time in years, since the day she'd told him she wouldn't marry him, that she'd initiated any conversation about his father. Another step. That one small gesture touched him like little else had. He waited for the feeling to ease; then he spoke, his voice gruff. "My old man was there."

Devon's gaze was riveted on him, and she stared at him, her eyes registering her alarm. Chase gave her a small, crooked grin. "Nice, huh?"

She stared at him, her expression intense. "What happened?"

Chase shrugged and looked away. "He had the papers all drawn up to sign the Bar M over to me."

"Oh."

Chase glanced at her, wondering about the funny inflection in her voice. She had her hands wedged between her thighs, and he could sense the tension in her. And a trace of fear. She looked so damned vulnerable, and so uncertain. She looked so much like the young, uncertain girl he remembered, and he simply reacted. Pushing his plate out of the way, he slid one arm behind her back and caught her across the thighs, pulling her legs across his. His fingers snagging in her unbraided hair, he pressed her head against his shoulder, then wrapped her up in a strong, secure embrace. She closed her eyes, and he heard her swallow. Chase shifted his hold. Spanning her jaw with his hand, he tipped her face up and brushed a soft, reassuring kiss against her mouth. "You are going to put me out of my misery and marry me, aren't you, Manyfeathers?" he whispered huskily.

Sliding her arms around his back, she hugged him hard, and Chase closed his eyes and hugged her back. "Come on, babe," he said, his voice gruff and uneven. "All you have to do is say yes."

She tightened her hold and pressed her face against his neck. He felt her chest expand, like a diver about to plunge off a high precipice. "Yes," she whispered, so softly that he could barely hear her. She took another deep breath, then tightened her hold even more. "Yes."

Chase turned his face into the silky tangle of her hair, his arms tightening around her torso, the wrench of emotion so profound that he felt as if something huge had opened up inside him. God, but it had finally come together for them. Finally.

It took a long time before he could ease his crushing hold, the fullness in his chest almost more than he could handle. Drawing an uneven breath, he caught her by the back of the head and pressed a kiss against the soft curve of her neck. Devon clutched him, and he realized that she was even more shaken than he was. Softening his hold just a little, he gave her a quick hug, trying to comfort her. "You sure as hell take your sweet time coming up with the right answer, Manyfeathers. I was beginning to think I was permanently out of the race."

She emitted a shaky laugh and gave him a light squeeze. "You were never out of the race, McCall. You're one of the most persistent people I know."

He grinned and gave her another quick kiss. "Damned good thing I am. You're a hard filly to corner."

She responded with a poke, and Chase grinned again, knowing full well that she hated those kinds of horse references. Giving her another firm hug, he rested his head against hers, experiencing a lightness that made him feel nearly indestructible. He had finally run her to ground, and she had said yes. Experiencing another surge of emotion, he closed his eyes and took a deep breath. He smoothed his hand up the full length of her back, molding her more snugly against him. "So," he said gruffly, "are we going to make a bunch of babies?"

She abruptly turned her face against his neck and tightened her hold, and he felt her chest expand unevenly against him. Cupping his hand under her jaw to nestle her head closer, he felt her swallow hard; then she nodded. Affected by her emotional struggle, Chase drew her deeper into his embrace and rested his cheek against the top of her head. "I do love you, Dev," he said huskily. "And I'm going to spend the rest of my life making you believe that." With all the gentleness he could muster, he lifted her head so he could see her face. She had her eyes tightly closed and her jaw clenched, but in spite of her battle to hold everything in, tears seeped out from beneath her lashes. His throat tight, he bent his head and kissed her face. "Just know that, okay?" he whispered gruffly.

Her throat worked, and she nodded once, then tried to turn her face against his shoulder. Chase maintained his hold, stroking the angle of her jaw with his thumb. "Look at me, babe." He felt her try to swallow again, then she opened her eyes and looked at him, the shimmer of tears adding a heart-wrenching vulnerability to her raw emotion. And for the first time she allowed him to see exactly what she was feeling. He wiped away the tears and smiled softly, his throat cramping. "You'd better speak up here, Slash, or I'm going to set a figure for all those babies that might scare the hell out of you."

She gave a shaky laugh through her tears, and he gazed at her. Tightening his hold on her face, he lowered his head and kissed her, closing his eyes when she opened her mouth and responded. Chase put all the tenderness, all the caring he felt for her into that slow, languid kiss, and finally the tension in her body eased, and she relaxed in his arms. Releasing an uneven sigh, Chase slowly withdrew, watching her come out of the sensations that kiss aroused, her lips moist and parted. Resisting the urge to take her under again, he brushed her hair with the backs of his fingers, smiling into her eyes when she finally opened them and looked at him. "How does an even dozen strike you?"

She stared at him, then gave him one of her dry, amused looks. "Excessive."

He grinned at her. "I don't know. I kind of like the thought of a bunch of babies lined up like a carton of eggs."

Straightening in his embrace, she gave him another dry look. "They're my eggs, McCall, and you aren't getting a dozen."

"I see."

"I'm glad that you do." She turned so she was straddling his legs, then leaned down and gave him a soft, lingering kiss. "But I'd settle for four," she murmured, licking his bottom lip.

Chase grinned against the softness of her mouth. "Four, huh? So if we work fast, we could get 'em here before I turn forty."

"You're *never* going to be forty, Slick. You're always going to be a big kid." She took his face in her hands and did some incredible things to his mouth. "And lack of speed has never been your problem."

His arms settling loosely around her hips, Chase let her explore and taste, reciprocating in kind, amusement warring with arousal. Lord, but she could turn him on. Realizing where all this was headed if he didn't put the brakes on, he massaged her hips and reluctantly drew away. She sat astride him, her arms resting on his shoulders, her tangled hair a wild tumble around her face. She looked soft, sensual and sexy as sin.

Smiling into her eyes, he gently tucked her hair back from her face, then touched the lobe of her ear. "We've got some talking to do," he said, his voice low and husky. "And if we keep this up, we're going to get sidetracked."

She gazed at him, her eyes dark and slumberous, her mouth still moist from their kisses, and Chase's pulse skittered and caught. He wondered if he would ever get enough of her.

Devon's gaze shifted to his mouth, and she wiped it dry with her thumb, then leaned down and moistened it again. "All you want to do is talk."

Chase gave a huff of laughter against her mouth, then pulled away. He leaned back and wedged his hands under her bottom, shaking his head slightly. "God, you just don't know when to quit, do you, Manyfeathers?"

She gave him a slow half smile that was a come-on if he'd ever seen one, but there was a glint in her eyes that wasn't at all sensual. She rubbed the back of his neck with her fingers, sending a tingle of sensation down his spine. "You're such a baby," she scolded huskily.

Chase grinned and shifted her hips forward. "So we're back to babies, are we?"

A sparkle of amusement appeared in her eyes, and she tipped her head to one side. "I guess we are."

Rubbing his thumbs against her hipbones, he maintained unwavering eye contact. "So when can I get my ring on your finger?"

She gave him a lopsided smile. "When do you want?"

"Tomorrow."

She laughed and leaned down and gave him another quick kiss. "Always quick out of the chute, aren't you?"

"You bet."

Lacing her hands together behind his neck, she studied him, her gaze turning solemn. "I do love you, Chase," she said quietly.

He had never doubted it. It had always been a matter of how far she was willing to go with it. He gave her hips a little squeeze. "I know you do, Dev," he responded gruffly. "It's always been a matter of working it out."

She looked down and ran her finger along his collarbone, her expression serious and a little pensive. Releasing a long sigh, she slid off his lap and sat cross-legged on the floor beside him. She toyed with a frayed thread on the cuff of her sweat suit, the light from the fire casting flickering shadows across her face. Finally she spoke, her voice quiet. "How do you feel about the business with the Bar M?"

Chase drew up his knee and studied her, his expression thoughtful. She was finally talking, but he wasn't sure where the conversation was headed. "I feel fine about it. Why?"

She looked up, an odd, perplexed look flickering across her face. "Are you going to be okay with it?"

Chase continued to study her, a funny feeling uncoiling in his belly. His eyes narrowed in contemplation, he didn't say anything for a moment, then he spoke, an edge to his tone. "I'm not taking the deal, Devon. Running the Bar M under my father's thumb is not my bag—never has been and never will. I thought you knew that."

She stared at him, and even in the dim light he could see alarm in her expression. She held his gaze for a moment; then she swallowed and looked away. "I thought maybe you'd move your operation up here."

The uneasy feeling in Chase's gut intensified, and his expression tightened. Working very hard at maintaining his relaxed posture, he responded, "It's not just my operation, Dev. I have a partner, and Ernie did time for aggravated assault. That's one reason we settled in Colorado—because he couldn't get a work visa in Canada with a criminal record."

"So you're not coming back here?"

"I have no way of making a living here. And there's no way I'd get into anything with my old man. I'd probably end up in jail for aggravated assault if I did."

Her head bent, she again plucked at the loose thread, rolling it between her fingers. "Maybe it wouldn't be that bad now." Annoyance flaring in him, Chase abruptly rose and went to stand in front of the window, his heart hammering in his chest. Bracing his arm on the window frame, he stood staring out at the darkened landscape, trying to get a grip on all the feelings that were churning through him. Forcing himself to let go of the tension in his body, he spoke, his voice flat. "Don't kid yourself, Devon. He hasn't changed. And neither has my mother. They'd make our life a living hell." He turned and looked at her, his expression harsh. "Do you have any idea what it would be like for our kids? My mother has a thing about half-breeds, and you can be damned sure it wouldn't make any difference if they were her grandkids or not. They'd be treated the same way Tanner was, and believe me, it wasn't pretty."

Devon stared at him, her expression stricken. She held his gaze for a moment; then she looked down, and Chase knew that he'd dealt her a dirty blow. He turned and stared out the window, hating himself for doing that to her, hating the fact that he'd had to do it to make her see what it would be like, angry with her for backing away just when he thought they'd put everything together. He released a heavy sigh and stuck his hands in the back pockets of his jeans, then spoke, his tone softening just a little. "I have to be my own man, Devon. I thought you understood that. And even if I could work things out with my old man, I still wouldn't feel right taking over the Bar M. If that goes to anyone, it should be Tanner." His expression reflective, he reached out and pressed a loose window molding in place. "I guess I figured that after all we've been through, you'd be willing to come with me," he said, his voice very quiet.

When she made no response, he turned, staring across the room at her. She sat with her legs drawn up, her arms locked around them, her forehead resting on her knees. He watched her for a moment, then spoke, his tone still quiet. "Now that I've told you where I'm coming from, I think maybe it's time you leveled with me, Devon."

She remained unmoving for a moment, then she lifted her head and stared into the fire, her face stark and expressionless. Silence stretched between them, and Chase wearily massaged his eyes with one hand, his other resting on his hip. Lord, was anything ever easy with her?

Releasing another heavy sigh, he raised his head and fixed his gaze on her. "Devon?" he prompted.

Without looking at him, she gave a dismissive little shrug. Chase waited her out, and as if realizing he wasn't going to let it go, she finally answered. "It wouldn't work," she said, her voice strained and uneven.

"Why?" She gave another little shrug, and Chase's temper flared. "Damn it, Devon! At least give me the courtesy of an honest answer. You're not hanging me out to dry without some kind of explanation."

She shot him a sharp glance, then she turned back to the fire, her jaw set. "So I'm just supposed to walk off and leave Sam high and dry—after all he's done for me? Is that it, Chase?"

His expression grim, Chase looked away, trying to rein in his anger. He waited a minute, then looked at her and spoke, his tone level. "You know damned well that Sam's ready to call it quits. He said as much to me. So don't use that as an excuse, Devon. It won't wash."

Even in the faint light, he could see her react, and she gripped her legs even tighter. She was clearly shaken, but she held it together, a bleak, determined set to her profile. She swallowed hard, then spoke, her voice unsteady. "Even if that is the case, what I do is here."

Chase watched her, a sick feeling unfolding in his belly. She hadn't been aware of Sam's feelings about the business; that was pretty damned obvious. But what made it even worse was that he'd stripped away a piece of her pride by dropping it on her the way he had. He had never intended to hurt her—but he had. Exhaling heavily, he tried to put things right. "You could train down there. You've built a big enough reputation that your customers are going to follow you."

She looked at him, a wounded look flickering in her eyes. "And just how am I going to do that? I don't have treaty status. So that means I'd have to get a work permit. First of all I'd have to find a trainer who'd want to hire me—one who would be prepared to go through all that hassle with immigration."

"We could build our own business down there."

"Do you have an arena? Do you have the necessary stall space? Do you have room for the extra hired help we'd need?"

Chase glared at her. "Damn it, Devon. Quit throwing up a bunch of stupid roadblocks. I said we could build our own business. That means from the ground up, if we have to."

She came to her feet in an agitated rush, and he saw the shimmer of tears in her eyes. "Stupid roadblocks? This is my life, Chase. It's not something that can be taken apart and put back together on a whim."

Frustration boiling over in him, Chase closed the distance between them. "What do you think I'm going to do? Take you down there and dump you, then take off?"

She stared at him, an awful, stricken look in her eyes, her arms clutched in front of her, and something hard and cold settled in the pit of Chase's stomach. He stared at her, then turned his head away and clenched his jaw in disgust. After all this time, he had never put it together until now. And he didn't like it one damned bit. He turned to her, his expression rigid. "You don't trust me," he stated flatly. "That's what this is all about, isn't it?"

She seemed almost frozen in place, her eyes wide and wounded, and he looked away and shook his head, his disgust compounding. He waited until he got a grip on the feelings building inside him, then he faced her again. "I'm not your mother, Devon," he said flatly. "I'm not going to walk off and abandon you, for God's sake."

She never said a word. She just stood there, huddled in the warmth of her arms, but he saw the answer in her despairing eyes as clearly as if she'd spoken. *But you did.*

Chase stared at her, then shook his head and gave her a cold smile. So this was it. There wasn't a damn thing left for him to say.

# Chapter 10

Stripped down to his shirtsleeves, his clothes damp with sweat, Chase stacked bales with the speed and precision of a robot, the ache in his shoulders turning hot and sharp. He wasn't going to think. He'd come out here to the hay shed determined not to, using hard physical labor as a vent for the undercurrent of bitterness that kept trying to pull him under. He'd got dressed and slammed out of the house after his big revelation the night before, and in another lifetime he probably would have got roaring drunk and picked a fight. But instead, he'd spent half the night driving down dark country roads, not wanting to acknowledge the sense of betrayal that was burning a hole in his gut. She didn't trust him. He had never once suspected that she just didn't trust him. She might as well have stabbed him in the back.

Sweat blinded him, and he stopped and yanked off his doeskin gloves, then pulled a bandanna out of the back pocket of his jeans and wiped his unshaven face. Stuffing the bandanna in his pocket, he tipped his head back and hooked his hands on his hips, trying to ease the burning tension in his shoulders. God, he hurt. From the inside out.

Exhaling heavily, he straightened, his expression rigid as he pulled his gloves on, the coldness inside the shed penetrating his sweat-dampened shirt. Ignoring the pain in his shoulders, he picked up another bale and swung it into place, his muscles taut and burning. He'd probably moved half a ton of hay that morning. And it wasn't helping.

The hay shed was closed in on three sides, but the open end faced east, the wide opening catching the rays of the sun, the climbing dust motes creating a shimmering scrim-like haze between Chase and the outdoors. A big gray barn cat materialized through the nonexistent barrier, like a shape coming through a waterfall, and Chase rested his hands on his hips, caught for an instant by the dreamlike effect.

The cat wound itself around his legs, and he stooped and lifted it onto a bale that was standing in the sun, rubbing it under the chin. "Looking for a little spot of sun, are you, old girl?"

The cat arched its back, then sat and began washing its face. She was fat with kittens, and Chase experienced an unaccountable thickness in his chest. His jaw tightening, he began heaving more bales into place.

"I've been looking for you, McCall."

He set another bale in place, then turned, meeting Sam's obvious agitation with an impassive expression. "What's the problem?"

Sam came over to him, his face mottled with barely controlled rage, his eyes hard as steel. He jabbed Chase in the chest, his expression hostile. "I don't know what the hell you've been up to, but I'll tell you, I've got one upset girl out there. She's trying to load six horses for that damned training clinic she's supposed to give today, and she looks like she's ready to fall apart." He jabbed Chase in the chest again, his fury making him tremble. "You blow into town, tear up her life, then blow out again. I thought maybe this time you'd come to your senses, maybe you would finally make an honest woman out of her. But damn it, it's just like every other time, only she's in worse shape than ever."

The older man flung a bale out of his way as if it weighed nothing, then paced back and forth, fury radiating from him in waves. His face stiff and expressionless, Chase watched and waited, not even trying to mount a defense.

Sam turned to him and leveled an accusing finger, the loose skin at his neck quivering. "You've been screwing up her life for too long, and I won't have it. She was seeing Jeb Cranston for damned near two years. Two years. And she was an inch away from marrying him, but then she goes to Vegas and runs into you. I knew the minute she pulled into the yard that you'd showed up again. She deserves a home and a family—she doesn't deserve you sniffing around like some damned dog. Why don't you clear the hell out once and for all so she can get on with her life? It ain't right."

Chase stared at him, his expression fixed and controlled; then, without a flicker of emotion, he picked up his jacket from one of the bales. He gave Sam one last look, then turned toward the opening. He answered, his voice flat, "It'll take me a couple of hours to round up my things."

It had taken him a lot of years to learn how to shut down and disconnect. But he had learned the lesson well. Disconnection was a little like riding a bronc. A good rider had to empty his mind of everything except sticking on, of holding on against every slick trick that old horse might throw at you. You had to focus. Focus. And it wasn't until the ride was over that the pain from a hundred old injuries would surface. This wasn't much different. He had to empty his mind. He had to stay focused.

Only this time there would be no eight-second horn to end the ride, no pickup man to get him off.

Sunlight glinted off the melting drifts of snow, the chatter of a flock of chickadees echoed in the clear still air, and off in the distance, Chase heard a door slam. The road to the bale shed was sheltered by a high, densely overgrown caragana hedge, and when he came around the end of it, he saw the familiar midnight blue rig backed up to the big doors at the south end of the arena. The truck was running, the driver's door ajar, and Chase could hear music coming from the radio inside, but the cab was empty. The horse trailer rocked slightly, and there were sounds of horses shifting around, but it was the peculiar stillness that caught his attention. His jacket clutched in his hand, he stopped walking and massaged his eyes, a nasty feeling settling in his gut.

Exhaling sharply, he clenched his jaw and swore, then angrily tossed his jacket onto the hood of the truck and went around to the back. Luke and Anne were both standing on the concrete apron in front of the big overhead door of the arena, looking confused and uncertain and more than a little helpless. A big roan stallion fidgeted on the end of a lead line, his sleek body quivering, a nervous lather forming on his haunches. Devon stood with her back to them, her elbow braced on the off corner of the trailer, covering her eyes with her hand. The air was brittle with tension, and Anne looked as if she was on the verge of tears.

Chase knew in a glance what had happened. The roan was one hell of a horse, but he was a rank loader—in fact, that was one of the reasons his owners had him at Silver Springs. Devon had trained him, and the stud had won nearly everything there was to win in pleasure and Western reining, but loading him was another story altogether. They had worked with him for two weeks, and the last few times, he'd gone in with a minimum amount of hassle. But obviously all that work had just gone to hell.

Chase released a weary sigh, then looked at Luke. "Just leave him and get me that can of molasses, then both of you get lost, okay?"

Luke gave him a relieved look and nodded, handing the lead line to Chase. "You got it." Chase waited until the two of them entered the arena, then led the stallion away from the trailer. It only took a few minutes for the horse to settle, then Chase led him over to the trailer. The roan started to balk, and Chase murmured to him, coaxing him along with the sound of his voice. Luke had set the container of molasses on the bumper, and Chase picked it up, unscrewed the top, then scooped up a handful of snow. There was an old saw about catching more flies with honey than with vinegar, and it was one that sometimes worked on horses. It was a trick Chase wasn't sure either Sam or Devon would approve of, but right then, he really didn't give a damn. All he wanted to do was get the horse in the trailer before everything fell apart.

Chase poured a small amount of molasses on the snow, then held it under the horse's nose. The roan didn't hesitate. Chase let the horse lick the snow from his glove; then he unsnapped the shank and crouched down. And the horse lowered his head. Once the stud had the scent, Chase poured a thin trail of molasses along the snow and up the rubber-matted surfaced of the ramp, then poured a healthy amount over the hay flake in the feeder in the trailer. After screwing the cap on the can, he set it on a snowbank, then went around the trailer to where Devon was standing. She hadn't moved. She looked so brittle and breakable, her arm against the trailer, her hand over her eyes—as if one wrong word would make her shatter. In spite of the new rift between them—in spite of how much had gone wrong—he could not walk away and leave her like that.

Tossing the shank on the side of the ramp, he caught her by the back of the neck, then pulled her into his arms. A muffled sob was wrenched from her, and she slid her arms around his waist and hung on, the awful tension in her body making him wince. Turning them so he was between her and the open door of the arena, he tightened his hold and tucked his head down against hers. "Hey, Slash," he murmured softly. "Don't get bent out of shape because he wouldn't load. It's not that big a deal."

She made another choked sound and turned her face against his neck, and he felt her chest expand against his. He knew this really didn't have anything to do with the horse;

this had to do with what had happened last night. And there was no easy molasses solution to that. He recalled what Sam had said about her long-term relationship with some guy he didn't even know, and his gut tightened into a hard, cold knot. No damned solution at all.

He felt the trailer rock, and he pulled away and spoke, keeping his tone light. "We've got something happening here, Manyfeathers. I think we'd better check it out."

His insides churning, feeling cold to the bone, he drew her to the back end of the trailer. He forced a smile. "Looks like old roany just loaded himself."

He saw Devon quickly wipe her eyes, then she managed an unsteady laugh. "I don't want to know how you did that."

"Nope. You don't."

Without looking at her, he picked up the shank and slid the ramp into place, then closed the door of the trailer. He gave it a light slap, then walked around to the front of the truck and collected his jacket. Her gaze fixed on him, Devon hesitated; then she finally climbed into the cab, closed the door and rolled down the window.

For the first time since he'd walked out on her the night before, Chase met her gaze. He stood with his weight on one hip, his hat low over his eyes, and she stared at him, a dark, haunted look in her eyes. All it would take was some indication from her, something to show she might be at least wavering, and he would stay. In spite of Sam's accusations. In spite of everything. But she swallowed hard and looked away.

It was as though he was looking at her through the wrong end of a telescope, and everything dropped away to nothing. Through a funny buzz in his head, he heard her put the truck in gear. "I'll see you later," she said unevenly.

He was so ripped up inside, he almost didn't respond. But he had promised her once that he would never leave without telling her. A final promise to be kept.

His throat tight and a hole where his heart should be, he spoke, his voice hollow. "No, you won't. I'll be gone when you get back."

He saw the sudden jolt of alarm in her eyes, and he saw her hands grip the wheel, but everything else was a blur. "Stay safe, Devon," he said, his voice gruff and unsteady; then he tossed the shank down by the molasses and started walking up the hill toward her house. He waited for her to call his name. He waited for the truck door to slam. He waited for something—anything. But then he heard the soft growl of the truck's engine, and just like that, she let him go. And suddenly, nothing mattered.

For the first few weeks after he returned to Colorado, Chase had stayed close to the ranch, hoping that maybe there would be some word from her, that maybe she would just show up, but there had been nothing. Not a letter. Not a phone call. Not a single word. Nothing. Zip. There had been three phone calls from Sam Creswell, which Chase had had the good fortune to miss and did not return. This was between him and Devon. Nobody else. When he'd finally faced the fact that he wasn't going to hear from her, bitterness settled in.

It had taken until the end of May before Chase could even see past the anger and the grinding feelings of betrayal. And it was then that he had to confront the jealousy that underscored all those bitter feelings. He had always been so dead certain that if Devon ever found someone else he would be able to cope with it, but when he was faced with the hard, cold fact that there *had* been someone else, he found he wasn't quite as big or as forgiving as he'd thought. Then most of his bitterness, most of his anger, turned inward, and that damn near brought him down. It was then that he had to face another hard, cold fact. He pretty much had it coming. He'd been callous and self-centered in the past, and he'd never really given her any reason to think the future would be any different.

The only person who knew the whole story was Tanner. Chase had phoned his brother when he got to Colorado and told him in as few words as possible what had happened. Tanner didn't say much; he didn't have to. Ernie was astute enough to put a few pieces together on his own. He didn't say much, either; he just got rid of all the booze, kept Chase away from anyone he didn't like and lined up enough backbreaking work around the ranch to drop an ox. Even feeling as bad as Chase did, Ernie's gruff fussiness was enough to wring the odd smile out of him, and he started calling his partner "mother."

By the first of June, Chase figured he had worked through the worst of it. He avoided traveling with the stock to the rodeos if at all possible, he quit listening to country music and he had to avoid certain things. There was one hair commercial on TV, featuring a well-known actress who had thick straight black hair, and that commercial tore him up pretty good the first time he saw it. So he stopped watching TV, as well. He started expanding their operation—started thinking about maybe building an arena so he could start training a few horses for roping. He spent hours on the phone setting up new contracts, and the place had never looked so good. All he had to do was make sure he was so busy during the day that he didn't have time to think, and that he was so tired when he went to bed at night that he was out before his head hit the pillow. Yeah, he had it back together.

Then he got the phone call telling him that Keith Nordstrom was in critical condition from a bad car wreck and had had to be airlifted to a trauma unit in Calgary. The prognosis was not good—massive head and chest injuries, and several broken bones. Chase got the call at five Thursday morning, and he was in the air by six. An old rodeo friend of his and Keith's had his own plane, and Doug flew in from east of Denver, landing on the gravel road running past the ranch, and they were airborne in under twenty minutes.

It was early evening when they walked into the IC unit. And Chase knew as soon as he saw Lisa sitting with Keith's parents in the waiting room that it was bad. Real bad.

By Sunday, there were no more options. Keith's parents, both in their seventies, were ravaged by shock and grief. Doug took them to Bolton, and Chase stayed with Lisa. He was with her Monday morning when they took Keith away for the organ donations surgery, and he was in the room with her later when they told her he was gone. But the worst had been when they took Keith up to OR. It had damn near been more than he could handle, watching Lisa, her body racked with sobs, kiss her husband goodbye one last time. He hoped to God he never had to go through something like that again—watching them wheel Keith away, knowing that he would never see his old buddy again. And it was nearly as bad when they came and told them it was over.

By the time they left ICU, Lisa had gone into a kind of shock. She was so pale, so cold, so numb, that nothing seemed to register, and he felt every grim step down that long, sterile corridor. It was over. Finished. It was the last road he and Keith would travel down together.

Numbness set in the next day. Funeral arrangements for Thursday. Notifying friends and family. Taking care of what had to be done. Trying not to think or feel. Acting as a bulwark between Lisa and a whole community of well-meaning friends and neighbors. He had never seen the kind of devastation he saw in her, and it was as if his presence was the only thing that kept her together. Her family arrived from Oklahoma early Wednesday morning, but she didn't want them with her. It was as though she didn't have anything left inside her to give, and she simply couldn't handle anything more. All she wanted was Chase and her girls. It was as though she was just trying to hang on long enough to get through the funeral.

The emotional crash came late Wednesday night. Chase heard her rummaging around in her bedroom, and he pulled on a pair of jeans and went down the darkened hallway. She had come completely unglued and was sobbing hysterically as she tore the closet apart.

He caught her by the wrist, then slid his arm around her middle, holding her immobile. "Hey, come on, stuffing," he said softly. "Come on. It's okay. It's okay."

She tried to pry his arm away, her movements jerky with desperation, her voice nearly incoherent. "I can't find it! God, I can't find it. And I promised him. I promised him a long time ago, and I can't find it. I can't find it."

Holding her firm, he turned her, locking her in a secure embrace. "Shh, honey. Shh. What can't you find?"

Violent sobs shuddered through her, and she tried to break free. "His belt. I can't find his belt."

His throat so tight he couldn't swallow, Chase rocked her, knowing that nothing could comfort her. "Shh, stuffing. Shh." He waited until she couldn't fight anymore; then he brushed her hair back, wiping her wet, ravaged face with his hand. "Maybe it's with his things from the hospital." She watched him with haunted, desolate eyes, and he gently tucked her hair behind her ear. "I'm going to sit you down in the chair, and I'll go get the bag from the front closet, okay?" She gazed at him numbly, her face awash with tears, looking at him as if she didn't quite comprehend what he was saying. He gave her a gentle shake. "Okay?"

She closed her eyes and hauled in a shuddering breath. Taking another breath, she nodded. Chase put her in the chair, then went to find the bag. When he returned with the white plastic bag with the hospital logo on it, fresh tears were slipping down her face, but that impenetrable, blank expression was gone, and her grief was open and exposed. He crouched in front of her and opened the plastic sack, his throat tightening even more as he lifted out the pair of jeans that were rolled up inside. He handed them to Lisa, and she closed her eyes and hugged them against her, fresh tears slipping down her cheeks. Chase looked away, his vision blurring. Resting his elbow on his thigh, he bent his head and massaged his eyes, trying to will away the awful pain clogging his chest.

Lisa touched him on the shoulder and spoke, her voice soft. "He loved to tell stories about all the scrapes the two of you got into." She smoothed down his hair, her gesture comforting and maternal, her voice going even softer. "And he especially loved the one about the big buck-off the two of you had in Calgary—he must have told it a thousand times."

Feeling raw to the bone, Chase dropped his hand and looked at her, and she gave him the softest smile. Taking his hand, she placed something cold and metallic in it. "If anything ever happened to him, he wanted you to have this." She closed his fingers, her eyes glimmering with tears, her brave smile unsteady. "And I want you to have it, too."

Chase stared at her, then swallowed hard and opened his hand. It was the silver belt buckle—the one from the Calgary Stampede, the one he and Keith had competed against each other for so many years ago. He bowed his head and covered his eyes with his hand, the loss finally just too much to handle.

Thursday dawned dismal and overcast, and Chase functioned like a man caught in a bad dream. The funeral passed in a blur, and by the time they reached the grave site, a soft rain was falling, enclosing the heavily treed cemetery in a gray mist, the scent of wet pines and damp earth mixing with the fragrance from the wreaths of flowers. He and Lisa stood shoulder to shoulder, her fingers laced tightly through his, the girls in front of them. The rain rustled in the tree branches above them, the dripping leaves shedding their water on the sodden ground, the solemn, sonorous drone of the minister's voice heavy and somehow final. He went with her when she laid a single red rose on the casket, and he gripped her hand even tighter and steadied her when he felt her falter and stumble beside him.

It was almost as though the rain kept them secluded and inviolate, safe from intrusion. So with her rigid and white-faced beside him, fighting valiantly to keep it together, he led her and the girls past the silent mourners, through the softly falling rain to the limo. He didn't give a damn what people thought. All he cared about was getting them out of there before the grim reality hit, before grief-riddled panic and despair swamped her again. That kind of anguish could never be shared. It was hers alone.

Chase checked into the Bolton Hotel that night. With all the public ritual of death behind her, Lisa was finally able to let go and turn to her family, and Chase was just as glad. He was so damned exhausted and beat up inside that he wouldn't have been much good to her anyway. He just wanted to crawl into a hole somewhere and lick his wounds. But beneath the numbness, beneath the exhaustion, rage had built to a dangerous level. Rage at the injustice, rage at the drunk driver who'd ended Keith's life, rage at the awful waste.

Lying on his bed, his arm draped over his eyes, Chase clenched his jaw and tried to empty his mind, but one emotion, one image, kept trying to surface. The emotion was intense, wrenching and so damned hollow he didn't dare let it take shape. And the image—it was even worse. Devon off to one side of the grave, standing alone in the softly falling rain, her face framed by the collar of a shiny raincoat, her expression stark with shock and sorrow. He wondered if she had ever grieved like that for him.

Swearing under his breath, Chase abruptly rolled to his feet and picked up his wallet and room key from the nightstand. He was going to need something a hell of a lot stronger than falling-down exhaustion to deaden his thoughts. Maybe, whatever it was, he could find it at the bottom of a bottle.

# Chapter 11

Devon Manyfeathers stood at the kitchen window watching the rain drizzle down, such an awful pain in her chest that she couldn't take a deep breath. The light was fading from the heavily overcast sky, and the yard lights had just come on, their luminescence doing little to dispel the deepening gloom. A chill crept across her skin from the open window, and she rubbed her upper arms, the fragrance of wet earth and cleansing rain wafting in on the light breeze. It had been so hot over the past few days. The kind of wind-driven heat that sucked the moisture out of the ground and withered the leaves on the trees. It was good to feel the rain, to smell it.

An image of a flower-draped coffin took shape in her mind, and she shifted her gaze, a recurring ache again constricting her chest. Keith. It didn't seem possible that he was gone. And Lisa and the girls. And Chase.

The ache climbed higher, and she abruptly fished a tissue out of her pocket and blew her nose, trying to detach herself from the feelings that kept threatening to break out.

Death had never touched her directly before. It had always been distant and removed—not her own personal loss. This one was personal, and she felt it right down to her soul. She didn't know how Lisa had held together like she had. She could only imagine what Keith's wife must be feeling—if she was even able to feel. A loss like that would go beyond ordinary pain.

Another chill feathered across her skin, and Devon turned from the window, her gaze catching on an envelope tucked behind the telephone. The writing on it was Chase's—just some idle scratching he'd made while talking on the telephone, but she hadn't been able to bring herself to throw it out. She reached out and touched the bold writing, her throat tightening even more. She kept seeing him standing by the grave, holding on to Lisa's hand, his other arm around both the girls, his grief buried beneath a hard exterior.

She had nearly gone to him—*would* have gone to him if he had lingered at the grave site, but he hadn't. He had left abruptly, taking the visibly trembling Lisa and the girls to the waiting limo, and she had stood in the falling rain and watched him go, experiencing the kind of guilt, the kind of regret, that had no dimensions.

Despair washing through her, Devon wiped her eyes with the side of her hand, so desperately lonely for him that she could barely stand it. She had felt as if she'd died inside when he had left in February, but seeing him again was even worse. It had nearly killed her when he had looked at her without even a flicker of recognition, as though she was a total stranger, and it was right then, for the very first time, that she was forced to recognize all she had lost when she'd let him walk out of her life. She had never been very good at being honest with herself. That took the kind of courage she just didn't have.

But something had happened today when she'd been standing by that open grave, Chase standing across from her, silent and isolated in the softly falling rain. She realized that she had been skirting a basic truth for a lot of years, and at an immeasurable cost. She had avoided making any kind of commitment to him because she was afraid. Afraid he would stop loving her, afraid he would someday walk out on her. Afraid he would discover she wasn't what he thought she was. He thought she was strong and independent and self-sufficient. But she knew, deep down inside, that she was none of those things. She never had been. She had simply learned how to hide what she really was. She'd been hiding it all her life.

And fear of discovery had cost her Chase. Before, she had always known at some intuitive level that he would be back. But this time was different. This time he wouldn't be. Her self-discovery had come too late, and she had lost everything because of her own insufficiencies.

Her vision blurring, she gently straightened the corner of the envelope, then swallowed hard and turned away. It would help if she could get his face out of her mind—a face scored with pain and marked by sorrow, and thinner. Much thinner. Her sorrow spilled over, and she covered her face with her hand. She had done that to him. That had nothing to do with Keith's death.

She went to the living room window, haunted by regret and guilt, wishing she could undo what she had done to him. She wondered where he was, if he was still at Lisa's or if he had gone to ground like he had when his grandmother died. The thought of him holed up somewhere alone, with no one to hold and comfort him, was more than she could handle, and something broke loose in her. Turning abruptly, she went into the kitchen and picked up the phone. She had to find him. She couldn't bear the thought that he might be alone somewhere. Not Chase. Never Chase.

There was the usual assortment of vehicles parked in front of the hotel, but in spite of that, the main street seemed oddly dark and deserted, the steady drizzle compounding the emptiness. Devon parked the truck and turned off the lights and ignition, then sat staring out the rain-splattered windshield, a sick, hollow feeling settling in her stomach. It had taken two phone calls to find him, but now that she was here, she felt almost paralyzed with uncertainty. She didn't know what she would do if he slammed the door in her face. But she also knew she would never forgive herself if she didn't try. Straightening her shoulders, she took the keys out of the ignition, then opened the door, her expression strained. The thought of walking into the hotel scared her to death.

There was no one at the desk in the small lobby, and her stomach knotted with dread. She had known she was going to have to get Chase's room number from the front desk, but now she was going to have to ring for service. Which meant Ida Urko, the owner's wife, would be the one to answer. And Ida was one of the biggest gossips in town. Composing her face, Devon drew herself up to her full height and pushed the bell.

Ida appeared from the suite tucked behind the lobby, her glasses hanging around her neck on a chain, her bottle-red hair held up with rhinestone combs, her eyelashes thick with black mascara. She gave Devon a saccharine smile. "Devon. What can I do for you?"

Devon used every inch of her height. "I'd like Chase McCall's room number please, Ida."

The rings on her fingers flashed in the overhead light as Ida caressed the edge of the ledger lying on the counter, and she gave Devon a small, knowing smile. She stared at her, a smug look in her eyes, then reached for the row of keys on the wall beside her. Devon knew exactly what was going through the woman's mind, and she knew Ida would have a field day with it if she let her get away with it.

She gave the innkeeper a tight smile. "I didn't ask for the room key," she said, her tone sharp. "I asked for the room *number.*"

The older woman's expression froze, and she broke eye contact and made a nervous, flustered gesture with her hand. "Oh, yes. Well. It's, um, room twenty-one."

Devon waited until Ida met her gaze again, then gave her another tight smile, letting her know she knew what Ida was up to. "Thank you."

That jolt of pure rage got her up the stairs and down the corridor, but her bolstering anger deserted her the instant she reached his door. Faced with the reality of her decision, she closed her eyes, her frantically beating heart caught in her throat, uncertainty sitting like a rock in the pit of her stomach.

Drawing a deep, stabilizing breath, she straightened, the mild flutter climbing higher as she knocked on the door.

There was no sound from within, and she turned her head and stared down the empty corridor, an awful, sinking feeling rushing in to replace the tense apprehension. He wasn't there. Now what? Did she stay, or did she go? Swallowing hard, she knocked again, compelled to try one more time.

She was about to turn away when the door swung open and she was suddenly face-to-face with Chase McCall. He looked completely wasted. He had on a pair of jeans, but he was still wearing the white shirt he'd worn to the funeral, though it was now wrinkled, loose and unbuttoned. He had that dark, dangerous gunslinger look, his jaw rigid and unshaven, his eyes narrowed in a steely-eyed squint. On the surface, he looked as hard as nails and almost threatening, but it was the tight compression lines bracketing his mouth and the emotionless expression in his eyes that made her heart falter.

He stared at her for an instant, then started to close the door, but she placed her hand against it, holding it open. She saw the muscles in his jaw tense, and for an instant she thought he was going to shove it shut anyway, but then he dropped his hand and turned away. It was then that she saw the bottle in his hand. His back to her, he went over to the window overlooking the street and stood staring out, his shoulders stiff. He lifted the bottle and took a swig, and a painful ache unfolded in Devon's chest. It wasn't until that moment that she'd realized just how badly she had hurt him. A sick feeling of guilt washed through her, and she swallowed hard and looked away. She waited until the spasm passed; then she looked at him, knowing she owed him one hell of lot more than sympathy.

Swallowing again, she eased in a steadying breath. "I'm so sorry about Keith," she whispered, her voice breaking a little. "I can't believe he's gone."

Chase bent his head and braced his arm against the wall, and Devon saw his chest heave. And she knew. Knew. Yanking the strap off her shoulder, she tossed her bag on the corner of the bed and crossed to him, a fierce, protective feeling welling up inside her. She took the bottle from his hand and set it on the window ledge, then put her arms around him. He tried to pull away, but she pressed her face against him and tightened her hold, her throat clogged with tears. It tore her to shreds, knowing she had hurt him so badly that he couldn't even accept comfort from her, knowing that he had no one to share his grief with. Needing to make him look at her, to acknowledge her, she caught his face and turned his head, her vision so blurred she could barely see. "Don't, Chase," she whispered unevenly. "Don't do that. For God's sake, let me hold you. Please."

He stared at her, his gaunt face set like stone, not even a glimmer of response in his red-rimmed eyes. For the first time in her life she felt completely estranged from him, and it terrified her. Despair washing through her, she touched his mouth, her tears spilling over. "I'm sorry, Chase," she whispered brokenly. "So sorry."

Something flickered in his eyes, as if he understood what she was really saying, and Devon touched his mouth again, her fingers trembling. "I was so scared," she whispered, trying to explain past the awful tightness in her chest. "And I didn't know how to tell you."

Chase stared at her for an instant longer; then he shut his eyes in an expression of immense torment, and Devon closed her eyes against a wrenching surge of emotion as his arms came around her in a desperate, crushing embrace. Holding on to him with every ounce of strength she had, she roughly turned her face against his neck and choked back a sob. She waited for the awful ache in her throat to ease; then she hugged him, closing her eyes tight against the swell of tears. "I can't believe he's dead, Chase. I can't."

Caving in around her, Chase tightened his hold and tucked his head against hers, and she felt him finally let go. Experiencing such a wealth of anguish for him, she cradled his head against her, giving him what solace she could, her relief nearly as wrenching as his grief. He had let her in, and right then, that was all that mattered.

It took a long time for the terrible tension to ease in him, but time didn't matter to Devon. She continued to hold him, her fingers splayed wide at the back of his head, so thankful for the small respite that little else registered.

She felt him wipe his face against the rough fabric of her jacket, and she reluctantly eased her hold, kissing his temple as she gently smoothed his hair. Releasing a ragged sigh, he lifted his head and loosened his hold. For one awful moment she thought he was going to turn away without even looking at her, but then he closed his eyes and rested his forehead against hers, and Devon could feel him try to pull himself together. She cupped the back of his neck, gently stroking him, and he released another unsteady sigh and shifted his hold. She heard him swallow, then he raised his head and looked at her, his eyes so bleak and tormented that it was all she could do to keep from responding. He held her gaze for an instant; then he shifted his attention and tucked a wisp of hair behind her ear. "I'm sorry," he said simply, his voice unsteady.

Her throat suddenly tight, she smoothed her hand across his ravaged face. "You have nothing to be sorry for, Chase," she chastised softly. "And never with me."

He started to speak; then he abruptly looked away, and she could see the glimmer of moisture in his eyes. Her eyes burning, she lowered her head and began doing up the buttons on his shirt, her fingers trembling so badly she could barely manage the task.

Shifting his hold, Chase caught her along the jaw and tried to raise her head, but she resisted, not wanting him to see the tears in her eyes. He rubbed her chin with his thumb, his voice very husky, very soft when he spoke. "What are you doing, Dev?"

She shook her head, needing time for the cramp in her throat to pass. He covered her hands, holding them still against his chest. "Would you lie down with me?"

Her throat cramped again, and she closed her eyes and rested her head against his, struggling against the swell of emotion. She didn't want to stay at the hotel. She felt too exposed here, with Ida downstairs, waiting and watching, trying to collect as much gossip as she could. Taking a deep, steadying breath, she turned her hand under his, then laced her fingers through his. Reaching deep for some control, she lifted her head and looked at him. "I came to take you home," she whispered brokenly. "I want to take you home."

He tried to turn away, but Devon saw how hard he was fighting to keep from losing it again, and she refused to let him go. Struggling with her emotions, she drew his head down against her shoulder, and he exhaled roughly and tightened his arms around her. She waited until she felt him take a steadying breath; then she gently eased away and took his hand in hers.

Ida was at the front desk talking to a regular patron of the bar when they came down the stairs, and her glance went from Devon to Chase, then she smirked and said something to the man standing at the desk. Devon ignored her. All she cared about was getting Chase out of there.

He never said a word on the drive to Silver Springs. He sat with his head tipped against the headrest, his eyes closed, the

dark stubble accentuating the hard set of his jaw. His stillness would have frightened her if it hadn't been for his hand
resting against the inside of her thigh. And for some reason
that one physical connection created such a load of emotion in her that she could barely function.

There was only a faint aura of light remaining on the
western horizon when she pulled into the yard, the headlights sweeping the blooming lilac hedge along the lane. The
fragrance drifted in through the open window, and moths
cast dancing shadows around the yard light. She ignored the
graveled parking area by the arena and pulled up to the back
of the house instead. She set the hand brake, then turned off
the lights and switched off the ignition. Smoothing her hand
across the back of his, she glanced at him, then slipped out
of the truck.

The house was dark except for the faint light from the
yard, and she paused in the back entryway, waiting for her
eyes to adjust. She heard Chase latch the screen door; then
he followed her up the stairs, and a nervous flutter unfolded in her chest. She went straight to the bedroom, but
when she turned to speak to him, he wasn't there. Her heart
lurching, she turned back.

She found him in the short hallway. He was leaning
against the wall, his eyes closed, and even in the faint light
she could tell that he was exhausted, both mentally and
physically. Her vision blurring, Devon approached him,
something painful happening to her heart when she realized how badly he was trembling. Quickly wiping away her
tears, she slid her arm around his waist. "Come on, Slick,"
she whispered unevenly. "Let's get you into bed."

For a moment she thought he wasn't going to cooperate,
then he exhaled unsteadily and straightened. Once in the
bedroom, Devon started to undress him. She very nearly lost
it when she recognized the big silver buckle on his belt, and
she locked her jaw against the raw emotion that washed
through her. Once he was free of his jeans, he stretched out

on his back, his arm over his eyes, the muscles in his jaw rigid.

He was still like that when Devon came back from the bathroom, and he never moved when she slid into bed beside him. Realizing he was in some kind of shock, she slid her arm under his neck and gently drew his arm away from his eyes. "Let me hold you, Chase," she entreated softly.

He didn't respond for an instant; then he exhaled sharply and turned into her arms. Closing her eyes against a nearly unbearable surge of feeling for him, she cradled his head against her breast and pressed her mouth to the top of his head. Chase shifted and draped his leg across hers, then pulled her flush against him. Devon swallowed hard and drew the sheet over his shoulders, then began slowly rubbing his back. It was as if all he needed was her physical warmth to let go, and he released another ragged sigh and turned his face against her, his beard rough against her skin, and the trembling slowly abated. His weight grew heavy against her, and she thought he had fallen asleep, but he tightened his arm around her and spoke, his voice thick. "Don't leave."

Resting her cheek on the top of his head, she hugged him against her and blinked back the sting in her eyes. "I won't," she whispered unevenly. "I promise."

Devon had never been so totally aware of him as she was that night. His weight against her, the texture of his hair and skin, the imprint of his arm around her, every breath he took. She lay awake long after he fell asleep, absorbing even the smallest detail, her chest so full of gratitude she could hardly breathe at times. He slept a totally exhausted sleep, something so vulnerable in his stillness, in the dead weight of him against her, and Devon experienced a kind of protectiveness that she had never experienced before. She wasn't going to let anything disturb him—anything. He was hers to keep safe, and she would stand guard all night, if necessary. The gift of sleep was one thing she could give him.

He finally stirred as dawn lightened the sky, the patter of rain on the roof permeating the dusky stillness. He shifted beside her, his beard scraping against her as he turned his head, his breath warm against her neck as he muttered her name. She knew he wasn't fully awake, and the sound of her name did unbearable things to her heart. With infinite care she smoothed back his hair and cradled his head against her, flooded with such tenderness that it made her chest hurt. God, but it had been so empty without him. And so very lonely.

He shifted his head, his breath warm against her neck; then, with drowsy languor, he smoothed his hand along her rib cage. Releasing a contented sigh, he slid his arms around her and gathered her up in an enveloping embrace, then spoke, his voice gruff with sleep. "Tell me I'm not dreaming."

Easing a breath past the aching fullness in her chest, she gave him a little hug. "You're not dreaming," she whispered unevenly.

She felt him swallow, and that one gesture set off such a swell of emotion inside her that she had to clench her jaw against it. Cupping the side of his face, she tipped her head and pressed a kiss against his forehead. Chase shifted and found her mouth, taking it in a slow, lazy kiss that sent her pulse skittering. Releasing his breath in an unsteady sigh, he tightened his hold on her face and drew away. "Are you going to let me make love to you, Slash?" he murmured, his voice gruff with emotion.

Devon opened her eyes and looked at him, far closer to tears than she wanted to be. Swallowing against the nearly unbearable fullness in her throat, she held his steady gaze and tried to smile. "You can do whatever you want, McCall." She almost pulled it off, but something happened and a sob escaped. She gripped his back and hid her face against his neck, fighting for composure.

Cradling her head against him, Chase used his other arm to pull her beneath him, his weight braced on his forearms as he hugged her against him. His hand tangled in her hair as he tucked her face against his neck; then he nudged her thighs apart with his knee and settled his legs between hers, securing her against him. He tightened his hold, brushed a kiss against her neck and spoke, his voice rough with emotion, gruff with tenderness. "I need you, Dev."

Of all the things he could have said, that was the one thing she needed most to hear, and she hugged him hard, struggling against the tears.

He buried his face against her neck, and Devon felt his chest expand. Abruptly, everything changed. She felt him against her, hard and fully aroused, and her breath caught on the sudden wild flutter in her chest. Closing her eyes against the explosion of need, she hung on to him, a heady weakness pulsing through her. On a soft sound of entreaty, she drew up her knees, and Chase tried to pull away. "No, babe. No," he whispered raggedly. "Once I'm inside you— ah, God, Dev—I won't be able to leave."

Shaken to the core by the agony of need in his voice, her body primed for the feel of him, she clutched at him, rubbing her wet heat against him. "It's okay," she whispered, her voice breaking from the frenzy of hot, surging desire. "I promise. It's okay."

Chase roughly tightened his hold and made a low sound, and Devon arched her back and lifted her pelvis. Chase went rigid in her arms, another low, ragged sound wrenched from him as he entered her in one despairing thrust.

There was no room for gentleness or patience. There was only room for urgency and a fever of need—and greed, a driving, desperate, frantic greed that consumed them, drove them, carried them to the very edge of an emotional precipice; then Chase clutched her and drove into her one final time. The blackness exploded into splintering shards of silver, and the release came—a blinding, paralyzing release that took them both under.

Chase held on to her, enveloping her in his strength and heat, his body shuddering against hers, and Devon clung to him, tears of raw emotion slipping down her temples, so shaken, so emotionally exposed that she felt stripped inside. It took a long time for all that emotional turbulence to settle, and the first things she was aware of were how close she was to sobbing and how securely he was holding her. She released some of the emotional overload by expelling the air in her lungs, then cradled the back of his head and hugged him fiercely, tears dampening her face.

Chase inhaled unevenly, then turned his head and kissed her on the curve of her neck. Devon could feel his heart hammering against hers. "Are you all right?" he whispered, his voice rough with emotion.

She nodded, burying her face against his neck. She waited for the pressure to ease in her chest; then she cupped the back of his neck. "Are you?"

Drawing one arm from under her, he braced his weight on it and looked down at her. With the dark stubble shadowing his strong jaw, his heavy-lidded eyes and his tousled hair, he looked dark and dangerous and very male. He gave her a slow, soft smile, a trace of amusement in his eyes. "You're pretty damned cute, do you know that?" He leaned down and kissed her, his mouth warm and moist and open against hers. "Yes, darlin'," he whispered huskily. "I'm fine."

Devon knew he was trying to lighten the mood, but she couldn't give him that yet. She remembered too clearly what kind of shape he'd been in last night, and she didn't want to diminish that. And she also remembered how much she'd hurt him, only she didn't know how to make it right. All she knew was that she didn't want him trying to cover up to make things easy for her. Like he always had. Her throat tight, she slid her hand up his neck and kissed him back, trying to give him all the emotional honesty he had given her. Holding her still, Chase eased away, then sighed and raised his head, his eyes dark and somber as he gazed down at her. Devon tried to ease the contraction in her throat, then spoke, her voice unsteady. "I'm glad you're here, Chase."

He shifted his gaze as he drew his thumb across her mouth, and she saw the muscles in his jaw bunch, then he looked at her again. There was a directness in his somber gaze that made her throat contract even more. "So am I," he answered unevenly. "So am I." He leaned down and kissed her again, then carefully withdrew from her. Using his arm as leverage, he lifted himself off her, then stretched out on his back and reached for her. "Come here," he said gruffly. "I need to hold you."

The ceiling was of open-beam construction, and the sound of the rain on the roof broke the stillness, the heavy dusk of the room lightening to an overcast gloom. Devon lay with her head on his shoulder and her knee tucked between his, the weight of his arm across her back holding her securely against him. She stared into the gray gloom, her hand splayed against his chest, listening to the counterpoint of his heartbeat and the rain on the roof, savoring the shared silence. Chase sighed and covered her hand with his, and Devon shifted her head a fraction and spoke, her voice quiet. "What are you thinking about?"

He sighed again and shook his head. "I don't even know. It's been a hell of a week."

"Do you want to talk about it?"

He rubbed his thumb against her palm, then shook his head again. "Not right now. I don't even want to think about it."

Devon could understand how he must be feeling, and she deliberately threw something at him that would catch him off guard. "You took my shampoo when you left."

Her forehead was against the side of his jaw, and she felt him smile. "What's the matter, Manyfeathers? Did somebody kick you out of the sandbox?"

Amusement flickered through Devon. That was one of her favorite things about him—the way he could put a twist on a rebuttal. Right from the first he had made her laugh, only she had always been careful not to let him see her do it too often. She hadn't wanted him to get a big head. She still tried not to laugh in front of him—mostly because it pleased him that she didn't. Her amusement deepened. They had been playing that game for a lot of years.

She poked her thumb in his ribs and smiled at the response she got. "What would you know about sandboxes, McCall?"

"Not much. Except they're full of sand."

She managed to keep her tone dry. "Not that you ever got kicked out of one, of course."

He gave her bottom a light squeeze. "Of course."

He smiled into her eyes, then smoothed his hand across the swell of her hips, his expression sobering. "It's getting late, babe," he said gruffly.

Devon knew what time it was, but in all the years at Silver Springs, she had never played hooky once. She figured Sam owed her. She gave him a lazy grin. "I don't cook. I don't do windows. And I don't go out in the rain."

The laugh lines around his eyes deepened, a sensual gleam appearing in his gaze. He ran one finger back and forth across her bottom lip, his touch erotic and sensitizing. The laugh lines deepened, and his gaze turned more intimate. "You don't say. What *do* you do, Manyfeathers?"

She stared at him, raised one eyebrow and gave him a slow smile. "Almost anything you want."

He laughed and dragged her on top of him. He looked at her, mischief and pure male sexuality sparkling in his eyes. His voice was like John Wayne. "Then show me your stuff, little lady." He shifted beneath her, then drew her head down and licked her bottom lip, murmuring, "And I'll show you mine."

Unable to keep from laughing, Devon caught his face and gave him a hard kiss, wondering if it was possible to love him any more.

Devon phoned down to the arena around nine o'clock and told them to finish chores, then take the rest of the day off. She knew that Sam would be scandalized when he found out, but she didn't really care. The bleakness was gone from

Chase's eyes, and she intended to make sure it didn't return, at least for today.

It wasn't until they went to bed that night and he was asleep beside her that the first tentacle of panic uncurled in her belly. She didn't know how to let go of the fear. She didn't know how to climb over the mountain of self-doubt. And she didn't know how she would survive when he walked out of her life again.

She had very nearly lost him once. She did not want to lose him again.

## Chapter 12

Devon leaned against the kitchen counter, her expression solemn as she watched Chase put the finishing touches on roast beef sandwiches. He had arrived Thursday night; it was now Monday noon, and he had been quiet and withdrawn since he had returned to town Saturday morning. She had taken him in to check out of the hotel and pick up the truck Tanner had loaned him. She had dropped him off and returned to Silver Springs, and he had spent most of the day with Lisa, helping her sort through Keith's papers. He had arrived back late Saturday night, his expression drawn, his mood preoccupied. She doubted if he had said more than fifty words since. She understood his silence, and she respected it. What troubled her was his stillness. In all the years she had known him, he had never been like this. That worried her, and it worried her that he had spent the past two days holed up in the house. That wasn't like him, either.

Not sure if it was wise or not, she took a deep breath and spoke. "Chase?"

He glanced at her, then lifted the sandwiches onto individual plates. "What?"

"Why don't you come down to the outside arena this afternoon? I'm going to be working a two-year-old colt that needs some corrective farrier work, and I'd like you to have a look at him."

Chase gave her an unreadable look, then pushed a plate of sandwiches toward her. She glanced at the sandwiches, then at him, a shot of apprehension making her stomach drop. She screwed up her courage and pursued it. "Chase?" He wouldn't look at her, and Devon's stomach took another nosedive. She swallowed against the flutter in her throat, then tried again, her voice soft and entreating. "Please."

He set his sandwiches on the table, then raised his head and looked at her, his expression guarded. He studied her for a moment, then exhaled heavily. "I won't go down to the arena," he said quietly. "Sam's not going to be very pleased when he finds out I'm here."

Devon stared at him, startled by his answer. "What?"

He held her gaze for a moment, then gave a small, dismissing shrug and sat down. "Just drop it, okay?"

Her expression thoughtful, she studied him, trying to figure out what was going on. Something had happened, but she didn't have a clue what it was. She *would* drop it with him, but she had no intention of dropping it with Sam. She had an awful feeling her boss had some explaining to do.

Wanting to ease the tension lines etched around his mouth, she tried to distract him. "You never put any mustard on my sandwiches, McCall," she said, her tone accusing.

For the first time in two and a half days she caught a flicker of amusement in his eyes. "For someone who doesn't cook, you do a pile of complaining, Manyfeathers."

She wanted very badly to get a real smile out of him. "I cook, Slick. Just not in the kitchen."

He rested his arms on the table and stared at her with a look that made her pulse falter, the glint in his eyes intensifying. "Feeling full of it, are we?"

She tipped her head and gave him a slow smile. "What's the matter, McCall? Getting too old to cut the mustard?"

He grinned at her and slowly shook his head, and suddenly she felt a whole lot lighter.

Lunch was never leisurely for Devon. And especially this week. She had a strict schedule for the horses she was training, and taking the day off on Friday had meant she had some catching up to do. She wanted to push Chase into going with her, but she had to find out what was going on with Sam before she said anything more. Chase had the faucet in the kitchen sink disassembled by the time she went back to work. It bothered her that he was staying in the house, especially since it was such a beautiful, balmy day. Chase hated being shut up inside, and she wasn't sure whether it was because he was still working through Keith's death or if it really did have something to do with Sam. She knew that, businesswise, summer was Chase's busiest season, but she had overheard one of his conversations with Ernie, and there didn't seem to be any problems there. But she did have the uneasy feeling that Chase's time here was limited. He wasn't the type to hang around if he wasn't welcome. And it was pretty clear that he didn't feel particularly welcome.

She was still mulling his comment about Sam over in her mind as she led three horses to the outside arena. A customer was leaning against the railing of the big round corral, watching Sam work one of the top ranked reining horses. She spoke to him as she walked by.

Anne opened the big gate for her, and Devon handed the reins of one horse to the girl. "Warm him up for me, will you, Anne? I want to talk to Sam for a minute." The girl nodded, and Devon tied the other two animals to the rail, then closed the gate and hitched it.

Her boots sinking into the freshly harrowed soil, she crossed to Sam, who was just dismounting. A small whirlwind swept across the ground, picking up dust and twisting through the leaves of the trees that sheltered the far end of the corral. Sunlight glinted off the horse trailer and truck parked beneath them, and she tugged the brim of her hat lower over her eyes. The gelding pulled at the reins in Sam's hands, and began cropping the lush green grass growing along the edge of the corral. The horse raised his head and pricked his ears as Devon approached, and she reached out and rubbed his nose, then looked at her boss. "Have you got a minute?"

His face was flushed, sweat trickled down his temples, and he looked hot and tired. He didn't ride as much as he used to, and Devon could tell by the way he was standing that his hip was bothering him. He swept off his hat and mopped his forehead, then replaced the battered straw Stetson, glancing at the horse as the animal tossed his head, then went back to grazing on the grass. "What's on your mind?"

Devon toed a clod of damp loam in the shape of a hoof, uneasiness turning over in her stomach. In all the years she had worked for him, she and Sam Creswell had never had hard words. And she didn't want them now. Not if she could help it. She looked at him, her expression unsmiling. "I don't know if you're aware of it or not, but Chase McCall is here."

Sam's head came up, his gaze riveted on her. "Here?"

Devon studied him. "Yes."

The older man scanned the area outside the corral. "Where?"

There was something in his voice that made Devon hesitate. "He's in the house." She paused, then continued. "He's been here since Keith's funeral."

Sam's gaze locked on her, a startled look registering in his eyes. "Since the funeral?"

The gelding lifted his head and chewed on the grass he'd cropped, his bit jingling, and she reached out and scratched him under the jaw. The truck Chase had been driving was parked in the shade of the weathered old garage by her house and wasn't visible from the arena. She wondered if Chase had parked it there deliberately. She looked at her boss. "What's going on, Sam?" she asked, an inflexible edge in her tone.

Sam let his breath go in a rush, a flush creeping up his face. "Now, Dev," he said, his tone placating.

"You said something to him, didn't you?"

He shifted his weight and looked away, then looked at her. "Well, yes, I did."

"What did you say?"

He gave her a sheepish look. "I guess I spoke outta turn, and—"

"What did you say?"

"Well, now, I guess I poked my nose in where I had no business poking it."

Devon looked away, her jaw fixed, the first flickerings of anger unfolding in her. She waited for the feeling to settle; then she turned and faced him. "I want to know what you said, Sam."

He released a heavy sigh and tipped his head. His voice was quiet when he finally answered. "I figured he was using you, girl. And it bothered the hell out of me. I didn't find out until later that I was dead wrong. I tried to call him a couple of times to tell him so, but he wasn't there."

Devon felt suddenly shaky inside, and she stared at him. "Just what made you think you were wrong?"

"Well," he said, shuffling his feet, "I said something to Tanner, and he put me right."

Devon continued to stare at him, a quiet rage taking hold. *Tanner* had put him right? Remembering the look on Chase's face when he'd told her about Sam, she gave Sam a furious look, then started to walk away. Damn it, why was it always Chase's fault?

Sam caught her before she took half a dozen steps. He grabbed her arm, pulling her up short. "Now just hold on a minute there, missy," he said gruffly. "I owe the boy an apology, and I'd like to deliver it before you stir up an ant-hill.''

Devon wouldn't look at him, anger still sizzling in her. An anthill? What did an anthill have to do with this? She tried to let go of some of the tension. Taking a deep, steadying breath, she spoke. "You had no business saying anything to him, Sam," she said, her voice uneven. "I can take care of myself."

Sam had the nerve to chuckle. "Well, I expect I didn't, and I expect you can. But lord almighty, woman, don't stick your chin out like that. Makes me think you want to scalp me."

Damn it, she didn't want him to make her smile. It wasn't funny. So she waited for the urge to pass, then turned to him, trying to look stern, but not doing a very good job of it. "You'd better make that apology a good one or you're in big trouble, Sam."

He looked at her, a bright gleam appearing in his eyes. "Now, Devon, you don't need to give me a lecture. I've been married for over forty years. I know how to stand with my hat in hand and toady under."

Devon was darned sure Sam Creswell had never "toad-ied under" in his whole life.

They were moving the cattle from the pasture into the corral to work the cutting horses when Sam and Chase came through the side gate. She experienced a nervous flutter in her chest and tensed, and the gelding she was riding tossed his head and sidestepped, flicking his tail in agitation. She let the reins go slack and touched the horse with her heel, cueing him to go through the gate. The dust from the moving cows rolled up, and she took her horse around the back of the herd, trying to stay out of the worst of it. She saw Sam unhitch the two horses she'd brought down earlier and lead them over to where Chase was standing. He said something and handed the reins of a neat little sorrel to Chase, then leaned against the corral fence. Chase hooked the stir-

rup over the saddle horn, listening to whatever Sam was
saying as he tightened the cinch. The sober look on his face
kicked off another flurry of uneasiness, and Devon motioned for Luke and Anne to take over the herd.

She rode across the outdoor arena, the saddle creaking
beneath her, the soft, warm breeze carrying the scent of silver willow and freshly mown grass. As she neared the two
men, she saw Chase give Sam a sharp look, as if warning
him about something, and the older man nodded once and
swung into the saddle. She wondered what that was about.

She reined in when she reached them, and Chase shot Sam
another quick look, then continued adjusting his rigging.
Not sure what to make of their silence, she tried to quell the
uncertain flutter in her belly. She looked at Chase. "Hi. Are
you going to ride turn-back for me?"

He glanced at her, and she knew by the expression in his
eyes that he didn't know whether to be amused or ticked off
over her going to Sam over him. Chase had never liked
anyone fighting his fights for him. She knew that, but
maybe that was part of his whole male charisma. The
thought made her smile. She gave him a taunting look.
"What's the matter, McCall? Did you get your tongue
caught in the garbage disposal when you were fixing the
sink?"

That made his eyes lighten up, and he looked back at what
he was doing, amusement tugging at the corner of his
mouth. "You've got a bad mouth on you, Manyfeathers.
Don't you know you're supposed be nice to your…
plumber?"

He might as well have said "lover." The insinuation was
certainly there. With Sam hanging on every word, she
wanted to pull her hat down over her eyes and disappear.
But in spite of the fact that she was an inch away from
blushing, she could not let him get away with it. "I'm never
nice to plumbers, McCall. They're always in a such a big
hurry to get the job done."

Chase's hands stilled on the latigo, and he slowly turned his head and looked at her, his eyes narrowing dangerously, a glint of reprisal appearing. He continued to watch her with that dark, heavy-lidded look; then he spoke, the husky timbre of his voice loaded with innuendo. "You want slow, sweetheart? I can give you slow."

Her insides dropped away into nothingness, and she stared at him, a giddy weakness sizzling through her. For an instant she thought she might slide right out of the saddle. Hot and cold and decidedly light-headed, she dredged up a mildly rebuking look and reined her horse around. "Get your butt in the saddle, McCall. And let's see some real action."

She caught the flash of color out of the corner of her eye, and she heard the squeak of the saddle. Sam rode off chuckling as Chase came alongside. She looked at him, laughter bubbling up in her, and he settled his hat low over his eyes, giving her one of those bad-boy grins that had always got her into trouble. "Wanna race?"

She looked at the open gate and the field beyond. And she looked at the two horses that were worth several thousand dollars each, and who were due to compete in two weeks. More than anything she wanted to fly with him like she used to—flat out, racing the wind, going hell-bent for leather—but somewhere along the line she had grounded herself. She had weighed herself down—with a sense of duty, with feelings of accountability, with uncertainty—and she had simply ceased to fly. She wondered when it had happened, when she had lost the wind beneath her wings. Chase's mount moved against hers, and she looked up, her eyes dark with the jolt of realization. Chase was watching her, an odd, contemplative look in his eyes. He reached out and caught her by the back of the neck, giving her a little shake. "You wanted to, Slash," he said huskily. "That's what counts."

She stared at him, suddenly dangerously close to tears. That wasn't what counted. What counted were all the things she didn't do, all the things she'd lost because she had become grounded and hadn't even realized it.

That discovery haunted Devon over the next few days. It was as if her whole life had been brought sharply into focus, and she was able to see things she had never seen before. It should have been enlightening, but it wasn't. It was unsettling. And it intruded, mostly on her concentration. She would find herself standing and staring at something with her stomach in knots.

And Chase only made it worse. He had needed her those first few days after Keith's death—really needed the comfort and solace she could give him. But that was changing. Every day his mood was a little less somber, and as his mood lightened, the more tense hers became. She would catch herself anxiously watching for the those old familiar signs of restlessness in him, and she would get restless herself. She knew his leaving was inevitable. And knowing that scared her to death.

She knew that any kind of association with his father would be disastrous, and Chase was right; without the Bar M, there was nothing for him here. Besides, he had built a whole new, successful life for himself south of the border, and he would be a fool to throw that all away. But knowing that wasn't going to make it any easier when he left.

She managed to keep up a front during the day, but at night—nights were bad. All the self-doubts and uncertainties and anxieties would rise up and drive her from her bed. She had turned into a midnight wanderer, and tonight it was worse than usual. Tonight, old memories were surfacing, as well—disturbing memories that made her cold inside.

She stood at the kitchen window, waiting for the kettle to boil, her arms wrapped around herself, the belt of her robe pulled tight. Cold. She remembered the cold. And she remembered the terror. The memory was from when she was six years old, and her mother had left her alone in a rundown shack somewhere—somewhere. It had been cold and rainy, and there was nothing to eat but some congealed macaroni. The wind and rain had made the old house creak and groan, and she had huddled on her mattress on the floor, too scared to go outside to the bathroom. And she remembered wetting the smelly mattress that was her bed....

"Kind of making a habit of this, aren't you?"

She was so far away and the sound of his voice so unexpected that Devon jumped, her heart slamming into high gear as adrenaline shot through her. Closing her eyes, she clutched her hand against her chest, not quite able to disconnect from the memory—that frightening, terrifying memory.

Chase came over to where she was standing and caught her under the chin, forcing her to look at him. He winced when he saw her face, then caught her by the neck and pulled her into his embrace—a warm, safe embrace. Devon turned her face against him and fought the feelings of abandonment, of fear, of shame. She had been six years old and she had wet her bed, and she didn't want to remember. She didn't want to feel what that child had felt. And she didn't want to cry.

Chase tucked his head down against hers and tightened his hold, then slowly rubbed his hand up and down her back. "It's okay, babe. I've got you. I've got you."

Of all the things he could have said, nothing could have been more devastating, more wrenching. It was as if he knew exactly what kind of emotional trauma she was experiencing right then and was there to lift her out of that nightmare memory. She shivered and pressed against him, her arms caught against his chest, and Chase tightened his hold. "You want to talk about it?"

Her teeth clamped against the well of unshed tears, she shook her head. He rubbed his cheek against hers and snuggled her closer. "Do you want to go back to bed?"

She shook her head again, and he smoothed his hand up and down her back, but he didn't say anything more; he just held her, his face tucked against hers. His warmth and physical closeness diffused the disturbing images, and

Devon clung to the solidness of him, her eyes tightly closed and her jaw clenched. It had come out of nowhere, that recollection. Without warning, it was just there.

"I think we're going to have to do a little two-stepping here, darlin'," he said, his tone soft. She started to pull away, but he held her secure. "Just over to the counter. That old kettle's boiling its little old heart out."

There was something in his Colorado drawl and his hokey phrasing that made her smile, and she turned her head to his shoulder. "Working the crowd, McCall?" she asked, her tone uneven.

She felt him grin, and he gave her braid a tug. "Well, hell. I was trying to impress you with my cowboy charm."

She smiled again. "I appreciate the effort." Feeling oddly vulnerable, she pulled out of his hold and went over to the counter, where she pulled the plug on the electric kettle. Fighting against the tight feeling in her chest, she opened the cupboard door and reached for the tea canister. "Do you want some tea?"

There was a brief pause; then he answered. "May as well."

She fixed a pot of tea and got two mugs out of the cupboard, then carried the pot and the mugs to the table. Chase was leaning against the stove watching her, his unbuttoned jeans riding low on his hips, his arms folded across his bare chest. He had an odd, intent look in his eyes, as if he were disassembling her piece by piece.

She set the teapot on a place mat and put the cups down beside it, knowing he was scrutinizing her and not liking the feeling. Finally he spoke, his tone offhand. "I don't suppose you're going to tell me what that was all about."

She shot him a quick glance, then began filling the mugs. She had never told him much about her childhood. At first she'd been too ashamed to reveal all she had hidden. She hadn't wanted him to know what it had been like throughout her childhood, and by the time she and her mother moved to Bolton, she had learned to take care of herself and how to cover up the situation at home. She might only have had one pair of jeans, but they were washed every night, and she made sure her clothes were clean and neat, her hair shampooed and shining. Then this dark-haired boy with the killer grin and the sexy eyes happened along. And her universe shifted. Right from the beginning, Chase McCall had made her feel special. He made her feel beautiful and smart and courageous and daring. She hadn't wanted him ever to see her as that hungry, dirty, neglected child—the one who wet her bed because she was too terrified to go outside, the one who ate dirty orange rinds because that was all there was to eat. She would have done anything to gain his respect, his approval. It had been so easy to be reckless with him, to take crazy chances, because he made it so obvious that her daring pleased him. That he was proud of her. And it was the first time in her whole life that anybody had felt that way about her. There was no pride in dirt and neglect and hunger, so she had never told him. Never revealed the shame.

"Devon?"

She looked at him, his steady perusal making her edgy. She shook her head and looked away. "No," she said, her voice uneven. "I'm not."

He came over to the table, pulled out the chair at the end and sat down. Bracing his elbows on the tabletop, he laced his hands together, his thumbs resting against his mouth as he continued to watch her. Her hands not quite steady, she set a steaming cup of tea in front of him, then sat down and cupped her hands around the hot earthenware. He watched her for a moment, then took a sip from his mug and set it on the place mat in front of him. He fingered the handle for a moment, then looked at her, his expression mild. "Why didn't you tell me you were trying to raise the financing to buy Sam out?"

She had her mug halfway to her mouth, and she abruptly set it down, tea slopping over the edge. She stared at him, her heart lurching in her chest. She held his gaze for a moment, then abruptly looked at her hands, caught so off guard that she couldn't even think. "How did you find out?"

"I saw the letter from your bank, and I read it. Then I mentioned it to Sam when we had our little talk."

She looked at him, trying to recover her equilibrium. "You had no business reading my mail," she answered abruptly.

He gave her a humorless smile. "Don't pull that crap on me, Dev," he said, a hint of warning in his tone. "It was lying loose in that pile of junk by the phone, and I opened it to see if I could write on the back."

Remembering that that was exactly where she'd tossed it after reading it, she looked at her mug. She wasn't sure why his question made her feel so exposed or so guilty—or so underhanded. She rubbed her nail along the base of her mug, then spoke, her voice uneven. "I discussed it with Sam after—" She took a deep breath, trying to fortify herself. "After you left this winter. I thought maybe we could work out some arrangement." She waited, a nervous flutter in her stomach, expecting a whole host of questions. But he didn't say anything at all, and finally she looked at him, certain she had lost every speck of color from her face.

He was slouched down in his chair, watching her, his head tipped to one side, his arms folded across his chest, and Devon looked away again. The silence stretched out between them, and she fidgeted with the corner of the place mat, trying to blink away the burning sensation in her eyes.

Finally he spoke, his voice quiet. "Why?"

Startled and confused by the question, she lifted her head and stared at him, her expression numb. "Pardon?"

He gave her a small half smile, his gaze dark and penetrating. "It's a pretty simple question, Dev. Why Silver Springs? There are a half dozen trainers around who would hire you on a minute, and probably cut you in on a percentage, besides." He paused, his eyes still fixed on her. "So tell me," he said softly, "why is Silver Springs so important to you?"

Devon didn't know where the sudden spasm of unbearable desolation came from, and she didn't know why that little girl had come out of hiding now, but suddenly her eyes filled and she sat staring at him, hurting so much for the child she had been. How could she tell him? How could she explain it to him, when she had only just rediscovered that wounded child herself? Tears spilled over, and she turned away and quickly wiped them, feeling ashamed and exposed.

Bracing his hands on the table, Chase rose, then reached across and caught her face. Tipping her head back, he leaned over and kissed her with such immeasurable care that more tears spilled over. Tightening his hold on her face, he slowly withdrew, then trailed his knuckles down her cheek. "When you figure it out and you're ready to talk, let me know, darlin'," he said huskily. He kissed her again, then straightened, giving her shoulder a little squeeze. "Finish your tea. I'm going back to bed."

Badly shaken by the shifting, disturbing images in her mind, she stared after him, his question sending a reverberation of a shadowy, half-remembered fear through her. It was as though her whole foundation had abruptly crumbled away and she was suddenly standing on shifting sand.

Resting her forehead on her upraised knees, she closed her eyes and locked her arms around her legs, trying to quell the heart-racing panic. She had never been good at facing ghosts or at self-analysis because she had never wanted to look back—looking back meant facing all that fear and hurt and shame. Devon tried to will away the panic, but it wouldn't let go. It was like a huge hand clutching her chest. Maybe this time there was no escape. Maybe this time she was going to have to go back through the maze before she could find her way out.

## Chapter 13

It was as if someone had picked a protective layer of scales off her body, exposing patches of sensitive flesh. The light seemed brighter, her skin more sensitive, sounds more intrusive. She was more sensitized to the movements and temperaments of the horses, more aware of everything that was happening around her. It was as if she had been suddenly cast adrift, then had resurfaced in a strange and unfamiliar place. That awful sensation of being disconnected from everything familiar left her feeling shaky and unsure and oddly exposed. And memories—disturbing memories—had begun floating to the surface of her mind, shadowy, indistinct memories that had no shape. But they weren't memories of things or places. They were memories of feelings. And in some ways, those were even worse.

She felt haunted, and it was nearly impossible for her to stay focused on anything. And Chase never made any reference to what had happened in the kitchen that night. It was as though it hadn't, and that made her feel even more vulnerable.

For three days she felt as if she was stripped naked inside, and that feeling was made even more acute by a situation that should have had no effect at all. It had been one hell of a day, and she had gone to bed early with a dull headache. A low-grade ache in the small of her back had awakened her. Careful not to disturb Chase, she slipped out of bed and went into the bathroom. The light in the small room seemed piercingly bright, and the heaviness in her belly made her feel slightly dizzy. But what finally broke her was the visual confirmation that her period had started. She hadn't realized how much she'd hoped she was pregnant, nor was she prepared for the wrenching sense of loss on discovering she wasn't.

She went back to bed and slid in beside Chase, curling herself around his back. He stirred and caught her arm, drawing it around him, then sighed and tucked her hand against his chest. It was such a small, unconscious gesture, but somehow momentous, and Devon molded herself against him and closed her eyes, struggling against a profound ache. Sometimes it was that kind of comfort she missed the most.

The headache was still there when she awoke in the morning, compounded by a heavy dullness that made every movement an effort. Chase was on the phone to his partner when she left for the arena, and for some reason that started the ache in her chest all over again.

The clouds on the western horizon were still undercoated with slate gray, while the upper eastern strata were burnished with orange and gold and deep, deep coral. Soft purple wisps trailed out behind those clouds like the wake of a boat, painting the sky with slashes of color. On most mornings like this, she felt that if she could take a deep enough breath, she would be able to absorb all the colors and hues, all the open-sky beauty. But today the magic didn't work for her, and she turned and started walking down the trail that led to the arena. The long grass along the path was wet with dew, and the boughs on the pine trees shed a heavenly fragrance along with beads of water. Devon noticed the cluster of wood violets in a hollow between two aspen, the waxy, heart-shaped leaves funneling dewy moisture to their roots. She crouched down and lightly touched the fragile white blossoms, a funny feeling unfolding in her chest. So exquisite, so delicate, and for all their fragility, they somehow survived. She wondered if they would survive transplanting. That startling thought made her heart skip a bit, and she rose, not wanting to consider the reason.

It was not a good morning. She decided to ride in the indoor arena because Luke was making some repairs to the fence on the outdoor one, and she didn't want any distractions. The first horse she rode was a two-year-old colt who had the breeding and conformation of a champion, but who had a bad attitude. He tried to buck off the saddle, he tried to buck her off, and then he wouldn't move at all. She gave up and had Anne pony him while she continued to ride him, and she kept at it until he finally decided to cooperate. Even so, it was a battle of wills, and her neck was wet with sweat when she finally dismounted. He was also wet with sweat, but he stood like a lamb. Then, the minute she turned away, he nipped her on the butt. She wanted to kick him.

The second horse, a veteran cutter, simply stepped out from under her. Just as she was swinging into the saddle, the stallion abruptly sidestepped, and she found herself face-down in the shavings.

Swearing under her breath, she got up and dusted the worst of the dirt off her chaps, wanting to kick him, too. She looked up and found Chase hanging on the gate, his elbows hooked over the top, a smile tugging at the corner of his mouth, and she could tell by the look on his face that he had been watching for quite a while. "Nice dismount, Manyfeathers," he said, a gleam in his eyes. "It's the first time I've ever seen anyone do a perfect belly flop in dirt."

"Shut up, McCall."

The glint intensified. "You've got dirt up your nose."

She gave him a foul look and wiped her face, then swept up her hat. "Keep it up and you're going to have something up *your* nose. Like maybe a fence post."

He grinned and tipped his chin at the horse, who stood quietly beside her. "Maybe the two of you could join a circus. It'd make a hell of an act. You could change your name to the Flying Martini or something."

Devon gave him another disgusted look. "This *is* a circus, McCall. And this whole show is an act." She bent at the waist, twisted her hair on top of her head and covered it with her baseball cap. Straightening, she gathered the reins and glared at him. "Why don't you find something to do? Like unload the manure spreader?"

Resting his chin on his folded arms, he stared at her, the lines around his eyes crinkling. "Why don't you show me your new bite mark instead?"

"Give it a rest, McCall," she said, her tone cranky. "The only thing I'm going to show you today is a hard time."

He continued to stare at her, a warm, sensual gleam appearing in his eyes. Devon could feel the sexual heat from ten feet away.

The gleam in his eyes intensified, and he gave her a slow, lazy smile. "A hard time, huh?"

Determined not to give him the satisfaction of making her smile, she stared at him, gave an exasperated sigh and spoke, her tone very dry. "Get your hand out of your pocket, McCall. This isn't playtime."

He grinned in response, his eyes alight with that same sensual glint.

"Hey, Chase. You're wanted on the phone!"

He kept his gaze fixed on her. "Thanks, Jimmy!" Then he smiled that slow, bad-boy smile of his. "Hey, Slash," he said, his voice low and husky and loaded with intimacy.

She could feel the heat of that bedroom tone right down to her toes, and her knees felt suddenly weak. "What?"

His eyes held hers, that same sensual look still there. "Just so you know..." She waited, wondering just how far he would take it. He smiled, the laugh lines deepening. "You still have dirt up your nose."

If she hadn't been caught in such a daze, she would have strangled him with the reins.

By midafternoon Devon was feeling so thickheaded and leaden that all she wanted to do was crawl into a corner and die. The headache was back, and the dull heaviness in her abdomen made her feel even more sluggish. Chase had been oddly quiet after he got the phone call, so she assumed it had something to do with Keith. But his somber mood left her feeling even more exposed, more weighed down.

Taking into account the mood she was in, she didn't even bother to get on her last two mounts of the day, knowing it was going to be a waste of effort for both her and the horses. Instead, she climbed to the second tier of the bleachers in the indoor arena to watch Chase make the first contact with a young filly that had been delivered four days before. She was a beauty—fine-boned, perfect head and wide, intelligent eyes. But she had been badly abused by her previous owner, and her new owners had barely been able to get a halter on her. By the time Sam and Luke got her from the back paddock and into the arena, she was lathered and quivering with fear, and as soon as Sam tried to approach her, she got a wild look in her eyes and spun away.

The new owner had sent her to four other trainers, and they had gotten nowhere with her. In spite of her stellar breeding and near-perfect conformation, she was a ruined horse. But this little performance was going to be Chase McCall at his very best.

Devon had never seen anyone do what Chase was going to try with her—and Sam had only ever seen it used once, years before. When he and Sam had first discussed it as an option, Chase had teased her that it was an old Indian trick, and maybe it was, but it bothered her nonetheless. But she also knew that this horse was so wild there was no other choice. They had to do something that wouldn't confine the animal, that wouldn't escalate her fear but would get the horse to approach a human. They had left the filly without water for the best part of two days, until there were signs of dehydration, hoping that thirst would overcome the horse's innate fear.

Now Chase was going to work his special brand of magic. Devon had seen him work it a hundred times in the past, but never with such extreme measures, or on a horse that was so governed by panic. Drawing up her knees and locking her arms around her legs, she sat motionless as she watched Chase walk to the middle of the arena with a big plastic dishpan of water in his hands, his back to the trembling horse. When he reached the middle of the arena, he turned and faced her and started talking, his voice quiet and soothing. "Come on, sweetheart. It's okay. Come on, little darlin'. Come on, sweet thing, nobody's going to hurt you here."

The filly spun away, and Chase kept turning to face her, talking to her the whole time. Devon rested her chin on her knees, trying to ignore the sudden tightness in her throat. So much fear, so little trust.

Left on her own, the horse finally settled down, and she turned to face Chase, her ears pricked toward the sound of his voice and the sloshing water. He kept talking and sloshing the water, coaxing her to him with her thirst and his patience. It took fifteen minutes, but the horse finally took a step toward him, and Devon held her breath. It was another ten minutes before she took another step. The crooning tone of Chase's voice never altered. Quiet, reassuring, soothing. The content, however, took on new color, and Devon found herself smiling.

"Come on, you damned piece of sass. Come on. Come here. Quit being such a snot. Come on. Game's over, little darlin'." The horse stretched out her neck in the direction of the basin and took a step. Then another. Chase sloshed some more water. "Come on, pretty girl. Come on."

Another step. Then two more, as if yielding to the collective urging of everyone watching. Sam, Devon, Luke, Anne, even Jimmy—it was like a force field, the absolute stillness, the tension, each of them silently willing the horse toward the water, knowing each step was a step taken in fear. A step toward building trust. He was offering the filly kindness in the form of cool water; she was reaching for it with hard-learned wariness. It was nerve-racking to watch.

The filly took another step and stretched her neck toward the basin, and Chase tipped it toward her, letting her see inside, talking to her, coaxing her forward. She pricked her ears, smelling the water, and they all waited with bated breath, urging her to take that final step.

Finally she did. She dropped her head and took a quick drink, then jerked her head up and shied back. Chase extended the basin and kept talking to her. It took another bout of coaxing in soft tones, and Devon had almost given up hope, when the filly took that critical step forward, dropped her head and drank deeply. Devon's throat closed up completely, and her jaw ached. It was so wrenching to watch, the building of that first fragile bond between man and beast. It was like watching a miracle unfold.

She expected the filly to wheel away as soon as she drank her fill, but she didn't. Continuing to talk to her, Chase very slowly lowered the empty basin and reached out his free hand. Devon again expected the horse to bolt, but the filly tossed her head and took a single step backward. Chase kept crooning to her and took a step toward her, his hand outstretched. The horse watched him, her ears flicking at the soft singsong tone of his voice. He took another step forward—and another miracle happened. The filly hesitated, then dropped her head and sniffed his outstretched hand. Suddenly blinded by feelings she couldn't even identify, Devon soundlessly slipped from the row of bleachers and headed outside. It was as if Chase had reached inside her and touched something that was raw and tender and hurting. Something she couldn't face.

She mounted the first horse she found saddled and headed to the back pasture, not sure what she was running from, but running anyway.

It was nearly five o'clock when she returned to the lower barn. It was obvious from the freshly swept alleyway and the state of the stalls that Anne and Jimmy had finished doing chores, and Devon experienced a dull sense of relief. The last thing she wanted was to see anyone. Almost too tired to move, she dismounted, then removed the saddle and put it in the tack room, every movement an effort. She led her mount to the side paddock and stripped off the bridle, watching as the horse found a suitable spot and rolled. Breaking one of her own rules about always putting tack away, she hung the bridle on a hook just inside the door, then started up the trail behind the arena. All she wanted was to avoid everybody, go home, have a shower and crawl into bed.

By the time she walked up the path to the house, her legs were aching and her head was thick and throbbing. She let the screen door slam shut behind her, and she knew before she even entered the kitchen that the house was empty. She found a note from Chase on the table, saying he'd gone into town and that he'd be home about six. She listlessly slid the note into a slot by the telephone, then headed toward the bathroom, rolling her head to ease the tension in her shoulders. Maybe an hour's nap would clear her head.

The feel of someone pulling the comforter up around her woke her, and she tried to swim through the gray weight of unconsciousness, her mind thick with sleep. It vaguely registered that she was huddled in bed with her hands under her face, trying to ward off the chill, her oversize T-shirt twisted up around her waist. Feeling as if she weighed a ton, she slowly opened her eyes, her body so heavy she couldn't move. Chase was sitting on the bed beside her, his hand on her shoulder, gazing down at her. "Packed it in, did you?"

She stared at him, feeling almost drugged. "Yeah."

He tucked the quilt around her shoulders, then drew her hair from her face, his touch warm and comforting. "Cramps?" he asked softly.

She nodded, and Chase shifted his hand and began rubbing the small of her back, a smile appearing in his eyes. "I don't imagine that face-plant this morning helped much."

She didn't even have the energy to smile. "Not much."

He snuggled the comforter around the back of her neck, then rubbed her collarbone with his thumb. "Still cold?"

She nodded, feeling just a little too close to tears.

"Would you like something to eat?"

Her hands still tucked under her face, Devon shook her head. "Not really. But I'll get up if you're going to fix something for yourself."

"I'm not. I had a hamburger in town." Withdrawing his arm, he stood up, and Devon thought he was going to leave. But he undid the buckle and removed his belt and hung it over the headboard. Taking the wallet out of the back pocket of his jeans, he laid it on the bedside table, then stretched out beside her. "Here," he said, sliding his arm under her neck, pulling her toward him. "Let me warm you up." He drew her head onto his shoulder, then kissed her on the forehead and wrapped both arms around her.

Devon closed her eyes and rested her arm across his chest, her throat suddenly tight. She had learned a hard lesson when she was very small, that she was the only one she could depend on to take care of her. No one was ever going to take care of her, or provide for her, or keep her warm—and because of that she had acquired a kind of internal toughness. She couldn't allow herself to be dependent or fragile; she would never have survived if she had. But right then, she simply didn't have any resources left to draw on. And he was there, sheltering her, providing her with warmth and strength, taking care of her and keeping her safe. It was as if he knew just how defenseless she was.

He brushed a soft kiss against her temple, then slid his arm around her waist and spread his hand wide across her belly, his touch oddly intimate as he tried to ease her discomfort. It was almost more than she could handle, and Devon tightened her arm around him and turned her face against his neck, struggling against the growing fullness in her chest. She didn't know what was wrong or why she felt the way she did. It was as if everything she'd built was collapsing around her, as if all her safety nets were gone.

"Dev, honey," he murmured softly, "do you have something you can take for this?"

It was almost funny. What kind of pill could she possibly take for this kind of confusion, for this sudden loss of balance—as though someone had turned her whole existence upside down? She waited for the ache in her throat to ease. "It's okay," she answered unevenly. "It'll pass."

He smoothed back her hair, then gave her head a little shake. "Determined to tough it out, huh?"

She nodded, then shifted her head on his shoulder and stared across the room. "Where did you go?"

Chase went still, and Devon realized what she had said. She had never done that before—asked him where he was or who he was with. If he brought up something, she would ask questions, but she was well aware that she had never initiated that kind of conversation or asked for an explanation before. She had sworn she would never pry. If she ever had, then that would open the door for him to... to what? Her heart went dead still, and she froze, a startled sensation filtering through her. Was it because she thought it was none of her business—or was it a case of guarding her own vulnerability?

Chase caught her along the jaw and tipped his head back so he could see her face. His gaze was intent, but there was an odd smile hovering around his mouth, as if she had said something that had saddened him. "It doesn't come easy for you, does it, Dev?"

Guilt unfolded in her, and she stared at him, unable to answer him. She wondered how many times she'd hurt him in their lifetime—and how many times she'd done it without even realizing it.

The expression in his eyes softened a little, and the corner of his mouth lifted with a trace of wry humor. "Don't worry, babe. I won't ask back."

It made her feel worse when she realized how clearly he had read her. And it made her feel even more guilty that he expected nothing back from her—as if he had resigned himself to her reticence a long time ago. She was still struggling with that unsettling thought when he drew her head against his shoulder. He didn't say anything, as if he was mulling something over in his mind; then he reconnected with a little hug and exhaled heavily. "I was in town talking to Milt. He phoned this morning, and he was pretty upset. I figured I owed him a few explanations, at least."

"Upset about what?"

"His life, my old man, my not taking the Bar M off his hands. I can't say I blame him. But I think we got some things sorted out."

"Like what?"

"Like the fact that the ranch isn't his responsibility. Like no matter what he does or how hard he tries, it's never going to be good enough. That he's got to say to hell with it and get out before it drives him nuts. He's actually pretty pumped up over this political thing, so we talked about that. I told him I thought he'd do a hell of a job if he got elected—and by the sounds of things, I think he stands a damned good chance. Maybe that'll be all it takes for him to break loose."

Lying on her side with her head on his shoulder, Devon stared across the room, thinking about Chase's brother. All his life, Milton had competed against Chase for his father's approval. It had to be so degrading—having every effort belittled and demeaned. At least she'd never had to endure that as a child—she'd just had to cope with alcoholic neglect. She blinked and shifted her head. "What's going to happen to the ranch?"

"Milt's got a new manager lined up. Someone who managed one of the big spreads in the interior of British Columbia. Who knows? Maybe my old man will end up selling it."

His comment left her with a hollow feeling in the pit of her stomach. She understood his feelings about the ranch, she truly did, but she'd always had this small, secret hope that the Bar M would someday bring Chase McCall back to stay. But it would never happen. Not as long as Bruce McCall was alive. And that was another reality she'd been skirting for a long, long time.

Chase tightened his arm around her back and began rubbing his hand up and down her arm. "Still cold?"

She shook her head.

"I'll fix you something to eat if you're getting hungry."

"No. I don't want anything."

The breeze from the open window rattled the blind, and Devon closed her eyes against the flutter of brightness. She could tell by the chirping of the robins and the angle of the light that the shadows were getting long. She liked this time of day—when it started to cool off and the shadows got long and the clouds would start to pile up against the jagged ridge of the mountains. It softened the landscape, somehow.

Resting his cheek against the top of her head, Chase continued to stroke her arm, and she settled deeper into his embrace and released a long sigh.

When she awoke the second time she was alone and dusk had infiltrated the room. She could hear the muted sound of guitars coming from the front room, and the fragrance of freshly brewed coffee pricked at her nose. She rolled onto her back and stared into the deepening twilight, trying to fight through the sludge in her mind. Heaving a sigh, she threw back the comforter and got up, the rush of movement making her sway. She waited for the sensation to pass, then shivered and picked up her robe from the end of the bed. Her eyes closed, she struggled into it, her actions awkward and uncoordinated. She felt as if her body was just too heavy to move. She went to the bathroom and splashed some cold water on her face and brushed her teeth. But that didn't help much. She still felt groggy.

She found Chase sitting at the kitchen table reading a newspaper, a cup of coffee by his elbow. A breeze from the kitchen window made her shiver, and she huddled into the warmth of her robe. "Hi," she said, her voice still thick with sleep.

He lifted his head and looked at her, a smile appearing in his eyes. "Well, hello. You took your sweet time waking up."

She hunched her shoulders and tightened her arms in front of her. "You wouldn't know a sweet time if it jumped up and bit you in the face, McCall."

The glint in his eyes intensified. "Ah," he said, his tone significant. "Feeling just a little cranky, are we?"

"I wouldn't push it if I were you, Slick. I'm in no mood for cute."

He watched her as she sat down adjacent to him, clearly amused by her irritability. "I can see that." He pushed part of the newspaper in front of her, then got up and went to the counter. He poured another cup of coffee and brought it to the table and set it down in front of her. He sat down again and went back to reading the newspaper. Devon didn't want to read the newspaper. She didn't want to be ignored. But she didn't want to talk, either, so she settled for the coffee. She could never remember feeling so contrary. Maybe she was just losing her mind.

She worked her way through half a cup of coffee, then drew up her knees and rested her cheek on them, her mind adrift, still more asleep than awake. She focused on Chase. "You need a haircut."

He ignored her.

"And a shave."

"Can it, Manyfeathers."

That made her smile. "What's for supper?"

He raised his head and responded with a long, steady stare.

She held his gaze, smiling at him. "You offered."

Chase continued to stare at her, then he dismissed her ploy with a malicious smile. "I did. But I'm not offering now."

Her head still resting on her upraised knees, she tried to entice him. "There are T-bone steaks defrosted in the fridge."

Studying her with a mixture of tolerance and amusement, he rocked back in his chair and hooked his thumbs in the pockets of his jeans. "Just out of curiosity, what do you live on when I'm not around? Crackers and jam?"

It caught her off guard, the little jolt of pain that went right through her heart. She didn't want to be reminded about what it was like when he wasn't there. It hurt too much.

Chase's eyes narrowed a fraction, and he stared at her; then he let his chair down with a thud. His gaze suddenly dark and serious, he leaned forward and rested his arms on the table. "We need to have a talk, Dev," he said softly.

Devon stared at him, a feeling of apprehension unfolding in her belly. Then he reached across the table and caught her by the wrist, silently urging her to her feet. He didn't say anything as he led her into the living room, but she could feel the tension in him, and her apprehension turned to dread.

He stretched out on the sofa, his back braced against the arm; then he pulled her down and settled her across his lap. He brushed the loose wisps of hair from around her face, then drew her head down against his shoulder. Devon tried to brace herself for what was coming, but nothing could soften the hard, cold reality of his words. "Ernie phoned this afternoon," he said, his tone quiet. "He's got some major problems down there, so I'm going to have to go back." He hesitated, trying to prepare her. "I was able to book a flight for tomorrow morning at eleven."

The chill of alarm went bone deep, and Devon closed her eyes against it, her heart suddenly too big for her chest. Not tomorrow. Not now, when her whole life was upside down. It was too soon. Much too soon. She made herself unclench her jaw, and she eased in an uneven breath, not wanting him to know how much his announcement had shaken her. As if sensing it anyway, Chase tightened his hold on her. "I'm sorry, babe," he whispered gruffly. "But I gotta go."

She closed her eyes tighter and swallowed hard. "I know."

Chase exhaled heavily and pressed his cheek against the top of her head. "You gotta understand that this time of year is crazy for us, Dev. Ernie's up to his armpits in alligators, and I've been gone too long as it is."

She slid both arms around him and hugged him hard. She hung on to him for as long as she dared; then she physically pulled herself together. She wasn't going to make a scene, and she wasn't going to make it any harder on him than it already was. She had made her choice. Now she had to learn to live with it.

She forced a droll tone into her voice. "So, Slick. Does this mean I get hash browns with my steak?"

He chuckled and gave her a tight squeeze. "Don't you ever stop thinking about your stomach, Manyfeathers?"

"Not if I can help it."

"God, but you're a snot." He ran his hand up her back, then hoisted her to her feet and came up behind her. "Up and at 'em, scout. No damned way are you going to get to sit this one out."

Devon somehow managed to disconnect from the hard, cold reality that Chase was soon going to be gone from her life again. She got through the meal preparation, and she got through the meal itself. She even managed to go to sleep after they went to bed. But there was no way she could make it through the night.

A disturbing dream captured her—a dream of out-stretched hands and a coaxing voice—and suddenly she was the little filly in the arena, wanting to go to the reassuring sound of the voice, wanting to approach, but a dark and disturbing fear held her back. Then the voice and reassurance dissolved into a yawning black hole, and she was trapped by it. And no matter how frantically she searched, there was no way out. Then suddenly she was falling, falling....

She awoke with a start, her heart hammering, panic gripping her. But it wasn't until she threw back the covers and stumbled out of bed that she realized she was trembling. Shaken and cold, she crept to the living room and wrapped herself in one of the Mexican blankets, then curled up in the corner of the sofa. She had never had any exposure to Indian spirituality, and she knew nothing of the lore, but she understood about dreams. She'd always understood about dreams. And she understood this one.

Every critical decision she had ever made in her whole life had been governed by fear. She had never wanted to admit that. Giving in to fear was a weakness, and she couldn't afford to be weak. She had struggled so hard to leave the shame and humiliation behind, to make something of herself so she would be respected. But the biggest reason for not wanting to admit the fear was that if she ever admitted it, she would have to face it straight on.

She didn't want to acknowledge what had happened between Chase and the little filly that afternoon. She had run rather than face it. She didn't know how many times—hundreds of them—she had wanted to reach out and take what he had offered, but fear had always outweighed the wanting. She remembered another dream—a terrifying dream from her childhood—and she still clearly remembered, in frightening detail, the precursor to that dream. She had been eight or nine, and she and her mother had been traveling somewhere with a man. They had stopped by the side of the road, and her mother had made sandwiches. There had been a field of thistles—sweet-smelling thistles, their old blossoms crowned like miniature ballerina dancers—and she had run around the edge, knocking the seeded blooms with a stick to make them fly. She had lain on the ground, watching them soar, fascinated by the hundreds of whirling seeds shining silver in the sun. Clouds moved in and it turned cold, and she went back to the road. But the road was empty. The car was gone, and she was alone, and scared, so scared.

She had been running down the road, her heart beating in her chest so hard she couldn't breathe, when they returned, drunk and laughing. That night marked the first time she had the thistle dream—where she was a thistle seed caught in the wind, floating in the breeze, whirling and dancing. But then the sky turned dark, and the wind carried her higher and higher, and she knew if she couldn't reach the ground and grab on to something she would be carried away and lost forever. Since then the dream had recurred with frightening regularity. It had terrified her so badly that she used to tie her ankle to the bed, so she would be anchored, so she couldn't be carried aloft and lost forever.

Sam Creswell and the Silver Springs Stables had been her anchor. When her mother took off when she was sixteen, Sam and Marj had taken her in. Sam had taught her everything he knew, and he had given her her first real home, a place where she belonged, and, in time, recognition and respectability. She was no longer the hungry, dirty waif of a child. She was a horse trainer with a respected reputation, a person with roots and self-esteem. Or so she liked to believe.

But Chase McCall was her nemesis. He had been right from the very first. He had tempted her and teased her and taught her how to fly. She wanted a life with him more than anything, but she was afraid to let go. He thought it was because she didn't trust him—and maybe, on one level, she didn't. Maybe she was afraid he would disappear like her mother had on countless occasions, and she would be caught aloft with no anchor, lost forever.

Hugging the blanket around her, Devon wiped her face and stared blindly into the darkness, every barrier she had ever erected in pieces at her feet. She had convinced herself that she couldn't leave Silver Springs because Sam needed her, because she owed him everything. But that had been her protective cover, her excuse, something to hide behind.

But she couldn't use that as an excuse any longer. She had stayed because she was afraid to let go.

Now all she could see was Chase's hand outstretched to the filly, coaxing her to come, to trust him. She wasn't sure she had that kind of courage.

## Chapter 14

The feel of callused hands cradling her face and a soft, moist kiss brought her awake, the scent of familiar aftershave making her want to curl into the warmth. Her mind weighed down with sleep, Devon opened her mouth beneath the pressure, savoring the warmth, the gentleness, the sweetness of the caress, the minty taste of toothpaste piquing her senses. The warmth roused her, and she yielded to the searching kiss, lost in a thousand sensations. So sweet. So warm. So unbelievably gentle. It was everything.

The hold on her head tightened and the pressure lifted, and an amused voice intruded on the floating sensation. "That's a hell of a way to kiss a man who just finished packing his suitcases, darlin'. Don't you know anything about playing fair?"

Feeling as if she were swimming through warm, swirling water, Devon reluctantly opened her eyes, not wanting to let go of the floating sensation.

Chase smiled a soft, lopsided smile, his eyes smoky with emotion.

Still more asleep than awake, she smiled back, loving the feel of his hands against her face. "Hi," she whispered sleepily.

The smile deepened. "What are you doing out here, Manyfeathers? Don't you like the company you keep?"

She gazed at him, so groggy that her mind refused to function. She managed a drowsy smile. "Who are you?"

He grinned; then he leaned over and gave her another no-nonsense kiss. "You're a real piece of sass, Manyfeathers. And a pain in the butt, to boot." He let go of her and leaned back, amusement glinting in his eyes as he slid his hand under the blanket and up her naked thigh, his touch making her shiver. "All snug and warm, are we?"

She yawned and rested her head on the arm of the sofa, unable to keep her eyes open. "Yep."

He rose, then, before she had a chance to protect herself, he snatched the blanket and yanked it loose, rolling her onto the floor. He stood with his feet braced apart, a tormenting grin on his face. "Well, now you're not."

She scrambled to her feet, trying to grab the blanket. "Damn it, McCall. Give me that blanket."

His grin broadened, and he tossed the blanket across the room, then stood so she couldn't get by him. "Not a chance." He caught her off guard again when he came at her and, in one swift, powerful move, hoisted her over his shoulder. "Game's over, Slash. Time to hit the shower."

She knew it would be a cold one if he ever got her through the bathroom door, and she fought against his hold, her loose hair blinding her. She got her fingers under his ribs, and he nearly dropped her, but he tightened his hold on her legs and hoisted her higher onto his shoulder. His voice breaking with laughter and exertion, he tried to drag her through the bathroom door. "That little piece of cheek is going to cost you big time, Manyfeathers."

Holding on to the door frame with both hands, she tried to kick free, her laughter weakening her. "Cut it out, Chase." Realizing that wasn't going to work and that she was losing her grip, she tried pleading. "Please. Please. I'll make you breakfast. I'll shine your boots. Anything."

Adjusting his grip on her legs, he grabbed one wrist and tried to break her hold on the door frame. "Too late. You're going in."

She knew it was only a matter of time. Laughing and out of breath, unable to see a thing for her hair, she used his back for leverage and bit him hard on the backside. His reaction was instantaneous. "Ouch! What the hell . . . !"

Before he could recover, she kicked loose and slithered down his back, landing in a heap on the floor. Knowing it wasn't over until she brought him down, she grabbed him around the calves and used her shoulder against the backs of his knees. He let out a yell and went down like a stack of hay bales. Sweeping her hair from her face, she looked at him, laughing and out of breath and feeling victorious. "Nice buns, McCall."

He rolled over onto his back, his chest heaving, laughter mixing with his shortness of breath. "Damn it, Slash, but you fight dirty. It was a figure of speech, you know—your being a pain in the butt."

She grinned at him. "Well, now it's not."

Smiling into her eyes, he reached up and grabbed a handful of hair and drew her toward him. As soon as she was within reach, he caught her around the back and pulled her on top of him. Trapping her against him, he expelled the last of his laughter in a sigh, then wrapped her in a companionable embrace. "That's a hell of way to start a morning, woman. You damn near killed me."

It was at that instant that it hit her. This was it. This was all the time she had left with him. In a matter of hours he would be gone, and she would be left with nothing bright and shiny in her life.

Closing her eyes against the sudden burst of pain, she slid her arms around his neck and held on to him, the sense of loss so intense that it made her shudder. It scared her to death, knowing she could be saying goodbye to him for the very last time.

As if sensing the change in her, Chase caught her by the back of the head and tightened his hold, his embrace suddenly rife with tension. "I'm going to miss you like hell, Manyfeathers," he said, his voice husky and uneven. "I don't know how I could have got through these past few days without you."

Her jaw locked against the ache in her throat, she tightened her arms, trying to will away the awful fullness burning in her eyes. She didn't dare think about what he'd been like that night in the hotel room, and she didn't dare think about what was ahead of her. She would never get through the next few hours if she did. Easing in a deep, tremulous breath, she turned her face against his neck, trying to absorb as much of his warmth and strength as she could. Enough to get her through this. Enough to hold her together.

Chase released a heavy sigh and smoothed his hand up her back, then turned his head and kissed her forehead. "Don't, Dev," he whispered gruffly.

Knowing what he was asking, she swallowed hard and gave him a little jab in the shoulder. "You lost, McCall. Which means you make breakfast."

He chuckled and rubbed his hand across her hips, pressing her firmly against his groin. "Hey. I figure I did all right for myself."

Reaching down deep for a smile, she raised her head and looked at him, gazing into his eyes. "Making lemonade out of lemons again, Slick?"

He grinned and slid his hand under the elastic band of her panties. "I never did check out your bite mark."

She gave him a dry, steady look. "Too bad. Now you've got one of your very own."

His gaze warm and intimate, he stared at her, his eyes alive with delight. Then something flickered in his eyes, and he looked away, his expression suddenly strained. "We'd better get up," he said, his voice husky. "It's getting late."

She got off him, and he rolled to his feet, then caught her by the hand and pulled her up. He stared at her, then carefully tucked her hair behind her ears. "You go ahead and get dressed. I'll make breakfast."

Feeling suddenly shaky inside, she swallowed hard and nodded, then turned away, her throat aching. *Please, God,* she thought desperately. *Just let me get through this without coming apart in front of him.*

By the time she came out of the bedroom, Chase had pancakes on the go and coffee perking. The last thing she wanted was anything to eat, but she would do it or die trying. This was part of keeping everything normal, part of pretending it wasn't happening.

They ate in strained silence, and Devon managed to get down three pancakes and a cup of coffee, but her stomach was such a ball of nerves, she wasn't sure how long she would keep things down. Striving for calm, she rested her elbows on the table and watched him mop up the syrup on his plate, the churning in her stomach making her hands clammy. She glanced at the clock, then back at him. "It's just seven. What time do we have to leave for the airport?"

Chase lifted his mug without meeting her gaze and took a swallow of coffee. It wasn't until he set the mug down that he spoke. "You don't have to go. I'm taking Tanner's truck back, and he's going to drive me in."

The rush of panic made her heart pound, and she sat there, clutching her mug. She glanced at his bags by the door, then at him, feeling as if every speck of warmth had been leached from her body. Too soon. It was too soon. She wasn't prepared to say goodbye. She had counted on the two-hour drive to Calgary. The panic climbed up her throat. He took the last bite of pancake, then washed it down with coffee.

Still without meeting her gaze, he got up from the table and took his dishes to the counter and set them in the sink.

He glanced at the clock, then wiped his hands on the dish-cloth and headed for the back door. She couldn't move. It was as if she were frozen in place, the dread so intense that it paralyzed her. A thousand images jammed up in her head, and she was once again that little girl in the field of thistles, sending the seeds whirling into the sky. She remembered the joy. A new, different kind of panic broke over her, setting her free, and she lurched to her feet, knocking her chair over in her haste. Fear and desperation propelled her, and she hit the back door at a dead run, the screen door slamming loudly behind her.

Mindless of the ruts in the path, mindless of the branches snagging at her hair, she dashed up the path leading to the weathered garage, afraid. So afraid.

She rounded the garage just as he was laying the garment bag in the back of the truck, and he turned, a startled look appearing in his eyes. She choked out his name, suddenly blinded by tears, and he caught her as she stumbled into his arms.

Gathering her up in a rough embrace, he caught the back of her head and held her tight against him. "What? What's the matter?"

She tried to answer, but she couldn't. There was just too much emotion breaking loose—old fear, new fear, desperation. It was as if his walking out the door had stripped everything away. And she knew she couldn't let him go.

He folded her in his arms and tucked his head against hers, one hand tangled in her hair. "What, babe? What's the matter?"

Devon hung on to him, her whole body shaking with emotion, suddenly experiencing the same soaring sensation she had experienced so long ago. This was right. He was her freedom. But he would also be her anchor.

"Dev? Please, baby. Tell me what's wrong."

"Don't go."

He tightened his hold, his voice gruff with regret when he answered. "I have to, babe. You know that."

Wiping her face, she lifted her head and looked at him, hope driving her, her tone urgent. "Just a couple of days, Chase. Just so I can get things straightened out around here. Then I'll come with you."

He went dead still and stared at her, the pulse in his temple suddenly beating double time. "What?"

It was like letting go of a secure handhold. And reaching out for something that might not be there. "Take me with you, Chase," she whispered, her eyes filling. She flattened her hand against his chest, her heart beating in frantic time just like his. "You can't come back here. I know that. So you have to take me, Chase."

He watched her with an intensity that made her heart climb up her throat and nearly stall. Finally he hauled in a deep, uneven breath and grasped her face between his hands, the look in his eyes fierce with emotion. "You would do that for me?"

"Yes."

He stared at her for an instant longer; then he closed his eyes and hauled her into his arms, his unchecked strength nearly crushing her. He didn't say anything for the longest time; he just held on to her as if he couldn't let her go, and Devon closed her eyes and clung to him, fear mixing with hope. She could do this. She could. Because anything else was too unbearable.

Finally he let all the air out of his lungs, and with unsteady fingers, he swept her hair back from her face. "Listen to me, Dev," he said, his voice rough and unsteady. "Listen. You need to think about this, babe. Don't do something you're going to regret later."

"Chase, no—"

"Shh." He hugged her closer, tightening his hold. "Shh, darlin'. Just listen to me. I'm not walking out on you—and I'm not putting you off." He inhaled roughly and slid his fingers around the back of her head. "I just want you to be sure this is what you really want." He took another deep breath, then continued, his voice so strained, so thick with emotion that she could barely hear him. "Because if I ever get you down there, you can be damned sure I'm never going to let you leave."

A thousand feelings washed through her, and she sagged against him, her face pressed against his neck. Chase stroked her back, molding her closer, his touch firm and reassuring. "You gotta know I love you," he whispered unevenly. "You gotta know that, babe."

She tightened her arms around his neck and nodded, focusing on the warm scent of him, the weight of his arms around her. Those were real and solid. And secure. He held her for a long time, rubbing her back, talking nonsense to her; then he swept her hair back again and tipped her face up. He gazed at her, his expression taut and solemn, then bent his head and kissed her—one of those long, wet, openmouthed kisses that made her senses swim and her body go weak. And Devon sank into it, tears seeping out from beneath her lashes, not sure how she was ever going to let him go.

Dragging his mouth away, Chase pressed his face against her neck and hugged her. "I gotta go, babe," he whispered gruffly. He kissed her again, then let her go. His face carved with strain, he threw his small duffel in the back with his garment bag, then climbed into the truck, started it and rolled down the window.

Chase had taught her a lot about saying goodbye. Don't linger, don't drag it out and don't make any promises you can't keep. He put on the sunglasses lying on the dash, then looked at her, a strained expression around his mouth. "I'll call you from the airport."

Hugging herself, her throat so tight she couldn't answer, Devon nodded.

He stared at her for an instant; then the muscles in his jaw bunched, and he looked down as he put the truck into reverse. With one final glance, he wheeled the vehicle into a sweeping turn, and with dust rolling around him, he headed toward the lane.

And Devon watched him go, her vision blurring, the pain in her chest nearly intolerable. She had left it too late, and it had taken her too long. And now he was leaving, and she hadn't even said goodbye.

It was an unpredictable summer. Cold and rainy, then hot and muggy, with some of the worst thunderstorms in recorded history. Devon barely noticed. They were running with a full stable of horses, and with Sam spending less and less time in the saddle, it meant she was doing most of the training. She started working a couple of hours at night so they could maintain a halfway reasonable schedule, and with all the horse shows, there were days when she was so busy she barely had time to eat.

But the nights were something else altogether. Loneliness like she had never known haunted her, an unrelenting loneliness that was compounded by a thousand regrets, even more self-castigations and uncertainties, and by the resurrection of more memories. The memories were devastating, but the loneliness was worse, and it got so she dreaded going to bed at night.

Chase had called her from the airport like he had promised, and he had called her again when he got to Colorado. But he never mentioned what had happened his last morning at Silver Springs. It was as if it hadn't happened. Devon felt emptier than she had ever had after he left, certain that he had given up on her and eased himself out of her life. He had no reason to believe her; he had asked her months before to marry him, and she had backed away. And after all the times she'd hurt him in the past, he had no reason to believe her now.

She started going to the arena every night to work with the little sorrel filly, partly because she couldn't stand being in the house alone and partly because there was something about the horse's wariness that drew Devon. And partly because of Chase.

He had so totally understood the animal's fear—better than she had, better than Sam. And it wasn't until late one night, after she'd sat in the middle of the arena for an hour, a bucket of oats at her feet, coaxing the filly to come to her, that it hit her why he had understood. She sat there hugging her upraised knees, experiencing such a rush of awareness that it made her heart pound. He knew. He'd done exactly the same thing with the filly that he'd been doing with her all her life. He had tempted her with all the things she craved—the speed, the danger, the excitement—and he had coaxed her to him, doing everything he could to get her to trust him. He knew. He had always known. It was as if that discovery freed something inside her, and she could take a deep, freeing breath. There was nothing to hide from him—because he knew it all.

She wrote him a letter that night—twelve pages—and she told him things she'd thought she would never tell another living soul. She told him about being six years old and being left alone, and she told him about the field of thistles. It was her unburdening, and she was an emotional mess by the time she was finished, but she felt lighter inside. She carried that letter around for days before she scraped up the nerve to mail it, and when that letter went through the slot, her heart went with it. It was her first step toward absolute honesty. He would know it all, every sordid, shameful detail, and that terrified her. She had let him see it all.

She was an even bigger mess after she mailed that letter. She wanted him to call, yet every time the phone rang, her heart dropped to her shoes and she dreaded answering it. She couldn't sleep, she couldn't eat, and there were times when she would have been out cleaning stalls at three in the morning if she could have gotten away with it. Then she got three hastily scrawled postcards from him. One from Oklahoma, one from Texas and one from New Mexico, and she realized he was on the road and probably wouldn't be back to his spread for weeks. She experienced such a jarring let-down that it took her two days to recover from it. The waiting was going to kill her.

It was the first of August when she got her second jolt. It was early Sunday evening, and she was in the tack room at the arena, putting the next week's training schedule on the blackboard. Sam came in, dressed in ironed blue jeans and a new shirt, his best straw Stetson angled on his head. Every Sunday night he and Marj went into Bolton for Chinese food, and without fail he brought her back a bag of fortune cookies. He set the brown paper bag on the corner of the battered old desk, then leaned against it.

She gave him a wry grin. "There had better be some good news in that bag, Sam. I'm in no mood for 'Confucius says.'"

He chuckled and crossed his arms. "I can see that."

She gave him a wry look, then she turned away from him and went back to writing out the schedule. "I'm taking the two Brecker horses out of the schedule, if that's okay with you. They've both gone a little sour the past two days, so I thought we'd turn them out in the pasture for a couple of weeks."

"Sounds good."

There was a brief silence, then she heard him shift behind her. "I just got an offer on the ranch."

Devon went stock-still. Her heart made a sickening rush to her shoes, and for one awful moment she thought her knees were going to give out. Tightening her hand around the piece of chalk, she made herself take a deep breath. "Someone from around here?"

"Nope. Somebody from the States who wants to get into the horse business."

Numbly, Devon looked at the shattered stick of chalk in her hand. "Was it a good offer?"

"Yep, it was. Wants me to stay on and manage the place for a while, and wants to sign you to a contract. Heard about you from several of our old customers."

Her insides churning, Devon rolled the pieces of chalk around her palm. "So what are you going to do?"

He sighed heavily. "Well, for starters, I thought mebbe we could talk about it."

She tossed the broken chalk in the garbage can, then wiped her hands on the rag she used to clean the board, her expression heavy. Silver Springs was home. And the thought of selling it made her stomach harden into a tight ball. Wiping the last traces of dust from her fingers, she laid the rag on the blackboard ledge, then turned. It took a concerted effort to meet his gaze. "It's your operation and your investment, Sam. This is up to you and Marj."

He stared at her, his expression thoughtful. "Well, now, I don't quite agree with you, missy. Marj and I see you as a damned sight more than a hired hand, and I figure you've got a fair chunk of time invested here."

She held his gaze for a moment, then looked down and rubbed some chalk dust from the tips of her fingers, her throat suddenly tight.

Sam didn't say anything for a moment, then he spoke, his voice gruff. "I figured mebbe we could strike a deal if you wanted to take over here."

Her gaze averted, Devon swallowed hard and shook her head. "Even if I could raise the money, I don't think I could make a go of it on my own. I'd have to hire another trainer, and there would be a drop in business if you weren't here on a regular basis. And with mortgage payments on top of all of that—I don't know."

His arms still folded across his chest, Sam tipped his head to one side and studied her. "What's happening with you and McCall?"

She gave a wan smile. "I don't know about that, either." Devon let go a long sigh and met his gaze. "Let's face it, Sam. There isn't a huge market for spreads like this. If you've got a solid offer, and you and Marj are satisfied with it, you'd be a fool not to jump at it."

"Would you sign on for a few months?"

She picked at a loose thread in the stitching on the saddle beside her, then raised her head and looked at him. "I guess—if you're going to be staying on. But there would have to be some very clear terms set down. I won't work for anyone who's abusive to horses, and I won't take orders from anyone but you."

Sam stared at her, a bright twinkle appearing in his eyes. "That's a good one. When in hell did you ever take orders from me?"

She gave him a lopsided smile. "I wasn't counting."

He chuckled and shook his head. "I guess you weren't." He stared at her, his expression turning solemn. "I'm sorry about this, Devon," he said quietly. "If it wasn't for Marj, I'd hang on for a few more years."

"I know that, Sam."

He sighed, a melancholy look appearing in his eyes. "It's been a hell of a ride, hasn't it?"

"Yes, it has." One hell of a ride. And it was going to nearly kill her to see it end.

Devon went on autopilot for the next six weeks. She worked, she ate, she slept. She didn't ask Sam anything about the sale; she didn't want to know, and she tried not to think about Chase, or what he was going to do when he read her letter. She put in at least eight hours a day in the saddle, and Sam had hired an extra hand to take up the slack. She got several more postcards from Chase, from all over the States, and she didn't want to admit what a sinking sensation she got from each one of them. And she tried not to think about why he hadn't phoned. She was able to disconnect from almost everything, but she wasn't able to disconnect from the loneliness. She had missed him before, but this time it was different. This time she was aware of his absence all the time, and there were nights when she wanted him so badly that she nearly climbed the walls. And there were other nights when she would have sold her soul just to have him in bed beside her.

The prospective buyer was due to arrive the second week in September to check out the place, and Devon worked everyone like dogs, making sure there wasn't so much as a straw out of place. She wasn't going to let anything reflect on Sam's reputation. The new owner was expected to arrive on Saturday, but she got a call very late Friday night from Sam, saying he had just arrived and had given Sam a certified check for the deposit.

She stared across the darkened kitchen, her hand clenched around the receiver, an awful sinking sensation unfolding in the pit of her stomach. This was it. It was going to happen.

"Devon? Are you there?"

She forced herself to relax her grip and moved the phone closer to her mouth. "Yes, Sam. I'm here."

"I was wondering if you'd mind slipping down to the arena. He brought four of his horses with him, and I thought we could put them in those stalls at the south end."

Her chin came up. She had a better idea where he could put his horses.

"Devon?"

She exhaled and rubbed the knot of tension between her eyes. "I'll see to it."

"Good. Good." The click of the disconnect startled her, and she pulled the receiver away from her ear and looked at it. He had hung up on her, and she didn't even know who she was dealing with here. Sometimes Sam could be so damned dense. She slammed the receiver in the cradle and turned toward the door. The last thing she wanted to do was be civil to whoever was taking over Silver Springs. Letting her irritation energize her, she yanked on her boots, then snatched a sheepskin jacket off a hook. She just had to keep reminding herself that this was what Sam wanted.

A wisp of wood smoke greeted her as soon as she stepped outside, the scent lingering from a pile of deadwood they had burned that afternoon. She turned up the collar of her jacket and stuck her hands in the pockets, the tang of autumn and the chill of frost mixing with the lingering smoke,

and inhaled deeply, savoring the smell. God, but she loved
autumn, especially like the one they'd had this year. A true
Indian summer with vibrant colors, clear skies and practically no wind to tear the leaves off the trees. It was her favorite time of year, but it was also the time of year when she
missed Chase the most.

She followed the trail through the copse of spruce and
aspen to the arena, the dry grasses beside the trail rustling
against her jeans, the glow from the yard light casting long,
eerie shadows through the branches. A wave of loneliness hit
her, and she huddled into the warmth of her jacket, her vision suddenly blurring. He would be back. She just had to
believe that, as soon as the rodeo season was over, he would
be back.

The dogs bounded up to meet her as she came through the
trees, and she snapped her fingers and gave them a soft
command to heel, a sick feeling washing through her when
she saw the outline of a big rig parked in the unlighted area
at the south end of the arena. She wondered if Sam would
leave the dogs.

Shutting off that thought, she pulled open the side door
and entered the long, still structure. Only one set of lights
along the shed row had been turned on, the scant illumination sucked into the high, wide blackness of the arena. A
horse nickered and stuck its head over the half door as she
approached, and she paused and scratched him under the
chin. "Checking things out, Dandy?" She found a crunchy
in her pocket and let him take it from her open palm, then
straightened his forelock.

Sticking her hands in her pockets, she started toward the
open box stall at the far end of the complex, a nervous flutter unfolding in her throat. Lord, she did not want to do
this. The thought of losing all this, especially on a lonely
autumn night like tonight, made her want to bolt.

A form appeared in the doorway of the box stall, and
Devon's heart skipped a beat. Standing in the shadows the
way he was, it was impossible to determine anything about

him except that he was wearing a black low-crowned Stetson and a shearling coat, his face hidden by the shadows. He rested one hand on the open stall door and watched her approach, something in his stance making her insides roll over. Arrogance. She could sense it from a hundred feet away. She kept walking, bracing herself for the first confrontation. This was the man who was going to be taking over her life, her home. She hated him on sight.

"You sure as hell took your sweet time getting here."

Devon's heart lurched to a stop and she closed her eyes, certain that her mind was playing tricks on her. It couldn't be. It couldn't. Her legs suddenly trembling beneath her, she swallowed hard and grasped a stall door for support, her heart hammering so hard that it felt like a stampede in her chest. Feeling as if she were suspended in some sort of dream, she watched him come toward her through the shadows, moving with a cocky swagger. "What's the matter, Manyfeathers? Cat got your tongue?"

Stunned and speechless, she watched him step out of the shadows, that old familiar cocky grin on his face, and a wave of stunning reaction slammed through her. Covering her face with her hand, she started to sob, the emotion too intense to hold in, relief and something raw breaking from her. He closed the distance, his voice going soft and husky. "I got your letter a few weeks ago," he continued. "And I gotta tell you, it shook me up. Then I got mad as hell at you for not telling me before." He walked up to her and caught her by the back of her neck, pulling her toward him. "Damn it, Slash, don't you know you don't need to hide anything from me?"

Shaking and crying because she was so glad to have him back, she slid her arms around his neck and hung on to him with every ounce of strength she had. She couldn't answer him; it was just too overwhelming.

He slid his fingers into her hair and drew her head against him, then began stroking her jaw. "Ah, darlin'," he whispered, his voice rough with emotion. "You also made me pretty damned happy." He hugged her hard, and she felt him grin. "So I said to hell with it and bought the farm."

She closed her eyes and hugged him back, happiness spiraling through her. The impossible had happened. Chase McCall had finally come home.

The autumn night breeze wafted in through the window, and Chase tightened his hold on her face, then kissed her with infinite care, moving slowly inside her. The loving had been urgent and out of control and completely unprotected, and Devon's breath caught when he moved against her, her body still supersensitized. Releasing a satisfied sigh, he broke off the kiss and looked at her, the light from the hallway highlighting the angles of his face. He gazed down at her, his eyes warm and intimate, softened by a glimmer of amusement. He smoothed his thumbs across her cheekbones, a smile tugging at his mouth. "So how does it feel to be in bed with the boss?"

She turned her head and kissed the palm of his hand, then gave him a wry grin and slid her hands up his naked back. "Don't get a big head about it, McCall. We haven't negotiated the terms of my employment yet."

He grinned at her, then leaned down and gave her another kiss. "God, but you're a snot. That's not going to get you many Brownie points, Slash."

She savored the moistness of his kiss, loving the feel of him still inside her. God, but it felt so good to have him back.

He heaved another contented sigh, then braced his weight on his arms and looked down at her, brushing a strand of hair off her face. He gave her that slow, lazy grin of his. "Maybe I'll keep you. You're not a half-bad kisser."

Gazing at him, she rubbed her hands across his taut shoulders. "You're not half-bad yourself."

His expression sobered, and he smoothed his knuckles along her temple. "Happy?" he asked, his voice low and husky.

Blinking against the sudden well of tears, she nodded. "Very."

His face grave with emotion, he cupped her head and drew his thumbs along her damp lashes. "Marry me, Slash."

The tears spilled over, and she swallowed hard. "Yes."

He stared at her, his gaze dark and intent, then a trace of amusement tugged at his mouth. "Scout's honor?"

She laughed through her tears, loving him so much she couldn't hold it in. "Is that another bad Indian joke, McCall?"

The amusement spread to his eyes, making his laugh lines crinkle. "Damned if I know."

She stroked his buttocks, absorbing the fact that he was really there. She had to wait a moment for the contraction in her throat to ease; then she spoke, her voice a husky whisper. "Why, Chase?"

He gazed at her, his expression turning solemn. He caressed her temple with his thumb, the warmth in his eyes as sensual as his touch. "You mean about buying this place?"

She nodded.

He held her gaze for a space, then started straightening some loose wisps of hair. Finally he spoke. "Your letter changed things for me, Dev," he said, his voice gruff with emotion. "And I started looking at things a little differently. I thought about how I would feel giving up my place—the life and business I'd built up down there, and I realized I didn't like the idea a whole lot. It was the first time I really realized what I was asking you to do." He frowned a little, his expression somber. "And I started asking myself a few questions. I knew all the reasons I didn't want to come back here, but I never stopped to think about all the reasons I did." He stopped fussing with her hair and met her gaze, his expression still solemn. "There was you, darlin', always you. But there were Tanner and Kate and the kids, too—they're my family. And there's Cyrus and Burt. And in spite of our differences, there's Milt."

"But why this?"

He stroked her cheek, his expression serious. "I guess because we can build a good life here. And because of you. Because I know this is the only home you've ever had. I didn't want to take it away from you."

"But you didn't have to *buy* it, Chase."

His gaze softened, and he smiled at her. "Yeah, I did, Slash. I wanted it, too. So I talked to Ernie and Sam, and we worked out a deal. Ernie and I were able to swing the down payment, especially when Sam decided he'd like to maintain an interest. Tanner put up some collateral for me, so it's a fifty-fifty deal with Sam, but we have the option to buy out his half in five years. Sam and Marj are going to stay in the house as long as they want, and we can live here until we outgrow it. It means I'm going to have to spend some time in Colorado, but I figured that was something we could both live with." He grinned at her, mischief twinkling in his eyes. "It's a hell of a mess, but Tanner's got it all figured out, so I just signed the damn papers."

Devon tried to smile, but emotion lodged in her throat, and she looked away as she tried to bring it under control. Finally she spoke, her voice still a little unsteady. "Why didn't you say something when I told you I would go to Colorado?"

Chase caught her under the chin and lifted her head, forcing her to meet his gaze, his expression unsmiling and solemn. "I didn't have it put together then, Dev," he answered, his voice gruff with recollection. "You blew me so far out of the water when you told me you'd come with me, it took me a while to get it back together. Then I got your letter, and that shook the hell out of me. I didn't know what in hell to do. And I have to tell you, I was damned ticked off at you for a few days for never telling me all that. Then bit by bit, this started making more and more sense, so I called Sam." His eyes dark and somber, he drew his thumb across her cheek, then eased in a deep, uneven breath. "And it was something I just couldn't tell you over the phone, babe. I needed to be here when I told you. I was afraid you'd think I did it for all the wrong reasons if I wasn't."

Touched by his confession, even more deeply touched by the solemn look in his eyes, Devon touched his mouth, her fingers not quite steady. "But you didn't have to do this, Chase," she whispered unevenly. "Not for me."

He looked at her, his gaze unwavering. "Yes, I did, Dev," he said quietly. "I did it for us. I didn't realize how damned much I missed being up here until I stopped and thought about it. And besides, I like this business. It's a good place to be. And I want to see our kids out there hanging on the corral, watching their mama ride."

Devon pulled her arms from around him and took his face in her hands, feeling such a rush of love for him that it made it hard to breathe. "I love you, Chase," she whispered brokenly. "God, how I love you."

Stroking the hair from her forehead with his thumb, he gazed at her, a heart-stopping smile in his eyes; then he lowered his head and kissed her, tightening his hold on her face. "That's what it's all about, babe," he whispered, his mouth moist and warm against hers. "That's what it's all about."

\* \* \* \* \*

# HE'S AN

## AMERICAN HERO

*Men of mettle. Men of integrity. Real men who know the real meaning of love.* Each month, Intimate Moments salutes these true American Heroes.

For July: THAT SAME OLD FEELING,
by Judith Duncan.
Chase McCall had come home a new man. Yet old lover Devon Manyfeathers soon stirred familiar feelings—and renewed desire.

For August: MICHAEL'S GIFT,
by Marilyn Pappano.
Michael Bennett knew his visions prophesied certain death. Yet he would move the high heavens to change beautiful Valery Navarre's fate.

For September: DEFENDER,
by Kathleen Eagle.
Gideon Defender had reformed his bad-boy ways to become a leader among his people. Yet one habit—loving Raina McKenny—had never died, especially after Gideon learned she'd returned home.

AMERICAN HEROES: Men who give all they've got for their country, their work—the women they love.

Only from

**ROMANTIC TRADITIONS**

Barbara Faith heats up ROMANTIC TRADITIONS in July with DESERT MAN, IM #578, featuring the forever-sultry sheikh plot line.

Josie McCall knew better than to get involved with Sheikh Kumar Ben Ari. Worlds apart in thought and custom, both suspected their love was destined for failure. Then a tribal war began, and Josie faced the grim possibility of losing her desert lover—for good.

October 1994 will feature Justine Davis's LEFT AT THE ALTAR, her timely take on the classic story line of the same name. And remember, ROMANTIC TRADITIONS will continue to bring you the best-loved plot lines from your most-cherished authors, so don't miss any of them—only in ▼ INTIMATE MOMENTS®

™ *Silhouette*®